Sharp Practice

Third in the Best Defence Series

Willie McIntyre

Others in this series:

SHARP
PRACTICE

William H.S. McIntyre

Copyright © 2013

www.bestdefence.biz

A good criminal lawyer seeks after the truth.
A great criminal lawyer makes sure the jury doesn't hear it.
~ Robbie Munro ~

Chapter 1

'In there.' The custody sergeant jerked his head in the direction of an interview room. 'And don't be long, there's a queue.'

Two thousand and twelve: Scotland no longer lagged behind such other bastions of human rights as Russia, Spain, Turkey, and, now that accused persons had the right to see a lawyer before interview, it made police stations much busier places of an evening; even a Friday evening.

'When's the interview happening?' I asked.

'Been there and done that,' the sergeant replied. 'He never wanted a lawyer. Your client is now officially huckled.' He opened the door for me. 'You've got ten minutes.'

Ten minutes was fine by me; I had other plans for the evening. I walked into the room and saw my new client had already been brought from his cell and was there waiting to see me.

Dr. Glen Beattie was young, gifted and hailed from the Black Isle. The latest addition to the local G.P surgery had arrived in our midst following the recent departure, feet first and in a box, of his predecessor: man of the people, hard-drinking, hard-smoking Dr Bill MacGregor, whose cold hands and warm heart had served the sick and ailing of Linlithgow for almost forty years.

The only time I'd ever had cause to consult the late Dr MacGregor in my adult life, was several years before

1

when worried about a suspected irregular heartbeat. Doc Mac had given me the benefit of a thirty second examination, asked me what beat I expected my heart to drum if I continued in a stressful job, drank gallons of black coffee and ate junk food. Following which sage advice, he lit up a smoke, showed me out and nipped next door to the Red Corner Bar for a swift half.

With old Doc Mac buried along with his mistakes, I suspected that there were women of a certain age all over Linlithgow dreaming up ailments that required the immediate and intimate attention of his young, handsome replacement; however, that particular night, Dr Beattie's sculpted features were pale and strained as he sat on a bolted-to-the-floor metal stool, shoulders hunched, elbows resting on an equally bolted-to-the-floor metal table. He brightened somewhat as I took a seat opposite and managed a strained smile. 'Mr Munro?'

'Dr Beattie, I don't think we've ever actually met,' I said as we shook hands.

'Your father is a patient of mine. I've heard him speak of you.'

'Dads; they love to boast about their children, don't they?'

What there was of a smile wilted. 'Yes... well... anyway...' Beattie cleared his throat. 'He happened to mention that you were a criminal lawyer. I'm new to all this and yours was the only name I could remember. I'm afraid I don't even know your first name.'

'Robbie.'

He pointed to himself, 'Glen.'

'Well, Glen,' I said, aware that time was marching on, 'bring me up to date on what's happened so far.'

He winced. 'The whole thing's mad. I'd just finished afternoon surgery today,' he glanced down at the bare wrist where his watch would have been, 'when Megan called to say that the police were at the house and wanted to speak to me.'

'About what?'

He clasped his hands at the back of his head and spoke to the ceiling. 'Pornography.'

'Child pornography?' Stupid question. So far as the law was concerned there was only one kind. 'And?'

'I was still on the phone and next thing I knew there were two plain-clothed police officers in the waiting room. They'd come to seize my laptop. I asked them what was happening and they said that I should go home immediately - so I did.'

'And I take it there were more cops waiting for you?'

'Lots. They've taken away my PC, printer, digital camera, just about anything with a silicon chip in it. They brought me here and said they wanted to ask a few questions.'

'And have they?'

'Yes.'

'Did they ask if you wanted a lawyer?'

'Yes, but I didn't think I needed a lawyer, I haven't done anything wrong.'

I'd started to laugh before I realised he was being serious.

'They only wanted to ask some routine questions,' he said, defensively.

Newsflash: the police never ask routine questions; they're busy people; sausage rolls and fudge doughnuts don't eat themselves. Any questions asked would have been for one purpose and one purpose only; to extract incriminatory evidence from the suspect, whether he realised he was incriminating himself or not.

'So you waited until after you'd been interviewed, arrested and told you were being kept in custody before deciding you wanted a lawyer?' I tried to keep the note of annoyance out of my voice. The law is no different to medicine, the sooner you seek advice from an expert the better; however, it didn't pay to be too critical of the paying clients, especially doctors; they were liable to take their Medical Defence Union hourly rate and go elsewhere. At the moment I was very much auditioning for the role of Dr Beattie's lawyer. After all, I was only there because of a conversation he'd had with my dad.

'I've never been in trouble before, not even a parking ticket. Can you get me out? Tonight?'

'I'll do my best,' I said. 'It'll be up to the duty inspector, though. If he says no, that'll be you until Monday. A lot depends on how much evidence they have. What did you tell them?'

'Nothing.'

When clients say nothing what they usually mean is not actually nothing as in an absence of words but, rather, things which in their non-legal opinion aren't important.

'Nothing? Really?'

'There was nothing much I could tell them.' Here

we go, I thought. 'I told them I didn't know what they were talking about and that's all.'

'Did they show you computer equipment?'

'Yes.'

'And did you confirm to them that it was yours and that you had owned it from new?'

He nodded slowly and with a faintly quizzical expression as though I was embarking on some kind of parlour-trick, guessing game.

'And they asked you and you told them that no-one else in the house used it?'

He nodded again even, slower this time, no doubt wondering how I knew this and where I was going.

'And then they asked if it was password protected?'

Nod.

'And is it?'

'Yes, but, who cares? I haven't done anything wrong.'

So in one short interview, my new client had confirmed to the police that if there were indeed any indecent images of children on his PC, there was no-one to blame but himself. That's called narrowing the field of investigation, eliminating other possible suspects. It's also called aborting an impeachment defence; one of the few defences open in computer-porn cases. The correct answers to the questions would have been, *no, I bought the PC second hand from a man wearing beer-bottle spectacles and a stained brown Mackintosh, people are always in and out my house using the internet and my password is 'password'*. An even better answer would have been, *I'm saying nothing until my lawyer gets here.*

'What is the password?' I asked, hoping it might

indeed be password, something someone else could have guessed and used to gain access to download porn without my client's knowledge.

'La Boehme, my favourite opera.'

My favourite opera was Aida but only because I heard somewhere that it was the shortest.

'Did I do something wrong?'

'The police like to use a process of elimination to show that no-one else but you had the opportunity to download any images. Leaving you—'

'Holding the baby?'

Well pictures of it anyway, I nearly said, but in times of falling prosecutions and the death by a thousand cuts of Legal Aid it didn't pay to be flippant with the private clients. 'You didn't help your case, let's put it that way.'

'I told the truth.'

'See what I mean?' I took a notepad from my briefcase and jotted down some details. 'Anyway, what's done is done. When they examine all the equipment they've taken away, what do you think they'll find?'

'Do you mean will there be any child-porn?'

I let him work that out for himself. I could see he was becoming just a teeny-bit ratty now.

'Absolutely impossible.'

It seemed less impossible to me; otherwise why was the young doctor banged up in a police cell on a Friday night waiting to join the ranks of Monday afternoon's custody cases?

A rattle of keys, the door opened and the custody sergeant poked his head into the room. 'You going to be much longer?'

I stood up, walked to the door. 'Is the Inspector around?'

'I'm sure Detective Inspector Fleming will make himself available - seeing how it's you Mr Munro.'

Dougie Fleming was the duty Inspector? Fleming and I had a long and acrimonious history. Our conversations were frequent, fraught and usually involved the disputed contents of his notebook, which, if ever published, would be found in the library under 'F' for fiction. I had a feeling that a long weekend on a hard mattress lay ahead for Dr Beattie.

Chapter 2

Linlithgow Sheriff Court was no more, or at least the centuries old building had been vacated and the court moved to the new and much larger town of Livingston, ten miles or so to the south. It made sense to move the administration of criminal justice closer to the criminals, but I missed the old courthouse. Yes, it had been a cramped warren of a building. Yes it had been run-down, indeed, downright unhygienic. The minute the decision had been made to build a new court elsewhere, the cleaning and maintenance staff at Linlithgow had downed tools; nonetheless, the old building, for all its faults, had great character. The new court was highly unimaginative from an architectural point of view, even if the amenities for court officials and punters alike were a huge improvement.

Monday morning; thanks to a jack-knifed lorry on the Avon Gorge, I was running late for the custody court. Throwing on my gown, I charged into Courtroom One where I met Paul Sharp, fellow defence agent and aficionado of the swinging Sixties. In a high-lapelled, four-buttoned black suit worn over a charcoal shirt with the skinniest of yellow ties, Paul was as dedicated a follower of fashion as Ray Davies could ever have imagined. 'No rush,' he said. 'They're going to do the summary stuff first before they close the court for your Petitions. Two in the one day? Not bad. How's your doctor client?'

'Innocent, apparently.'

Paul laughed. 'Same as all your clients then? Would he still be so innocent if the Fiscal reduced the case to summary? Hugh Ogilvie's doing the custodies and you know what he's like these days. Only bothered about keeping up the conviction rates; any plea will do. Speak to him nicely - you never know your luck.'

Speak nicely to the Procurator Fiscal? There was a first time for everything I supposed and, it was true, an early plea of guilty on a summary complaint and Glen Beattie could say ta-ta to his medical career but at least he wouldn't go to jail. Maybe I should sound the Fiscal out, keep my client's options open.

Ogilvie was sitting at the table in the well of the court across from the defence agents, waiting for the Sheriff to come onto the bench. As though he'd read my thoughts, he came over and dragged me aside, away from the other agents. 'I just want you to know that I'm prepared to keep this whole thing very quiet,' he said.

'What thing?'

'The petition hearing for Dr Beattie. I'm doing my best to keep it away from prying eyes and ears.' He threw an irritable glance in Paul's direction. 'You know, in the *circumstances*.'

'That's very nice of you,' I replied, not sure why Ogilvie was being so reasonable; it wasn't like him. 'What's the evidence?'

'We got a tip-off, end of last week, that there were images on your client's PC. The sex crime unit is looking at them right now.'

'How many images and what level?'

'We'll have to wait and see what comes back from

the High-Tech boys.'

'If there's only a few and they're low-level pictures, what are the chances of the whole thing disappearing? You know – in the circumstances,' I added, although, other than my client being a doctor, I wasn't sure exactly what those were.

'Hmm. Not so easy. Kiddy-porn is zero-tolerance and if it's level four or five, it'll definitely stay on indictment. Anything lower and for a quick plea I'll drop it down to a summary. Can't say fairer. Until then you can tell your client and...' he tapped the side of his nose with an index finger, '*other interested parties*, that I'm keeping this case under wraps, at least for the moment, best I can do.' I still had no idea what he was talking about. The PF turned to the rest of the waiting solicitors. 'Anyone looking to plead?'

Paul Sharp came forward. 'I think you'll find we're all open to persuasion.'

How things had changed even in the ten years or so I'd been a defence agent, *or a stakeholder in the criminal justice network* as the bureaucrats at Holyrood preferred now to refer to us hacks. The Scots legal system, once the envy of the world, now, so far as the Scottish Government was concerned, merely an expensive nuisance. The politicians had come to the conclusion that most of the cost of dealing with crime could be attributed to two things; firstly, a bothersome concept called the presumption of innocence, which led to people standing trial and the resulting cost of lawyers, witnesses and court time, not to mention those inconvenient findings of innocence. Secondly, there was the horrendous expense of sending people to prison.

Forty grand a year to keep someone banged-up? You could just about fund an MSP's taxi fares for that. The answer was obvious: more accused persons needed to plead guilty and less sent to jail. Simple. Why had nobody thought of it before? Lawyers were now obliged to tell their clients that guilty was good. An early enough guilty plea and an accused could expect a third off his or her sentence, so a maximum Sheriff Court sentence of five years, quickly became forty months on a plea of guilty. That discount brought it under the four year limit which meant a further full one-half remission. So an accused facing five years would be out in twenty months and out in ten or even less if released home on electronic tag. You didn't have to be guilty to be tempted by an offer like that, and there was no incentive for your lawyer to bend over backwards to establish your innocence; not if you were a legally-aided client. Legal aid fixed-fees meant that more or less the same paltry sum was paid whether the accused pled guilty or not guilty. Why carry out a painstaking investigation, rack up hours waiting in court, go twelve rounds with some dour-faced Sheriff, all for an extra hundred quid? Why not chuck in the towel at the first bell and still pocket most of the purse?

Fortunately for me, and thanks to the never-ending series of G.P. pay-rises, Dr Beattie was my very own private patient and there'd be no fixed-fee. I'd be charging out my work time and line and at a proper hourly rate. Plead guilty? He'd be pleading guilty over my dead body. Hugh Ogilvie could shove his *circumstances* – whatever they might be.

'You never told me,' Beattie said, as, after his brief

appearance in court, we stood in the entrance hall of the court, me clutching my briefcase and my client his freshly signed bail papers. 'If I'm found guilty - am I going to jail?'

This was where it got even tougher, especially for an innocent man. The possession of indecent images of children was an offence often committed by middle-aged men with no past record of offending. Filling the jails with teachers, bank managers and Scout masters was a waste of prison resources, so the Appeal Court had laid down a few sentencing guidelines. If a person accused of possessing child-pornography was a first offender, did not have the images for commercial purposes and, here was the rub, pled guilty: the court was expected to impose a non-custodial sentence, which meant the imposition of a large fine or, more likely, the requirement to carry out a number of hours unpaid work as part of a community pay-back order. Go to trial and the sentencing gloves were off. In front of a jury on child-porn charges, the accused started the game a couple of goals down. Unless the defence scored a hat-trick it was jail-time. Many a man with a perfectly stateable defence opted for the definite no custody route rather than maintain his innocence and run the risk of prison. Given his fragile condition, and the size of my overdraft, I thought it best not to set out my client's options in any great detail at this early stage of proceedings and, anyway, his declarations of innocence had been strong enough.

'You're innocent,' I said. 'Remember that.'

He looked out at the lone newspaper photographer who'd been wandering around since before lunchtime.

Given the PF's assurances of the matter being kept hush-hush, I wondered how the snapper had managed to get wind of the case.

'Is there another exit, a fire escape or something we could use?' Beattie asked.

I straightened my tie and took hold of my client by the arm. 'They can't use your photograph at this stage and only guilty men sneak out the back. We're leaving by the front door so hold your head up high and smile for the camera.'

Chapter 3

Like being wrapped in warm cotton wool. That's how Tanya
Lang had once described the joy of heroin to me. I'd
represented her in court on several occasions; nothing
serious, mainly shopliftings. Junkies deal or steal to
feed their habits. Tanya was a stealer and seemed to get
caught a lot. It was hard to tell if she was really bad at
nicking stuff or if she stole so much that the times she
was caught counted as merely a small percentage of a
much larger total. Her endeavours were probably
hindered by her appearance. Tanya was a pretty girl,
but the fact that her father was Jamaican didn't help her
blend in with the crowd, not in a place like Linlithgow
where anyone whose skin wasn't white was either a
tourist or had spent too long on the sunbeds.

Teenage Tanya's favourite method of raising funds
for the Afghan poppy-growers and their local
intermediaries was to plunder the supermarkets either
end of town; nothing fancy, no high value goods, just
the usual junkie items that were easy to shift: jars of
coffee, packs of cold meat, batteries, razor blades;
everyday things that the bloke in the pub felt quite safe
to buy without fear of detection. Everyone likes a fry-up
and the cops are unlikely to beat down someone's door
in search of a missing packet of bacon.

But my young client's days of being wrapped in
warm cotton wool were over. Now she was cold and
wrapped in a white mortuary sheet, lying on a stainless

steel dissecting table, a drain between her heels and myself and forensic pathologist, Professor Edward Bradley, either side of her.

The Professor pulled back the sheet to reveal the young woman's mortal remains. The body had been examined by the Crown the previous day and all the necessary dissecting had been carried out and samples taken. The smell hit me. I took a step back.

The Professor sighed. 'Chalk up one more victim of the magic pixie-dust. Am I right, Robbie?'

Tanya had died sometime late Friday evening when, following my brief interview with Dr Beattie, I'd attended a leaving do for a cop who was retiring after thirty years' service; the last five spent keeping the peace at the Sheriff Court. All areas of the criminal justice system had been represented: Fiscals, defence agents, Clerks and, of course, a large contingent of cops including D.I. Dougie Fleming, fresh from refusing my request to release Dr Beattie. Even my dad had made a cameo appearance. It was hard to believe that while we'd all been eating, drinking and recounting anecdotes, some of them true, that young Tanya was lying dying on her livingroom floor.

It was Sunday before Tanya's body was found. The Crown autopsy had been performed first thing Monday morning. It was now Tuesday afternoon. I put my hand over my face and mouth, wishing I could breathe through my ears. What made a doctor want to be a pathologist? I wondered, not for the first time. At what point during the long medical training does the young pathologist-to-be decide, 'you know I think I'll spend the rest of my career carving up dead people'?

'I don't know how you can do this for a living,' I said, no pun intended.

The Professor stretched a latex glove over one hand, a puff of talc escaping as he snapped it over his wrist. 'Quit complaining. Young Tanya here is quite fresh.' He pulled on the other glove. 'You should have been in the Balkans after the war. A few of us were shipped out to the mass graves. Now that was what you call messy. Anyway,' he looked down at the remains of my former client, 'won't be much to see here. Healthy enough I expect, apart from being dead, of course. The toxicology report is going to tell you more than I can about cause of death.'

'That's not why you're here,' I told him. 'I want you to check the girl for injury. I need to rule out any suggestion that she was forcibly injected.'

'Have there been any such suggestions?'

'Not that I'm aware of, but I like to cover all the bases.'

'And net a wee defence post-mortem fee from the Legal Aid at the same time?'

Everyone's terribly touchy about legal aid money – until they find themselves in the dock and suddenly the defence preparations should be no-expense-spared; however, the Professor's concerns about the public purse were unfounded. The Scottish Legal Aid Board had long since stopped paying defence agents for attending autopsies.

'You're the only one getting paid here,' I assured him, 'but just because I don't get paid doesn't mean I stop being thorough. I'm not having the girl buried and then the Crown springing a surprise about her having been held down and jabbed with a syringe.'

'Cynical.'

'Experience is the mother of cynicism.'

'Hope your client appreciates you.'

Unlikely. My client, former boyfriend of the girl on the slab, was not one to express his gratitude for anything anyone did for him. He was a drug-dealing ned called Brandon Biggam, who'd gone out with Tanya Lang just long enough to introduce her to a raging heroin habit and knock her up, before disappearing off on yet another stretch for selling smack. That particular window of opportunity had allowed Tanya's family to get involved and book her into rehab. They didn't want the next generation arriving with withdrawal symptoms and looking for a fix; not the kind of rattling they had in mind for baby Lang. Tanya had been back in town less than a month when Brandon was released early from his sentence and now she was dead.

'I see she'd not long had a baby,' Professor Bradley said, reading from a clipboard.

'A wee boy,' I confirmed.

'Heroin addict with a young child? Social work nightmare. Is the kid okay?'

'Why? Are you looking for another post-mortem fee?'

'Touché.'

'The child is missing. You must be the only person in central Scotland who doesn't know. It's been all over the newspapers.'

'I try not to read them,' he said. 'So, can I take it your client is implicated in this young woman's untimely death?'

'The Crown say it's culpable homicide because he supplied her final fix. They're not happy because he's not helping them find the child.'

'Can't say I blame them. What's your client saying about it?'

'Nothing.'

The Professor snorted his derision at my client's decision to exercise his right to silence.

'All I'm interested in for now,' I told him, 'is showing that Tanya's death was no-one's fault but her own; although I wouldn't put it past the Crown to up the stakes anyway they can. If she has so much as a bruise on her they'll say it's evidence that she was forcibly injected. From there it's only a small step to allege that he did it so that he could abduct the child or something.'

'And did he?'

There is a popular misconception that accused persons make a clean breast of things to their lawyers. From my experience, guilty or innocent, criminal clients have the decency to provide their lawyer with a defence or at least a denial. I'm sure this is because there is an equally misconceived idea amongst guilty accused persons that a lawyer who thinks their client is innocent is going to try a lot harder than one who knows otherwise. Experienced defence lawyers don't really care and, in fact, would rather not know. Their interest is in the evidence and there was plenty of that to suggest Brandon Biggam had given his girlfriend the tenner bag that killed her, but none, so far, to suggest that he had intended to harm her or that he had abducted her son.

I shrugged in reply to the Professor's question.

He set down the clipboard. 'You must have an idea? I mean, it must have crossed your mind.'

'He tells me he doesn't know where the child is. Until he says otherwise I have a job to do and so do you.'

The Professor looked down at the body and sighed. 'So that's my remit, is it? Check for external traumata?'

'Recent bruising, grip marks, you know the sort of thing.'

If the defence could rule out any signs of force then I felt it was a reasonable argument to say that in supplying heroin to an experienced junkie, like Tanya, there had been no recklessness sufficient to prove a charge of culpable homicide and that what we were actually dealing with was a straightforward supply charge - notwithstanding Tanya's untimely demise. In that case, matters could proceed in the Sheriff and not the High Court. Brandon would plead guilty to social supply on the basis that Tanya knew what she was doing and the risks involved. Even though the court wouldn't ignore the consequences of Brandon's actions, neither could it pin Tanya's death on him.

Professor Bradley lifted an arm and commenced his examination, first visually and then running his hand over the skin, checking for contusions that might not have shown up as bruises if inflicted at the time of death. I took another step back and glanced over at the clock on the wall. I had custody cases calling at two and after that a trip to Polmont Young Offenders Institution, where Brandon Biggam had started his seven-day-lie-down the day before. He'd be up for full committal the following Monday. If I went to court armed with a favourable autopsy report from Prof. Bradley my client might be in with a remote chance of bail despite his horrendous record.

'There's no need for a detailed report at this stage,' I said. 'Just a few words to confirm what seems to be the obvious: self-inflicted heroin O.D.'

Prof. Bradley had started on the other arm. He stopped, looked over the top of his glasses at me. 'I'll tell you what seems *obvious* once I've finished my examination. What does the Crown expert say?'

'Won't get the report for weeks. That's why you're here. Anyway, I'll leave you to it. If you could fax me a letter ASAP that would be great.' I walked to the door, glad to be going and yet unable to resist a parting shot. 'You will send me a note of your fee won't you?'

'Don't worry,' the Professor said, moving on to inspect the neck area, 'and might I just say that I'd sooner have my job than yours – one meets a better class of person.'

Chapter 4

'Have you found that wean yet!'

On the way to the office next morning, I dropped by to see my dad. He might have been dying of 'flu but it didn't seem to have affected his vocal chords.

'No!' I yelled back at him. 'Where did you say the stock was?'

'The fridge!' I opened the refrigerator door and stared at the occupants of the white-walled cell: a block of cheese, a litre of milk and some eggs of an uncertain vintage. In many ways the contents were not dissimilar to my own; perhaps the cheese was less fusty.

'If it was me I'd have beaten it out of him by now!'

My dad, an ex-cop, liked to take an unwelcome interest in my clients and their cases and held old-school views on interview techniques.

'I can't see any stock in the fridge!'

'Not in the fridge! On top of it!'

I eventually found a Pyrex bowl under a tea towel in the middle of the kitchen table. It was filled with a semi-jelly of chicken stock, chunks of meat held fast like flies in amber.

'Just pour it into the pressure cooker and add the veg. And don't bother skimming the fat off the top – that's what gives it the taste!' he roared.

I went through to the livingroom where the old man was sprawled on the couch in a tartan dressing gown, a patchwork quilt about his burly shoulders.

'So what's the score with that dead lassie's wee boy?' he asked.

'Dad, let's get this straight. I'm not discussing my cases with you and I know how to make a pot of soup.'

'Aye,' he muttered through his normally bushy moustache that today was droopy and sorry-looking. 'So long as there's a tin-opener involved.'

'I should go to my work and let you starve.'

'On you go then. Away back to your baby-killer. Give me five minutes with him and I'd find out where his bairn was.'

There was no talking to him. I withdrew again to the kitchen and confronted the bowl of stock. I skimmed the layer of fat off the top, better in the bin than in his arteries.

'And barley! I like plenty barley in my soup!'

I chopped some turnip, leek and potatoes, rinsed the starch from half a mug of pearl barley and chucked it in as well or I'd never hear the end of it. Once it was all in the mix and I'd clicked the lid of the pressure cooker into place, I turned the gas on full and I turned my attention to the kettle which had just boiled.

'Where's my tea?' came the cry from the livingroom. You could have gone to Ceylon and picked the leaves yourself by now!'

'Sri Lanka.'

'What?'

'Nothing! It's just coming!'

I carried the tea through to him on a tray and saw him open his mouth to speak. 'Yes, I did warm the pot first.' He closed it again. Other than whisky the only other thing my dad would drink was tea and it had to be tea leaves. Not only that, but he had this thing about mugs – he didn't like them. He liked china cups. The problem with cups, though, was that they were too small and he always needed a second, which was a pity because, apparently, the second cup poured was never as good as the first. One day I'd spied a huge tea cup and saucer in a charity shop window. It held about a pint of tea and must have been intended as a novelty item. I'd bought it for a joke. My dad thought I was being serious and absolutely loved it.

'Robbie...?' he said, lifting the enormous cup from the equally enormous saucer and taking a sip, his voice quieter, more friendly now.

'No!'

'Aw go on. Just a drop. Help me sweat out the lurgy.'

From the couch I selected one or two of the throw cushions not being crushed under my dad's immense bulk and looked under them.

'What you doing?' he complained, as I shoved him over a bit and pulled a depleted whisky bottle out from where it was jammed between his side and the arm of the couch.

'I think you've been sweating enough. Do you never listen to what the doctor tells you?'

'The new boy? What does he know?'

Even my dad, whose ear was usually pretty close to the ground, didn't seem to have heard of Glen Beattie's recent court appearance.

I grabbed my coat. 'When the pot starts screaming, turn the gas down and let it simmer –'

'For twenty minutes. I know. I taught you how to

make soup - remember?'

'You're sure you'll be all right yourself?'

'I've never died a winter yet. And if you leave that bottle where it is I'll be in perfect company.'

'Not a chance. I'm taking it with me. I'll bring it back tonight when I've finished work. I'll make you a toddy.'

At the mere mention of putting hot water and honey in a precious Islay malt, my dad's face flushed and he collapsed into a fit of coughing that almost allowed me to make it to the door before he could bark out his next order. 'Bring a loaf of bread with you when you come back!' I slipped out but could still hear him shouting as I walked away. 'And make sure it's a plain loaf, none of that pan rubbish.'

Chapter 5

I arrived at the office, back of nine, to be confronted by my secretary, Grace-Mary, dressed in her usual work wear of tartan skirt, green twin-set and spectacles dangling from her neck on a gold chain.

'Nice of you to drop in,' she said. 'It's been like the Marie Celeste without the party atmosphere around here lately.'

Andy Imray, my former assistant, had been made an offer from a firm in Edinburgh and gone off to work there. I felt like a second division football team. Train up the player and just when he starts to bang in the goals, some big Club comes in and whisks him away on a Bosman. It meant that it was down to Grace-Mary to put the Co. in Munro & Co.

'The life of a court lawyer,' I said, sifting through the basket of mail that Grace-Mary presented to me each morning so that I could dig out anything red hot that needed my urgent attention. 'If I was always in the office and never out then we'd really be in trouble. Maybe we should get an office cat or I could always buy you a dog to keep you company.'

'That'll be right,' Grace-Mary said, 'I've enough to do clearing up behind you without house-training a puppy.' She plonked a stack of old files down on my desk. 'Where am I supposed to put these?' I lifted the letter that looked least like a bill from the basket and tilted my head at the corner of the room where bundles of closed files were stacked waist high, threatening to tip.

'Oh, no,' Grace-Mary said. 'If that lot falls over they'll kill someone. You need to spend some money and send all those old finished files away to storage.'

That wasn't going to happen; not even if the Law Society and Scottish Legal Aid Board had ganged up to set down regulations for file storage. Apparently, I was supposed to keep summary criminal matters for three years and solemn cases indefinitely, meaning a minimum of ten years. When they made storage costs a chargeable item on a legal aid account I might pay a warehouseman to keep my old files. Until then they were going no further than the corner of my room.

Grace-Mary tutted. 'I don't know what your clients think when they come in here and see all those old files piled sky-high.'

Most of my clients had more to worry about than the state of my room, the rest were too spaced-out to notice.

'Here.' Grace-Mary handed me a yellow-sticky, which, when not shouting at me, was my secretary's usual method of imparting important information.

'Dr Beattie? What's he want?'

'Didn't say.'

'I've hardly been on the case five minutes. I hope he's not expecting me to have done anything. Was there a message?'

Grace-Mary inhaled deeply, took the note from me and cleared her throat. 'Dr Beattie called,' she said in a clear, crisp voice. 'He would like you to go down to the surgery to see him sometime today. Urgent. That was the message.' She slapped the yellow-sticky into the palm of my hand. 'You can go after court.'

I reached for the court diary. 'Anything juicy?'

Grace-Mary knocked my hand away. She lifted the court diary and rapped it against the top of my computer monitor. 'It's all there in your electronic calendar. The one that I'm constantly updating while you insist on using this.' She waggled my big red paper diary at me accusingly, opened a drawer and threw it inside.

After all that, there was only one case in court. A client up on a charge of racist conduct. Grace-Mary fetched me the file from the cabinet and then went off to do something vitally important elsewhere. Court didn't start for forty-five minutes. Barring more traffic hold-ups, I had just enough time to finish my coffee, read over the case file and drive to court. I found the charge sheet. Sixty-two year-old Maureen Rooney was alleged to have contravened section 50(A) of the Criminal law (Consolidation) Act 1995. Maureen had been arguing with one of her neighbours whose children were forever leaving their toys on the communal path. There had been a slanging match, some words of ancient-Saxon origin were swapped, but the heinous crime for which my client had been summoned to court was describing her neighbour's children as, 'wee black toe-rags.' No big deal one might think, everyone with any common-sense knew that 'black' was often used to describe someone or something as being dirty or grubby, *I'll need to wash my hands, they're black from gardening,* but it was a mistake to confuse common-sense with Crown Office policy. The present dictat stated that Procurators Fiscal were to proceed to prosecution in all cases in which racism was even suspected and certain words used as adjectives; black being one of them. Zero-tolerance meant that not the police, the alleged victims or the Procurator Fiscal had any say in the matter. So keen in fact were the Lord Advocate and Parliament on the idea of people being convicted of racism, that section 50(A) had been introduced into Scotland, lifted from an English statute. Crown Office policy no longer distinguished men in white bed-sheets, pointy hats and carrying fiery crosses from elderly women having a barney with their next-door neighbours about their mucky children.

Grace-Mary returned carrying another wire-basket, this one full of freshly typed letters. 'And make sure your trial finishes before lunch,' she ordered. 'None of your showboat cross-examination. Just get on with it. Dr Beattie's a busy man. He'll have a two o'clock surgery and remember you've a visit booked for three o'clock at Polmont with that ned who killed his girlfriend. For goodness sake find out where the child is.' She placed the basket in front of me. 'These are all first class. Sign them before you go.' I took a pen from her and started to sign away. No need to check the letters, Grace-Mary didn't do typos.

'You'll have to lock up,' I said, dashing off a final scrawl. 'I've shopping to do for my dad.' I handed her back the basket. 'He's under the weather. The cold or he thinks it could be flu'.'

Grace-Mary recovered her pen before I could tuck it into the inside pocket of my jacket. 'He's a man,' she said. 'Trust me - it's the flu'.'

Chapter 6

There may have been a new courthouse, but some things about the administration of justice in West Lothian never seemed to change. One of those permanent features was Sheriff Albert Brechin, a man who tried to avoid using words like 'not' and 'guilty' in the same sentence.

'Let me guess, Mr Munro,' he sighed, as my elderly client was guided into the dock by the Bar Officer, 'your client adheres to her plea of not guilty?'

He knew me so well. 'That's correct,' I said and sat down again.

Sheriff Brechin turned to his right and looked down at the Procurator Fiscal depute. Joanna Jordan was a new recruit to the local Crown and Procurator Fiscal Service, young, keen and eager for scalps. With a convicter like Bert Brechin on the bench she'd have a whale of a time in West Lothian. 'And given the nature of the charge, no need to ask your position Madame Fiscal.'

'The matter will be going to trial later, M'Lord,' she confirmed to the man in the wig.

While the day's other cases were being called over, I had a chance for final discussions with my client in the corridor outside the courtroom. Maureen was determined to declare her innocence. 'I'm no' a racist Mr Munro. Anybody will tell you. I had a wee black girl living down the street from me for a while there, and she never got any hassle from me, even though she was a junkie, nae offence to the lassie, she's deid noo, but they were coming an' going at all hours and you know what it's like with junkies: you've got to keep your door locked or they'd steal the peas oot your mince. Anyway, that wee black neighbour of mine—'

'Tanya Lang?'I thought I'd recognised the address on Maureen's complaint.

'Aye, wee Tanya. Her boyfriend killed her I was telt. Anyway, I was always round there making sure she was all right. I used to put some silver in the wean's cot for luck, you know? Didn't do much good mind. The wee thing's gone, probably murdered, though how that could of happened with all they social workers and health visitors checking on her, I don't know. The point I'm trying to make...' I was glad to hear there was one, 'is that I had nothing against her, even if she was a Paki or whatever she was and let me tell you they get everything paid for them: rent, council tax, the lot. I told the police when they were door-to-dooring that the social workers better not be getting the blame. They did everything for that lassie. Even gave her a darkie health visitor. 'Course they should never let a junkie keep a wean. Wouldn't put it past some of them to sell their babies for drugs like the Africans, except they do it for food, poor souls—'

'Mrs Rooney, I think it's time for the trial,' I said. The court officer had opened the door to the courtroom and caught my eye. We walked into court, passing a few lawyers who were on their way out. Though we'd not actually talked tactics, I'd already decided that I was letting my client nowhere near the witness box.

All the other cases that morning had gone off for

one reason or another: non-appearances, missing witnesses or late guilty pleas, leaving Maureen's the only trial going ahead. Brechin looked grumpier than ever. No doubt he'd been clinging to the hope of an early finish and a chat with his chums over a brandy and soda at the New Club. He opened the front cover of his big blue notebook as though it were a slab of concrete. All going well, he'd be away by lunch-time and yet the job he was being paid a six figure sum a year to do seemed such an effort for him. Is that what being a Sheriff did to you? Listening to countless pleas-in-mitigation, presiding over summary trials where the offences libelled were often nothing more than examples of political incorrectness. I supposed it would take its toll on even the best-intentioned Sheriff. I looked up at Brechin. He slowly unscrewed the lid from his fountain pen and tested the nib on a corner of his notebook. No, I decided, he'd always been a tosser.

The first witness was Maureen's neighbour. She was a tired-looking woman, who could only have been in her early twenties. The cuffs of her trackie-top were frayed at the edges, like her nerves, I suspected, with three kids under seven to cope with and their father(s) AWOL.

According to my client, she and her neighbour were best of pals again and Maureen was once more helping out with baby-sitting, just as she had before the brief spat that had brought them to court. The mere fact that the neighbour no longer wished the prosecution to proceed made no difference to the Crown's position. Racism was racism, even when it wasn't, and had to be stamped out.

'And what colour are your children?' I asked the witness once she had been led reluctantly through her evidence in chief by the PF and it was my turn to cross-examine.

'Eh, white, I suppose,' the witness answered.

'All of them?'

A warning rumbled from the bench.

'Yes,' the witness replied.

'And all-over white – there are no wee bits of black anywhere?'

The Sheriff bellowed. 'Mr Munro!'

'Yes M'Lord?'

'Where do you think you are going with this insulting line of questioning?'

Hopefully, I was heading in the direction of a rare acquittal from his lordship. 'M'Lord, if it helps, there's no dispute over what my client said to this witness and as I understand it the witness gave as good as she got.' I looked to the young woman in the box. 'That's right isn't it? You called Mrs Rooney a nosy old cow didn't you.' She smiled coyly. 'And I don't suppose you thought you were being ageist or disrespectful to the Hindu faith?'

'That's quite enough, Mr Munro!' Sheriff Brechin's red face contrasted vividly with his white-starched collar and fall.

'This prosecution is ridiculous,' I said. 'My client is charged with racially motivated conduct which means that her remarks were intended to cause distress wholly or partly due to her neighbour's race or nationality.'

'Thank you for that dissertation Mr Munro, but you can take it that I am quite familiar with the provisions of section fifty A. I am the master of the law in these proceedings.'

'And master of the facts in the absence of a jury,' I countered. 'The fact that the witness has confirmed the colour of her children's skin must surely give your lordship cause for a reasonable doubt even at this early a stage.' I nearly added, 'for once in your life.'

'That's quite enough,' Brechin said. 'The test is a subjective not objective one and the time for speeches is after the evidence. Now are you finished with this witness or do you have any more *questions*?'

I had several more questions, all centring on the fact that my client's remarks about the blackness of her neighbour's children were not based on the melanin content of their epidermis, but the fact that they were a grubby bunch, a fact conceded by their mother on a kids-will-be-kids basis.

After evidence from a passer-by who'd heard the altercation, and because I wasn't letting Maureen loose to testify, it was time for closing speeches. The PF's summing-up was basically a case of saying to the Sheriff, *that's the evidence - I've done my job - now you do yours*. I simply reiterated my earlier remarks, only louder. Then we waited. Unless it was convicting or sentencing an accused, Sheriff Brechin always did things grudgingly. If he was granting bail it was with *great hesitation* or *against my better judgement*. Even after having presided over what was clearly an absurd prosecution he could only bring himself to return a not proven verdict *by the narrowest of margins.*

'What a farce,' the PF depute said across the table to me as the Sheriff rose from the bench and was led back to his chambers by the Bar Officer. 'Zero-effing tolerance. Just makes us all look stupid.'

'You've got a mind of your own,' I told her. 'You could have accepted a plea of not guilty.'

'Thinking for yourself is not Crown policy,' she said.

'What? You're not permitted to exercise your discretion even in a stupid case like this?'

'Exercise it? Not even allowed to let it warm up when it comes to racism.'

'But this wasn't racism,' I reminded her. 'This was about an elderly woman slagging off her neighbour's kids for being mocket.'

She dropped the folder containing her case papers into a big canvas satchel. 'I know that and you know that, but presumably the idiot at my office who marked the case didn't, and once a trial is set on a charge of racism it goes ahead, or else the trial depute can start looking for another job.

'As a matter of fact I'm looking for someone at the moment,' I said. 'My last assistant left to work in Edinburgh.'

'I know. Andy Imray. He was in my year at Uni.' She buckled the satchel, pulled on the straps. 'Yeah,' she smiled, 'he told me all about working for you.'

'Plenty of opportunity to exercise your discretion at Munro & Co.' I said. 'Just so long as you do what I tell you.'

She smiled. 'And the pension?'

'Non-existent,' I replied but you can keep all the brown envelopes you get - just so long as the client's on Legal Aid.

A voice behind me. 'You looking to get struck off?' I turned to see Paul Sharp. Today's tribute to the Sixties was a slim-fit grey suit over a white shirt with a rounded collar, the knot of a thin black tie held in place by a single gold bar.

The Bar Officer wanted to lock up the court, there being no more business that day, and we all walked out of the courtroom together. The young PF depute parted company with us in the hallway.

'Thanks,' I said to Paul as we stopped outside the agents' robing room and he held the door open for me.

'Think nothing of it. Manners are of more importance than the law.' He followed me in. 'So it can be done - a not guilty from Brechin?'

'It was a not proven and if I'd lost that case I'd have hung my gown up for good.' I threw Maureen Rooney's case file onto the big table in the centre of the room. 'New court: same old Sheriff. Brechin's a joke. He should have bombed that case out from the start, instead he let it run on just in case he could think up a reason to convict that the Appeal Court wouldn't kick into touch.'

'That wouldn't be hard,' Paul said. 'Pushing against the allegorical open door there. Talk about bending over backwards to uphold a conviction? The Lord President could limbo under a lavvy door.'

They called it murmuring judges and it was a criminal offence, but criticising the judiciary was a popular everyday pastime for the average criminal lawyer.

I took off my gown and rolled it up. 'I mean, what's the point of having a Sheriff when all he does is rubber stamp whatever the Fiscal puts in front of him?'

'All that is necessary for evil to triumph is for good men – or women – to do nothing.'

'You don't say? Why is it you're still here? Have you not more important things to do than follow me around quoting Edmund Burke?'

Paul removed his jacket and folded it carefully across his arm. The sleeves of his white shirt were encircled at the bicep by a pair of gold, elasticated armbands. I remembered my dad used to have a set when I was a boy. He kept them in a little blue cardboard box that was embossed with a gold Crown on the front and only wore them on special occasions. Whenever I tried them on they kept slipping off. I hadn't seen a pair in nearly thirty years.

Paul draped his jacket over the back of a chair, sat down and jerked a thumb at the notice-board. In between the usual circulars and notices was an advert. It was headed: Judicial Appointments Board for Scotland.

'What about it?' I asked.

'I need referees.'

'You? A Sheriff?'

'They're looking for ten new ones. One hundred and thirty K per annum, a pension you'd have trouble spending and tons of holidays, I mean, writing days.'

'You're serious? You're actually going to apply?'

'Yeah? Why don't you?'

'Same reason sane people don't do the lottery – and, anyway, you're way too young.'

'They made Mandy Morrow a Sheriff at my age and now she's being touted for a temp Judge.'

'You are aware that she used to be a Fiscal and her dad is the Crown Agent?'

'Are you saying that's not just a coincidence?' Paul adopted a look of mock horror.

'I'm saying that a defence lawyer who makes it to the bench is usually either related to someone in the judiciary or is the owner of some highly dubious photographic material of someone who is.'

'Can I put you down as one of my three referees?'

I could almost hear the bottom of the barrel being scraped. Fact was Paul would have made an excellent Sheriff. 'Sure. Better put me last, though maybe they won't read that far.'

'I've only got you and Sheriff Dalrymple so far, but thanks and, you know, you should seriously think about it.'

I shook my head. No chance. I enjoyed my independence too much. Being my own boss.

My phone buzzed. The office. Grace-Mary. 'On my way,' I said.

Chapter 7

Down at Dr Beattie's surgery I was confronted by a hatched-faced receptionist for whom a see-the-doctor-without-an-appointment scenario clearly didn't compute. She studied the big diary for my name.

'No,' you're definitely not in here,' she said, as though I had argued otherwise.

'Yes. I know. I don't want to see the doctor—' She snapped the diary shut as though my head were between its heavy covers. '*He* wants to see *me*.'

There were a few remarkably fit-looking patients sitting behind me and I could hear them shift in their seats at the very idea I might be trying to jump the queue.

'Dr Beattie called me this morning. I'm sure it won't take a moment. If you could just let him know I'm here.'

An elderly man got up and shuffled forward to join me at the counter. 'I've got the first appointment - two o'clock,' he said, pulling a screwed-up tissue from his pocket and blowing his nose lest he be taken for a malingerer.

The receptionist stared from the old man to me and then opened the diary again. 'I can give you half-four on Friday.' She flicked over a few pages in rapid succession. 'If that's no good we're well into next week.'

The old guy sneezed. Some if it hit his tissue. Suddenly I realised why there was a glass partition between patients and staff. As I recoiled from the airborne germ attack, the door to my left opened and out came the doctor wearing corduroy trousers, a soft-cotton shirt open at the neck and a tweed jacket with leather elbow-patches. Only the stethoscope slung over one of his shoulders suggested he was a doctor and not a teacher dodging double geography.

'Good afternoon, Mr Munro,' he said, holding the door open for me. 'Come through will you?' He caught sight of the old guy, tissue clamped pathetically to his nose. 'Mr Jamieson, I'm sorry to keep you waiting.' The doctor tilted his head at me. 'Bit of an emergency case.' The old man took a step away from me as though I might be highly-infectious and blew again, loudly, into his soggy tissue. Beattie turned to the receptionist. 'Nancy, see if Mr Jamieson would like a glass of water. It's always best to keep up your fluid balance when you're poorly.' With that, he smiled around at the other patients and ushered me down the corridor to his examination room.

'Thanks for coming,' he said once the door was closed and we were seated.

'No problem,' I assured him. 'I have to say, I wasn't sure if you'd be back at work.'

He grunted. 'I'm hanging on in there, although I am expecting a call from the General Medical Council at any moment. I may be presumed innocent in the eyes of the law, but it's likely I'll be suspended until my guilt or innocence is finally decided.' He sighed. 'Until then I still have patients to see. Word doesn't seem to have spread yet about my court appearance. I'm hoping it stays that way.'

Not much chance of that, I feared. 'Anyway,' I said, 'while I'm here could I have a word with you about my dad?'

'He drinks too much and needs to alter his diet.'

'I know. I keep telling him—'

'I really wanted to talk about my case.'

I had nothing new to tell him. 'The High-Tech crime unit are examining your computer equipment right now. I'm afraid we'll have to wait for the results.'

He looked at me, his face a mixture of dejection and disbelief. 'Mr Munro, Robbie, I want to assure you that there can be no indecent pictures on my home computer.' He said it quite aggressively, like I was the person bringing the charges against him. 'Sorry.' He leaned back in his chair and pressed the knuckles of his clasped hands against his forehead.

'I know how difficult this must be for you,' I said, 'but we have to wait until all the evidence has been disclosed so we know exactly what we're up against. Until then speculating about the Crown case is really a waste of time – and of your money,' I added, to remind him that Munro & Co. wasn't a charitable institution.

'But what if they do find images on my PC? I know they can't but what if they do?'

We were going round in circles. Still, I'd warned him and, if he wanted to play guessing games at two hundred an hour, I was his man. 'Let's look at some possible ways images might have ended up on your PC. Do you have a family?'

Beattie shook his head. 'I live with my partner. Megan's the reason I came to Linlithgow. I'm from Conan Bridge in Ross-shire. I studied in Aberdeen and worked there until I came down to Edinburgh to take a diploma in public health. I met Megan at a conference. We hit it off straight away. We'd only been on a few dates and I tried to impress her by taking her to a production of L'étoile by Chabrier. That's an opera,' he spelled out for me because I had no idea what he was talking about. 'I loved it, she hated it, and afterwards we moved in together; on the understanding,' he laughed, 'that I never take her to the opera again. When Doctor MacGregor died, Megan suggested that I apply to replace him. And here I am. Great job, great girl and about to go to prison.'

'You live with your girlfriend?'

'Fiancée. We rent a place in Edinburgh, take the train into work together every morning. She's a health visitor based here in the surgery.'

'Very cosy.'

'We like it. Or, should I say, liked it? Megan's left me. When I got home from court on Monday afternoon she was gone. I don't even know where she's staying. She left her father a message saying she'd be gone for a while and telling him to make sure I stayed away from her.'

'Could she be the one who tipped-off the police about images on your PC?'

'I've already told you there were no—'

'Perhaps she misunderstood. Do your diploma studies include any aspect of paediatrics?'

'I think Megan would know the difference between a medical photograph and a porn picture. She is a paedophile after all - if you use the proper meaning of the word - a lover of children. Anyway, all my work is on my laptop, I seldom use the PC except for my home email.'

'And what about your laptop. You said the cops took it away too.'

'Yes, that's a real bugger, because it's got all my public health qualification data on it. I've a twenty-five thousand word dissertation to present at the end of the year.'

'Could there be anything incriminatory on that?'

'Definitely not.'

'Not even accidentally? You don't, for instance, surf the net between patients?'

'Mr Munro, I don't have time to surf the net between patients.' He jumped to his feet, crossed the room and opened the door wide so that I could see down the length of the hallway to the sickly folk who were probably wondering what the hold-up was. 'You've seen my waiting room. I can assure you that my laptop is used for work purposes only. There's no way there can be any illegal images on it.' He sighed 'Mr Munro... you believe me when I say I'm innocent don't you?'

After a few years in my job, you begin to realise that a belief in a client's guilt or innocence is an irrelevant detail. I gave him the reassuring smile that was all part of the service for one of Munro & Co's private fee-paying clients. 'Of course I do.'

'Then why is this happening? I'm a doctor. The police, the prosecuting authorities, they must know what effect allegations of this type will have on my career.'

I could understand his concern. Personally, I was all

for castrating convicted paedos, but I also knew that the hint of a rumour was sufficient to convict an accused in the eyes of the general public. The Procurator Fiscal's petition, even if it never led to a formal indictment, was the equivalent of the pointing finger and cries of *witch, witch* from the middle-ages. Once the accusation was made, the result was pretty much inevitable whether the accused sank to the bottom or floated to the top of the judicial duck pond. For a family doctor like Beattie, it was game over.

I glanced at the clock on the wall. I had a prison visit in under an hour and still had to walk back to the office to collect the file, drive the seven miles or so to Polmont and book in. I got up to leave.

'Robbie, I do have one theory.'

I sat back down.

'I take it you know who Megan's father is?'

The new doctor had only set up practice in the town a couple of months before. I had unread mail on my desk that was older than that. Why he should assume that I'd be familiar with his ex-girlfriend's family tree, I didn't know.

'Kenneth McIvor.'

'The Justice Secretary?' I knew Kenny McIvor all right. Everyone in the town did. He was Linlithgow born and bred. Though McIvor hadn't lived in the town for many years, he still declared his undying allegiance to the Royal Burgh and his grip on the local electorate was such that his Linlithgow constituency was considered the safest of seats. The smart money was on him to become First Minister now that the present incumbent was stepping down to take a seat on the

Board of the European Commission. The contest for leadership of the party was on-going, a straight fight between McIvor and his colleague, Angus Pike.

'I think you should know that Kenny's not too happy about me instructing you,' Beattie said. 'He says it's too potentially high-profile. Doesn't want it turned into some kind of three ring circus. His words not mine.'

Kenny McIvor needn't have worried. People knowing that you act for paedophiles wasn't a particularly effective form of advertisement. Who wanted to be seen going into the offices of the *beasts' lawyer*? 'Believe me,' I said, 'I'll be trying to keep things as low-profile as I possibly can.'

He seemed happy enough with that. 'Good. If word gets out, I'm finished here. I know that. Even suspicion is enough to put paid to my future in the town and, given my relationship to him, it's likely to be a major blow to Kenny's political prospects as well.'

That must have been what Hugh Ogilvie, the Procurator Fiscal was going on about. He was putting a lid on Beattie's case, the *circumstances* being the ensuing bad publicity were word of the case to leak out. It wouldn't do Ogilvie's career any harm to have aided the Justice Secretary in this small but important way.

'Kenny tells me the Authorities have agreed to keep things under wraps for the moment,' Beattie said. 'However, if I'm convicted, it's open season. Do you think—'

'That he might put in a good word for you? Get the charges dropped? Risky for him, given his position, but definitely worth a try.'

'No - that someone is out to get me because of our connection?'

'What do you mean?'

'Politics is a dirty game.'

'Oh, you mean throw mud at you and hope some of it sticks to your prospective father-in-law? Seems unlikely. If someone's planting evidence, why not plant it on him?'

'Because I'm an easier target.'

'But you're not related to the man, may never be, and, even if the prosecution does continue, the leadership contest is only a few weeks away. Your trial won't take place for months.'

Beattie ruffled his hair furiously with both hands. 'I'm sorry. I know it must sound to you like a mad conspiracy theory. I've hardly had any sleep, racking my brains, and that's the only thing I can come up with.'

I sympathised. 'There's no point getting all worked up about things. You say the cops won't find any images. Maybe the whole thing's a terrible mistake, a technical glitch, a malicious prank.'

He smiled. That was probably all he'd asked me to come see him for; reassurance. A crumb of comfort to sustain him over the weeks, months of uncertainty to follow. 'Thanks. I'll just have to keep telling myself that.'

He stood up, a signal that our meeting was over.

'Before you go,' he said, 'is there anything you can do? I really need my laptop back as soon as possible.'

I told him I'd do my best, although I knew that he was liable to be in for a long wait.

'Which reminds me.' He opened a drawer in his desk and brought out a small but very thick Olivetti computer notebook. 'It was only after the police left that I remembered this. Dr. MacGregor's old laptop. He kept it in the safe.' Beattie opened the lid and blew dust out of the keyboard. 'It's pretty antiquated. I've never even switched it on. Do you think I should tell the police? They did ask for any laptops that were in the surgery, but I never even thought of this. When I came here there was only one laptop in use. It was quite new and so I just started using it. There wasn't much on it, just Doc Mac's NHS email account and some patient data about drug trials, that sort of thing, and now, of course, my dissertation.'

I took the old laptop from him. 'I better have it examined.'

'Why?'

For one thing it made it look like I was actually doing something. If Beattie's pseudo-father-in-law was keen to instruct some other lawyer, it wouldn't do my chances any harm if I could show that I was taking a proactive roll. 'Assuming the search of your laptop is negative, the police might come back,' I said.

'But it belonged to Dr MacGregor.'

'You're charged with possessing indecent images of children. Doc Mac's dead. You're the person in possession,' I brandished the laptop at him, 'of whatever is inside here.'

'But why have it examined?'

'If it's clean – great. If it's not, even better. We use that to our advantage.'

'In what way?'

In a pin-the-blame-on-the-dead-guy sort of a way was what I meant. I explained. 'Let's say it might open up a possible defence of incrimination.' *Straws and how to clutch them by Robbie Munro.* 'The main thing is that you take the initiative away from the police. You don't want them coming back and finding you in possession of anything remotely incriminating, especially if it looks like you hid it from them when they first came.'

'If you think it's for the best.' He rummaged in the drawer and pulled out a power cable. He coiled it around his hand and held out to me. 'How quickly can you have it done?'

'I'll get onto it straight away.' I asked him about the screen and keyboard on his desk.

'The computer terminals here all run off a network server. Nothing on there except patient records.'

'But you can still access the internet?'

'When I have to – for professional reasons. No surfing the net between patients,' he added, which seemed to remind him that his surgery should have started twenty minutes ago.

'My fees,' I said. 'I take it the Medical Defence Union is picking up the tab?'

'Yes, I'll have to intimate the claim to them. Sorry, should have done it by now. Money is the least of my worries at the moment.'

I loved it when people said that. The only problem was that, after the other worries had disappeared, I noticed how money suddenly became very important again and I was perturbed to hear that my work to date had not been covered by the MDU.

'There'll be some initial outlays,' I said. 'Expert fees,

that sort of thing.' I held up the ancient laptop. 'Could you let me have, say, a thousand up front?'

I'd no sooner said the words than he was dashing off a cheque in a clear, bold, most undoctor-like hand. He tore it out of the book and handed it to me. 'What age are you?'

'Thirty-five.'

'That's right,' he said, as though perhaps I'd just made a guess at it. 'I was reading your medical notes before you came in – there's not many of them.'

'That's good isn't it?'

'Y complained to Dr MacGregor about an irregular heart-beat and then – nothing. No further appointments, no referral to a consultant, no ECG - he didn't even send you along to a Well Man clinic.'

'I stopped drinking coffee for a couple of weeks and cut down on chinkies, I mean, Chinese food. I read somewhere that too much monosodium glutamate could make your heart go a bit funny. Seemed to work.'

'Good, very good,' he said absently, studying me closely. 'Tell me, what weight are you?'

'Difficult to say really.' At least it was if you never weighed yourself.

He glanced to the corner of the room where there was a set of serious looking scales.

'Look, I've really got to be going and I know you've a lot of sick people to see.'

'They can wait a little longer.' He took my elbow and encouraged me towards the scales. 'Step on. This will only take a moment.'

Chapter 8

When not supplying illegal drugs, though largely because of it, Brandon Biggam spent a lot of time in Polmont Young Offenders Institution, on the outskirts of Falkirk, and just because he was locked in a cell with his own games console, didn't stop business as usual.

Contrary to popular belief, there are no Godfather type figures in prison, living in penthouse cells, surrounded by soft furnishings and piling up cash from sales of drugs and tobacco. Drugs are, it's true, widespread, entering the system by various means: brought in by visitors, bent screws or up the backsides of those recently sentenced; however, very little money changes hands in prison. There's not a lot of it around. Payment for drugs supplied inside is collected on the outside from the prisoner's nearest and dearest. That's when an inmate knows who his friends are, because there are other means of settling debts - not all of which come approved by the Financial Services Ombudsman.

I was shown upstairs to where Brandon was already waiting for me in one of the glass-fronted interview rooms.

'S'appening?' he asked.

'First things first, Brandon. Where is he?'

'The wean? I wish you'd stop going on about it.'

'If you know where the baby is, anything you tell me is strictly confidential. If need be I'll make an anonymous call to the social work—'

'Tanya's mam probably took it. Fear't I'd want custody or something. Ask her. I'm not interested in the wean. What I want to know is when I'm getting out.'

'Not for a while whatever happens,' I said. 'Even if everything goes to plan, you're stuffed so far as a supply charge is concerned. They've got digital scales and a tick list from your house and then there's the wrap found in Tanya's flat: the cling-film is a match for a section ripped off a roll in your kitchen.'

'Supplying? That's nothing. Just do what you did the last time.'

Brandon's last sentence had been for drug supplying too. I'd done a deal with the P.F. so that he pled guilty to social supply rather than commercial and for a shorter time period than originally libelled. It had led to a much shorter than expected sentence, helped by the fact that Sheriff Brechin was off on a writing day and they'd drafted in a floater.

'This is different than the last time,' I told him. 'The Fiscal is still trying for culpable homicide, saying you should have known that by giving Tanya heroin she might O.D.'

'I just gave her a tenner bag. I thought she was going to sell it on.'

'But if you were there when she took the hit—'

'I wasnae.'

'Well, if the Crown accepts that, maybe they will drop it to supply only.'

'When?'

'It's not guaranteed. But, if it happens, you'll not go to the High Court, you'll go guilty in the Sheriff Court and get a discount for an early plea.'

'How long'll I get?'

'Depends a lot on who the Sheriff is. Of course, if I could give the Crown the baby safe and sound it would make things a lot easier. The cops are taking heavy flak about it.'

He leaned forward, arms folded on the table between us. 'How the hell do I know where it is?'

'Because you were one of the last two people to see it, him, alive and the other person is dead. Tell me where he is and I'm sure I can cut you a great deal.'

'How many times do I have to tell folk?' The prisoner threw himself back against the chair, snarling, pretending to pull his hair out. He was either telling the truth or baby Lang was dead and buried somewhere.

'Might make it easier for you in here too. Are you getting a hard time about Tanya and the baby?'

Brandon looked at me and crossed his eyes. 'Eh, naw.'

I hadn't really thought so. It was generally true that those charged with harming woman and children didn't have a happy time inside and had to seek out the sanctuary of the protection wing, but that was because most beasts were loners, often first offenders, inadequate individuals, unused to prison and ideal targets for those who needed little excuse to rip the face off someone. With a smuggled two-inch screw from the workshop, a plastic tooth brush handle and some welding with a cigarette lighter, it was child's play to fashion a highly effective chib. Prisoners like Brandon Biggam, however, could have murdered the contents of a school bus and then raped the mums on the PTA for all the difference it would have made to their security in prison. Brandon was connected. He wasn't Mr Big by any means, but half his gang were inside Polmont with him and the other half on the outside selling smack. A beast was only a beast if he was vulnerable. Mess with the likes of Brandon Biggam, even with the best of intentions that a warped prison mind-set could provide, and the hyenas would soon surround you and you'd be collecting bits of your body from the floor by lock-down.

Visits to Polmont were booked in advance and in short supply. Time slots of half an hour were the norm and by the time I'd been processed through security, sat in the waiting room for a while and been led to the interview rooms upstairs in the new wing, I had about fifteen minutes left to speak to my client.

The door partially opened and a screw stuck his head through the gap to give a five minute warning. I thought I might as well have another bash at the mystery of the missing baby. 'Do you have any idea where your son is?' I thought that by reminding him I was talking about his own flesh and blood he might show some signs of interest, though the last thing I wanted was him telling me the kid was at the bottom of Linlithgow Loch in a weighted-down carrier bag.

'You're worse than the cops,' he said.

'How was he the last time you saw him?'

'Okay, I'll say it one more time. Write it down so you don't forget. Tanya phoned me wanting money for nappies or something. I went round. I gave her a tenner bag and told her to sell it and buy nappies with that. I think the wean was there but I cannae mind exactly. Geordie Lyon was wi' me. We were only there two minutes and then went back to his place. Geordie will go a witness to that.'

I knew Geordie Lyon. He was an outrageous smack-head with a readily identifiable Brillo-pad of frizzy, ginger hair and, as such, a regular at court for anything from shoplifting to housebreaking. Whenever they needed to print Geordie's schedule of previous convictions they had to chop down a tree. In the witness box his testimony would be about as credible and reliable as an MP's expenses claim form.

'Hopefully, we'll not need to trouble Geordie,' I said. 'Once I hear back from the pathologist I'll talk to the Fiscal about taking a plea to a supply charge.'

'Tell the PF if he drops it to a supply I'll sign the section right now.'

Section 76 of the Criminal Procedure (Scotland) Act 1995 allowed an accused to speed up the prosecution process, if he intended to plead guilty, by the signing of what was known as a section 76 letter. Obviously, Brandon was thinking that if he was going to serve a sentence he'd do it with the perks that came with convicted prisoner status, rather than staying banged-up twenty-three hours a day on remand; even with SKY TV and a PlayStation.

'Have they buried Tanya yet?' he asked.

'Her body's not been released.'

A final rap on the glass of the door. The screw opened the door. 'Biggam. This way.'

Brandon kicked the leg of the table. 'Trust that stupid bitch to die on me. 'Can you get me out for the funeral? Better than being stuck in here.'

'Tell me where the baby is, and if he's okay, I bet I

could get you out of here tomorrow on bail.'

He pointed a finger in my face. 'I'm warning you.'

Ah, clients. You didn't have to like them: you just had to do your best for them.

Chapter **9**

At the tender age of thirty-five, I couldn't remember a time before computers - but that didn't mean I had to like them. I'd seen what recent I.T. upgrades had done to the courts and prosecution service; half the work done in double the time. The only allowances I'd made at Munro & Co. were internet access and the introduction of email. As far as I was concerned that was the top of a very slippery silicon slope. Which meant that, on matters involving information technology, I was forced to turn to the experts.

'What exactly am I looking for?' asked ex-Detective Constable Jimmy Garvie, once, and briefly, of Lothian & Borders High-Tech Crime Unit, now I.T. gun-for-hire. We were sitting in Bistro Alessandro, better known to its patrons as Sandy's Café. Dr MacGregor's prehistoric laptop was sitting between us on one of the small, round, rubberwood tables. Jimmy was not much older than me, dressed like my dad and smiled about as often as he put his hand in his pocket.

'What do you think you're looking for?' I said. 'Dirty pictures of children, of course.'

'On this? You'll be lucky.' He turned the old Olivetti laptop this way and that, checking the sides and underneath. 'There's no Wi-Fi, no slot for a PCMCIA card, not even a port for an external modem.'

I let that wave of jargon drift on by.

'How do you expect to download pornographic

images if you don't have access to the internet?'

An elderly couple at the next table bent their heads in our direction.

'Just check it, will you?' I said.

'Whose is it?'

'The owner is dead and the new owner wants to make sure there's nothing funny on it.'

'Why? He's not going to use it is he? It's a piece of junk.'

'Jimmy,' I said. 'You're not a cop any more so you can stop asking stupid questions and leave that to us lawyers. Just take the back off this thing and run it through your scanner or whatever it is you do.'

It was always a good idea when dealing with experts to sound like you hadn't a clue; something, to be fair, that wasn't difficult for me to do where computers were concerned. Start sounding knowledgeable and I've found your average anorak can become a tad touchy.

'Okay. Okay. I'll give the hard-drive the once-over with EnCase and see what we come up with.'

Sandy materialised, tea towel draped over a shoulder.

'So, what-a-you-having, boys?' he asked, deploying his best faux Italian accent; mid-morning the place was busy and he liked to keep up appearances. He took a spiral notepad from his breast pocket and a pencil from behind his ear.

Jimmy unscrewed a small plate from the base of the computer. 'Coffee,' he said, not looking up from his work, 'and a Danish - peach if you've got one.'

'If I've got one?' Sandy smiled smugly and glanced

over at his beloved and well-stocked cake stand. All chrome and glass it looked like a penthouse for pastries.

'And let me see, Robbie. You'll have...' He pressed two fingers against his temple and closed his eyes. 'Americano, two shots of espresso, and a crispy bacon roll. Just the one do you?' He jotted down the order, ripped it off his pad and laid it on the table.

Jimmy looked at the bill and turned to me, screw driver in one hand, laptop in the other. 'Could you get that, Robbie? I've got my hands full, here.'

'Actually, Sandy,' I said, remembering my visit with Dr Beattie and the results of my weigh-in, 'I think I'll just have a mineral water. In fact out of the tap is fine.'

Sandy looked at me and blinked hard. 'Water?'

Sandy pushed the notepad back into his shirt pocket. He swished his pencil around in the air. 'No coffee?'

'No, you see —'

'No nothing. You want water go swim in the loch.'

'All right, all right. I'll have a cup of tea.'

Sandy sniffed. 'What about the bacon roll? I got the stuff you like, Ayrshire. Crisps up so much you could cut your tongue if you're not careful.'

'I'm not sure,' I said.

'Not sure? It's all you ever eat.'

It was true. When I thought of the number of pigs that had laid down their lives...

Sandy returned the pencil to behind his ear. He laid a hand on each of my shoulders and stared into my eyes. 'Is something wrong?'

'No,' I said, 'It's just that...' I patted my stomach.

'What?' exclaimed, Sandy. 'You're not fat. Your bones are big. You need to keep your energy levels up, boy. You can't get folk the jail on an empty stomach.'

I relented. 'I'll have toast. Okay? But not too buttery.'

Sandy looked down at his notebook and shrugged. 'Okay. Tea and toast it is. The customer, even you, Robbie, is always right.'

'How's your dad?' Jimmy asked, after Sandy had sloped off to the kitchen. Was there a cop in the land, even one who'd served for only a few years before discovering the Force was not a route to riches, who didn't know ex-police sergeant Alex Munro?

'Dying—'

Jimmy stopped working at the laptop. 'What?'

'Of the flu'. He is managing to keep his fluid balance up though.'

Jimmy tapped the side of his nose with a finger. 'The water of life. It doesn't cure a cold but it fails more agreeably than anything else. Which of the eight sisters of Islay is he favouring this weather?'

'The most unpronounceable.'

'Ah,' said Jimmy returning to his work, 'Bunnahabhain. Your old man always had an educated taste in malts.'

Jimmy slotted the hard disk from Dr MacGregor's laptop into a cradle device and connected it to his own laptop. Using EnCase Forensic software an image of the doctor's hard disk was taken, the beauty of it being that, for evidential purposes, while that image could be examined for incriminatory data files, no deletions could be made from it nor any new files added. The whole process took only a few minutes and was over by the time Sandy returned with our refreshments.

'I'll just have my coffee, then I'll stick the hard drive back in the laptop and you can take it away again,' Jimmy said. 'I'll run some tests on the EnCase image, see what's on it and let you have a report in the next few days. How's that sound?'

Before I could answer, Sandy returned. He set down a mug of coffee and a side plate in front of me. On the plate was a bacon roll. 'Tea and toast,' he laughed. 'Nearly had me there.'

I lifted the top half of the roll. The lid had been lightly-fried in the bacon fat.

'Something wrong?' Sandy asked.

'Obviously,' I said, handing him back the plate. 'You've forgotten the brown sauce.'

Chapter 10

My dad was still under the weather and in his place I'd gone to visit his pal, Vince Green, who had cancer and was now resident at St Gideon's, a privately-run hospice set in the West Lothian countryside between Linlithgow and Edinburgh; a sort of VIP departure lounge for the terminally-ill. Apparently, Vince's twenty-two years of being bitten by sand-flies in Belize and shot at by the Provo's hadn't been a complete waste of time because his Army insurance was footing what had to be some pretty extravagant care costs. Vince was my dad's best mate and had been since they were boys. He was a rubber ball of man and, as a child, to see Vince come bouncing down the garden path to our house always meant big laughs and a pocketful of sweets. It was quite a shock to think of him as ill. He'd seemed cheery enough during my visit, although obviously tired and drained. We chatted for the best part of an hour, mostly about my dad or football, and I'd laughed uncomfortably at the wee man's brave attempts to make light of his situation.

I was strolling back to my car when I heard the click of high heels behind me and turned to see the hospice's chief administrator coming through the gloom of the small car park, dimly lit by two rows of ornate wrought iron lampposts. I'd met Fiona Scott before, at some of the charity do's my dad and Vince used to help organise to raise funds for another local hospice, St

Michael's, a charitable organisation, and to which events I was usually dragged along and made to buy raffle tickets and cakes of tablet. Designer clothes, perfect hair: Fiona Scott, like St Gideon's, presented the glamorous side of palliative care. The administrator was forty and extremely foxy.

'Vince seems in good spirits,' I said after I'd let her catch up with me. How long... how long do you expect...'

'Him to live?'

'To be here, I was going to say.'

'It's the same thing.'

'He won't be going home?'

'No chance.'

'But his treatment. He said it was helping.'

'He isn't getting treatment. Palliative care only. That's why he's here. This is a hospice.' She smiled patronisingly, as though she knew there was a village somewhere missing an idiot.

'How long has he got?'

'Has he family?'

Vince had a daughter, Jill, who had been in the year below me at school. She'd only been in her early teens when her mum up and emigrated to Canada, but old enough to know that she wanted to stay in Scotland. Teenagers, I knew from experience – I used to be one - could be very reactionary. They liked to think they were cutting edge in fashion and music and ready to change the world, but ask them to up sticks and leave their pals behind and suddenly it's all tears and slamming doors. So, instead of taking the route to the Rockies with her mum, Jill had stayed behind with her dad and gone on to study pharmacy at Heriot-Watt University. She now lived and worked in Edinburgh.

'He's got a daughter.'

'Oh, yes, I think I've met her.'

'And an ex-wife in Canada.'

'Then,' she said cheerily, 'I'd tell her not to delay booking a flight.'

I wasn't convinced the former Mrs Green would be jetting across the North Atlantic anytime soon. Jill, I knew, visited frequently, as did my Dad.

Fiona Scott took a car key from her handbag.

'Does Vince know?' I asked, as she pressed the key and a nearby yellow sports-hatchback squawked in reply, orange indicator lights flashing. It was small, fast and French and parked next to my beat up, ancient Alfa. 'Does he know he's not long to live? Has anyone told him? He seemed so well tonight. I thought, maybe, he was in remission or something.' I suddenly realised how little I knew about mankind's great killer.

Fiona sighed. 'Mr Green is a trooper. He has good days and bad days. It's the job of my people to make sure there are more good than bad. She gave me a friendly punch on the shoulder. 'It's tough. Don't worry. We'll take good care of him.' She turned to her car and then to me again. 'Glen Beattie - I hear talk, you know what Linlithgow is like, Chinese whispers: *send three and four-pence we're going to a dance.*' She was talking quickly now. The cheery note, as she had suggested Vince's ex-wife book a flight to his funeral, had been replaced by a tight, nervous giggle. 'What's the goss?'

I shrugged apologetically. I assumed she knew that

I was Beattie's lawyer and should have known I couldn't discuss his case. I changed the subject to the sudden demise of Dr. MacGregor.

'Yes, Doc Mac was quite a character. It's certainly a loss.' She made it sound as though he was simply one less medical bean for her to count. 'But Doctor Beattie...' she moved closer, leaning in. I could smell her perfume. 'I've heard rumours,' she whispered, 'about child-pornography and there was something in the papers, not the local rag, I think it was The Scotsman. No name was mentioned just that it was a Linlithgow man and putting two and two together... is it true?'

I couldn't deny it and if I said nothing then she'd infer the truth anyway.

'I'm a friend. I'd ask him myself,' she added before I could make that very suggestion, 'but it's not the sort of thing one brings up over coffee and a bun and, anyway, I'm sure it's not true. What confused me even more though was that the newspaper said that Glen, or whoever it was, had made no plea and I wondered why. If he's not guilty, why wouldn't he just come out and say so?'

'It's not what you think. At the outset of a serious case an accused isn't asked to tender a plea of guilty or not guilty. When an accused makes no plea it just means that there are no preliminary objections, say, to the competency or relevancy of the charge. I don't think the newspapers actually know that's what it means, they just print it.'

She looked troubled. 'Is it true then? Has Glen been charged?'

'How well do you know him?' I asked.

'Small town, same profession, we talk back and forth.'

'A pleasant change from Doc Mac?' I took the conversation down a slip-road again.

'Bill MacGregor was quite a character, but a good doctor nonetheless.'

'I didn't mean to speak ill. My dad wouldn't hear a bad word, still, when it comes to bedside manners, I suppose Dr Beattie might be more to many people's liking, don't you think?'

She didn't answer, just smiled and opened the door of her car, careful not to bash it against mine. When I asked questions in court I was always on the lookout for the slightest change in a witness's demeanour. It was part of my job to discern any crack in the evidence that I could prise open in search of a reasonable doubt. I felt sure that with Fiona my comments had struck a raw nerve.

She sat down sideways in the driver's seat and put the keys in the ignition, bringing the car headlights and sound system to life.

'What's the chances of Vince getting home? Even for a wee a while?' I asked over the strains of a soprano belting out a song I'd never heard in a language I didn't know.

'Chances?' Fiona cast a glance at my car. 'About the same, I should think...' she swung her shapely legs inside, 'as you getting that heap through its next MOT.'

Chapter 11

The Crown had asked me to agree the evidence of Thomas Fairbairn, Tanya Lang's grand-father and witness in the case against Brandon Biggam. I'd been sent a draft Joint Minute of Admissions which I was expected to sign, agreeing that Mr Fairbairn had visited Tanya on the morning of her death and that she was alive and not under the influence of drugs when he left her to catch the one o'clock bus.

Agreeing prosecution evidence was not something I liked doing, but apparently the old guy was taking Tanya's death very hard. There was already other evidence to confirm that she was alive as late as six o'clock, which was around the time Brandon Biggam had gone to visit her, so it didn't seem like a big deal to sign the JM and save Mr Fairbairn the trauma of giving evidence; however, I wanted to know why Fairbairn could say for certain that his grand-daughter had been drug-free when he'd visited her and to see what other information I could find out from him.

Grace-Mary had arranged for me to call on Mr Fairbairn as my last job of the day, and I was heading over the Flints on the road to Bo'ness, when she phoned to say that Glen Beattie had called to ask how the defence preparations were progressing. Rather than confess that preparations into the doctor's defence had so far involved opening a file and sticking a label, 'HMA –v- Beattie', on the front cover, my secretary had arranged a breakfast consultation for the next morning.

'Seven o'clock!'

'He's a doctor. He's used to not having much sleep,' Grace-Mary said, presumably harking back to the days before NHS Direct, when doctors actually got up in the middle of the night to visit sick people and didn't leave the practice of medicine to a call centre.

'It's Saturday. Why can't he have a lie-in like everyone else and see me later?'

'He's a private client,' said Grace-Mary, firmly. 'If he says seven o'clock, seven it is.'

I battered on and ten minutes later was standing outside a block of flats. Inside, I encountered a group of boys sprawled across the stairs. They were too busy rolling a spliff to take notice of me, that is, until I took out my notebook to check the address.

'Polis!' yelled one of the youngsters and they all jumped to their feet.

'He's no' the polis,' said the smallest and most discerning of the group. He was wearing a grubby white tracksuit, red trainers and Burberry baseball cap.

'I'm looking for Fairbairn,' I said, but their lips were sealed. 'Look, the wee man's right. I'm not the polis.'

The boy in the Burberry baseball cap raised a hand and pointed a finger further up the steps.

'Top landing,' he just managed to get out before a much bigger lad slapped him hard on the back of the head, sending his baseball cap flying.

'Diddy!' the bully yelled. 'The polis always say they're no' the polis so that numpties like you will tell them what they want to know.'

'If he's the polis how come there's only wan of

him?' the wee boy countered, tears welling. Fair comment I thought. The others were less inclined to debate the point, clattering off downstairs and out the front door. I picked up the fallen baseball cap and handed it to him. 'Are you all right, wee man?' I asked, and, in answer, he snatched his cap, flashed me the prongs and disappeared after his mates.

Three floors later, I pressed the bell on the door marked 'Fairbairn' and a woman not much older than myself answered. I took her to be Tanya's mother.

'You the lawyer?'

I gave her my business card. She took it but didn't read it. 'He's not here.' She handed the card back.

'Show the laddie in, Jinty,' a voice called out. The woman hesitated and then took half a pace back, allowing me passage along the hall to a livingroom where a man sat in a chair by the fire, reading the evening paper. There was a pair of walking sticks propped up against the hearth. When he saw me come in, he folded the paper and stuffed it down the side of his chair.

'I'll not get up, pal. I've a spot of bother with my pins these days. Have a seat.'

I sank into a ludicrously soft armchair that enveloped most of my lower body and looked about the cosy little room. On the mantelpiece was a framed photograph of a little girl in a party frock. Mr Fairbairn noticed me staring at it.

'Tanya,' he said, and turned to look out of the window, across the grey vastness of the River Forth to the smoking stack of Longannet Power Station.

There was another photograph on the mantelpiece:

a black and white shot of a footballer, carried shoulder high by his team mates and holding aloft a silver trophy. I thought I detected a faint similarity between the young man in the photograph and the old man sitting opposite.

With a struggle I managed to escape the clutches of the armchair and took down the picture. 'Is that you?'

The old man sat up a little straighter. 'It is indeed. I was ten year with the Thistle. I didn't score many goals but I hit the winner that day.'

'My brother was a footballer,' I said.

He looked at me closely. 'Munro... are you not big Malky Munro's brother?'

I told him I was.

'I thought I recognised you. I'm Tam Fairbairn,' he said as though I wasn't already fully aware of the fact. 'I used to play with Malky. At the end there I played in the juniors, Kirkintilloch Rob Roy, after that Linlithgow Rose then finished up with Bo'ness United. On my way down from the seniors I met Malky on his way up, so to speak. I never hung my boots on the peg until I was thirty-eight. Did you ever see me play?'

'He's a lawyer not a student of ancient history, Dad,' said Tanya's mother, who was still haunting the doorway.

'Wheesht hen and bring the boy a cup of tea. So, as I was saying, you'll maybe have seen me play?'

I probably had, my dad and I had been Rose supporters forever. Unfortunately, I had no recollection of the man in the chair opposite.

I played the odds. 'Mid-field?'

'Aye that's right,' he looked pleased.

I rolled the dice again. 'Right side wasn't it?'

His smile wilted slightly. 'Left-mid.'

I crossed my hands one over the other and tried to look confused. 'Of course, on the left. A bit tasty as I recall.' He was hardly going to dispute that.

'Aye, well you were allowed to tackle folk back then. Shame about your brother though. Bad injury. Hate to see that happen.'

I pointed to the walking sticks. 'Looks like you've not escaped the wars yourself.'

'My football legacy - all those cortisone injections. Too many jags with the Jags. Back then it was no play, no pay.'

Tanya's mother came through carrying tea and biscuits on a tray. 'Would you listen to yourself? It's your own fault you ended up a cripple. If you'd kicked the ball more and other folk less, your legs would be fine.'

'Tell you what, hen,' Mr Fairbairn said, 'You pour tea, I'll talk fitba'.'

She set down a tray of Rich Teas and digestives. There were no chocolate biscuits going to waste on the lawyer who was acting for the scum-bag who'd killed her daughter.

'Mr Fairbairn...'

'It's Tam or Tommy.'

'Tam, you do know why I'm here, don't you?'

'Is it about Logan? Have they found him?' he asked excitedly.

I'd almost forgotten that Tanya's child, his great-grand-child, had a name. I saw the light in the old man's eyes. Mrs Lang's face flushed in excitement. I hated to think that my arrival had raised false hopes.

'Not yet,' I said. 'Sorry, I'm here to take a statement from you. I'm Brandon's lawyer. I don't want to upset anyone. I just would like to know how Tanya was on the day she died.'

Tanya's mother had taken up her position by the livingroom door. She scowled. 'The day she was murdered you mean?'

It took some time and persuasion but eventually Mrs Lang left her father and me alone.

According to the old man, there had been ructions in the Lang household when Tanya first started going out with Brandon Biggam and she'd left home and ended up with my client in homeless persons' accommodation in Glasgow. The family had tried to talk her into coming home and failed. Mr Lang, who worked for the Roads, knew someone who knew someone in West Lothian Council's Housing Department. They'd tried and failed to have Tanya allocated a flat of her own in Linlithgow where the family could have kept a closer eye on her.

'That's where I stepped in,' Mr Fairnbairn said with an air of pride. He pointed to the mantelpiece. 'Friends in high places.'

I took down the team photograph.

'Recognise the keeper? He was the baby of the team. Left us to go to Uni. No money in the game back then. In those days you didn't give up a good day job far less the chance of an education for fitba'. What's wrong? Do you not recognise your own MSP?'

'Kenny McIvor?'

'McIvor the Diver we used to call him.' He laughed.

'The only folk who dived in the penalty box were goalies when I played.'

'So, did he help out?'

'He was brilliant. Got her into LEAP and then a flat of her own. The man was a total star.'

I knew just how difficult it was to find someone a residential place on the Lothian and Edinburgh Abstinence Programme. Some serious strings must have been pulled. As for a Council tenancy, that couldn't have been easy either, though it would have helped that Tanya was pregnant, something she discovered not long before she'd been sent off to rehab, and which happily coincided with the start of her boyfriend's last sentence. With Tanya back in the fold, more or less, the family hoped that by keeping a close eye on things they could keep her free from drugs and Brandon until the baby was born.

According to Mr Fairbairn, on the morning of Tanya's death he had gone to see her mid-morning and caught the bus home about lunch time.

'How did she seem to you?' I asked.

'Fine. She was definitely not using. I could tell. The wean was fine and happy too. She told me that Biggam was calling into see her from time to time, but promised there was no chance of her taking him back and she was definitely off the drugs for good.'

'And you believed her?'

'Why not?'

'Well... you know... she'd been a heroin user. I suppose she'd lied to you and her parents before? About needing money for this and that – money she used for drugs?'

Mr Fairbairn shifted in his armchair. 'It was going to be different this time.'

I was noting all this down when I heard the front door open and someone shout. 'Hurry up, Janet, I've got the works van parked outside and I'm not wanting to take my eye off it with they neds hanging about the place.' Footsteps in the hall, whispered voices, the livingroom door was thrown wide. Tanya's father, JayJay Lang was big, black and very angry. He stared at me accusingly. 'What's this all about?'

Mr Fairbairn started to say something, but the big man cut him short. 'I'm talking to him,' he clarified by jabbing a finger at me.

'Your father-in-law's a witness,' I said. 'I'm here to take a statement.'

'You're that wee shite's lawyer then?'

It was an enquiry that would usually require some narrowing down, given my client base, but on this occasion I knew exactly to whom he referred. I didn't answer and got up from my seat. Time to leave.

'Anyway,' I said, 'thanks for your help, Mr Fairbairn.' Tanya's grandfather, very much aware of his son-in-law's malevolent presence, grunted non-committally. I was putting my notes inside my jacket pocket when Tanya's father tried to grab them. I pulled my hand away.

'Give me that,' he growled. 'You're not taking anything away from here that's going to help that bastard.' He lunged for me. I side-stepped.

'Leave him!' I heard Mr Fairbairn shout. The big man swung a punch. I ducked. The blow glanced painfully off my left ear. He went to swing again, but I dipped my shoulder and rammed a fist under his ribs. He gasped, stepped back. Aware that he was about to come at me again, I tried to put some furniture between us. Moving backwards in the cramped room, my heel caught on the fireside rug. I stumbled. The big man saw his chance and was almost on me when a wooden walking stick ricocheted off the back of his head. He turned in anger to see his father-in-law holding the second stick in one hand and clinging onto the mantelpiece for balance with the other. 'I said leave him!'

Mr Fairbairn moved in on his son-in-law, sliding his free hand along the mantelpiece, steadying himself. As he did so he knocked the framed picture of young Tanya and it fell, the glass front smashing to pieces in the hearth. I scrambled to my feet. Mr Fairbairn, feet planted, swaying slightly, gripped the walking stick batter-up style. JayJay Lang glared from his father-in-law to me and back again, not sure, it seemed, who to deal with first. The wee girl in the summer frock smiled happily up at us through the shards of broken glass and splintered wood. JayJay rubbed the back of his head, stared down at his dead daughter, dropped into the armchair I'd recently vacated and, head in his hands, began to cry.

Chapter 12

Quarter past seven on a Saturday morning. I was sitting in a private dining room across a stiffly starched white table cloth from Dr Glen Beattie in a small and exclusive hotel at the foot of the Royal Mile.

I'd decided against the full Scottish fry-up, something of a first for me, but was unable to lower my cholesterol sights as far as the bowl of muesli and prunes that my G.P. client seemed actually to be enjoying.

'Thanks for coming, Robbie,' he said. 'You've no idea how worried I am about everything. It's all the waiting and the uncertainty. How long did you say the process could take?'

'You're on bail, so the Crown has eleven months to serve an indictment – that's if they don't decide to drop it to summary complaint.'

'Would that help if they did?'

It was difficult to say. Summary procedure was for less serious cases and consequently attracted less serious sentences; however, there was no jury: only a Sheriff and, from my experience, juries tended to be more prone to reasonable doubts than the average Sheriff. The exception to that generality was probably Perth, where the jurors always seemed to be members of the local landed gentry, better-dressed than the lawyers and entering the jury box with a united air of disapproval. It was a jury of peers only if the accused was a retired colonel with a subscription to the Daily Mail. That said, no matter where in the country you went, on a charge of possessing child-pornography, the defence was always going to be sledging up hill.

'It would certainly help you avoid the jail if you were convicted on a summary complaint rather than on an indictment,' I said.

'Any conviction is completely out of the question.'

I turned to see the source of the voice: a man, in his late fifties approaching at speed from my left. Big and burly, clad in a tweed suit over an open-necked, checked shirt, Kenny McIvor MSP, looked more like a ruddy-faced farmer than Scotland's Justice Secretary. I could imagine him as spokesperson for a Perth jury. Beside him was a younger man in a dark suit, the peaked cap of a chauffeur tucked under his arm. He had a military bearing that suggested he wasn't only paid to drive. From his pocket the younger man removed an object the size and shape of a transistor radio. Without a word he set it down in the middle of the table and extended a long silver aerial. When he pressed a button on the side, a vertical row of lights flashed once and then stabilised, three illuminated, one green two red.

McIvor pulled a chair out from the table, took off his jacket and draped it over the back. 'Just let Chris do his stuff. He won't take a minute.'

'Do you have a cell-phone, sir?' the man in the dark suit enquired of me. I did. He took it, deftly removed the back and knocked out the battery onto the palm of his hand. He set the two parts of my phone on the table beside what I assumed was a pocket-sized bug-detector.

The device now showed only one green and one red light. The chauffeur turned to Beattie. 'Sir?' he held out his hand, presumably ready to receive and dismantle another phone.

'That's all right,' McIvor said. 'Wait in the car, I'll not be long.' Chris the chauffeur withdrew. McIvor sat down beside Beattie and rolled up his shirt sleeves. When the waiter hoved into view ready to lay out an extra place setting, McIvor shouted, 'just coffee!' and waved him away. 'So, you're Robbie Munro?' He fixed his eyes on mine, like a poker player assessing the opposition, trying to spot my tell. 'I've heard a lot about you.'

I smiled politely, with all the modesty I could muster at that time of the morning.

'You have a knack for rubbing people up the wrong way. Bloody nuisance, is about the best I've heard said.'

I'd been told McIvor was no loss to the diplomatic corps. I let the jibe evaporate and cut into a poached egg, watching the golden yolk spill across my Finan haddie.

Beattie stopped chewing his horse-food and looked for a moment like he might interject on my behalf.

McIvor leaned across the table at me, the fingers of his hands interlocked. 'Bring me up to speed.'

I selected a slice of toast from the rack and speared a ball of butter with the tip of my knife, glancing over at Beattie as I did.

'Well?' McIvor said.

Undiplomatic and impatient. I ignored him and continued to spread butter on my toast.

'Please feel free to talk openly,' Beattie said.

'What? About your case? Really? He's the Justice Secretary,' I reminded my client. 'His Government is prosecuting you.'

'The Lord Advocate is the prosecutor, a role entirely independent of the Government,' McIvor said.

'And yet the Lord Advocate tends to follow whatever policy the Government and its advisers – that is the tabloid press - feels appropriate. I'm afraid I don't see a great deal of independence in practice.' If there was a wrong way to rub McIvor I hoped he felt thoroughly rubbed.

'Kenny's not here as Justice Secretary. He's here as a friend,' Beattie said.

McIvor nodded gravely. 'I only want to help – in any way I can.'

A lot of his earlier bluster seemed to have departed and yet I didn't like how things were shaping up. There was no way Beattie could stand up to Kenny McIvor and if McIvor decided I wasn't the man for the job, I'd be for the sack. It went against the grain to discuss my client's case with anyone else, far less the Justice Secretary, but I relented. I could see it from my client's point of view. He was practically related to the man. How could he possibly ignore such a strong ally?

'There's really not much to say at this stage,' I said, in between munches. 'You'll know how these things work. The Crown carries out its investigations and the defence doesn't really get a look-in until the prosecution case is fully prepared. The problem with a high-tech type of offence like the one we're dealing with here,' I said, skirting around any mention of child-porn, 'is that it's not the same as a good old assault or a theft charge, where I can start digging about. At the moment all the evidence is in the hands of the police.'

'Have you done *anything*?' McIvor spluttered. 'This man's career is at stake.'

'It's only been a few days,' I countered. 'The Crown won't know what evidence there is yet, far less have got around to sending it to me.'

McIvor's face was redder than ever. 'You're Glen's defence lawyer and you sit here telling me that so far you've done absolutely nothing to try and establish his innocence!'

'Kenny,' my client said in a timid voice, 'there's no need to be so hostile. Robbie has been very helpful so far.'

'Really? What's he done?'

I was beginning to wonder why I'd bothered coming, apart, that is, for being paid private rates to eat a tasty breakfast, though judging by McIvor's attitude I couldn't see too many more breakfast meetings in my future.

'Well?' McIvor's question was directed at me.

I dabbed my mouth with an enormous starched-linen napkin. 'Did you know Dr MacGregor?'

'Of course I knew him. I went to school with Bill MacGregor.'

'Well I'm having his laptop examined in case there's been some sort of mix-up.'

'I thought you said the police took the laptop away.' McIvor said to Beattie.

'They did,' the doctor replied. 'They took the new one, the one I use. I found another, an old one, in the safe.'

McIvor looked confused.

'Robbie thinks that if the police have traced porn to a surgery laptop and it's not on the one I use – which I can assure you it isn't - then maybe it's on Bill MacGregor's old one. If so, there's obviously been some kind of mix-up.'

McIvor snorted. 'Bill MacGregor a paedophile? Impossible.' He looked at his watch and then around the room. 'Where's that bloody waiter?'

'I wish you sounded so certain of my innocence,' Beattie said.

McIvor looked uncomfortable. 'Of course I believe you're innocent, Glen. But you have to face the facts. The police went to your home, not Bill McGregor's. You're the only subject of enquiry.'

'Sounds like you've been making your own investigations,' I said to McIvor.

'I don't care what it sounds like to you Mr Munro.'

'Well here's what it sounds like to me,' Beattie pushed his bowl of oats to the side and harked back to our earlier discussion at the surgery. 'I think the Lord Advocate is out to get you.' He pointed his spoon at McIvor. 'And he's doing it through me.' He prodded himself in the chest, leaving drops of milk on the front of his shirt.

McIvor turned to look out of the window and shook his head. 'Nonsense.'

Beattie was quite adamant. 'How can you say that, Kenny? You know the LA hates you.'

The current Lord Advocate, Scotland's Chief Prosecutor, was a hang-over from the last administration. It was no secret that McIvor wanted him replaced and although, so far, he had been over-ruled, the Lord Advocate's duffle coat was on a shoogly peg. If McIvor became First Minister it would fall right off the wall.

'The Lord Advocate wouldn't have the nerve to do something like this,' McIvor said.

'Why not?' Beattie looked to me for support. 'It's perfect. Isn't it, Robbie? Nothing has to be proved. They keep me on the hook for a month or two. Just long enough for the rumour and innuendo to blacken my name and rub off on you, Kenny. Then they say, oops, there wasn't any porn on your PC after all and drop the case. Too late for my reputation and one or two unattributed comments float about saying that my fiancée's father used his position to make everything go away. Suddenly your position is untenable and the LA is safe. It's classic political smear tactics.'

Although I didn't want to leap immediately onto the tailgate of my client's conspiracy-theory bandwagon, I had to admit that, with the election looming, the allegations against him had come at a fortuitous time for McIvor's opponent in the leadership race. Sooner or later word would leak out and an association made between Beattie and his prospective father-in-law.

McIvor stared hard at Beattie from under a pair of ludicrously-bushy eyebrows that had tendrils spreading out everywhere. 'Is this his idea?' he asked, turning his withering gaze onto me. 'Because I'm telling you right now that I don't want any of this conspiracy nonsense being bandied about, understand?'

'No!' Beattie yelled. 'I don't understand!' I had

never imagined the usually so sedate young doctor could get so angry. The waiter who'd arrived, jug of coffee in hand, stopped and backed slowly away. Beattie took a deep breath and lowered his tone. 'What I understand is that I'm innocent and I'm being fitted up. Is it purely coincidental that this is all happening to me, now, right on the eve of *your* leadership vote?' The waiter cleared his throat. Beattie paused while McIvor's coffee was poured and then continued. 'Face it, Kenny, you're the problem, but you're also the solution. Tell the Lord Advocate that his position is safe or make him a judge or something, that's what usually happens, isn't it? Sort out your differences with the Lord Advocate and I know this will all stop.'

McIvor shook his head and took a sip of coffee. 'This isn't the movies, Glen. It's not even Westminster. I hate to tell you, but, in Scottish politics, we're really not all that devious. What you need right now is some action from your lawyer and at the moment I see a distinct lack of animation. Perhaps Mr Munro will be good enough to tell us what he proposes to do. Apart, that is, from charging a huge fee and trying to wring every drop of publicity out of this whole unfortunate affair?' He turned his bushy eyebrows in my direction. 'I'm told you enjoy seeing your name in the papers.'

'It's something we have in common,' I said, raising a forkful of fish to my mouth.

McIvor got up. He reached across the table and grabbed my wrist causing the flakes of smoked haddock to fall back onto the plate. 'Eat later.'

I pulled my arm free.

Beattie leaned back in his chair and said in a tired

voice. 'Kenny - you're not helping matters.'

The older man sat down again and took another drink of coffee. 'Why did you choose him?' he demanded from my client, speaking about me as though I wasn't there. 'This is a very important, high-profile case and he's an unimportant, small town lawyer. Are you telling me this is the best the Medical Defence Union can come up with? A legal aid lawyer?'

Just about all criminal defence lawyers are legal aid lawyers. There aren't that many rich criminals around, or at least they're not the ones who get caught: which is probably why they are rich. Poverty is the big reason people become criminals. Run a criminal defence practice for rich clients only and you'd starve. Which meant that when a rich person was accused, while they might find comfort in instructing one of the big corporate firms, the case was often sub-contracted out to a so-called legal aid outfit, who actually knew what they were doing. From McIvor's attitude, I could tell which way the wind was blowing and that it was going to carry my client off with it.

I set down my cutlery. 'Mr McIvor, who would you like to represent Glen?'

'There must be plenty of good firms, with respectable solicitors, who would take on the case.'

'Like Caldwell & Clark?'

'Why not? Caldwell & Clark is a fine Scottish Firm, an institution. Has been for—'

'Over a century.'

'There you are then.'

'That's it settled,' I said to my client. 'Glen, I think you should get onto Caldwell & Clark straight away.

Ask to speak to Margaret Sinclair, she's senior partner.'

'But Robbie, I thought—'

McIvor was straight in there. 'Mr Munro has seen sense. It's time you let the experts take over your case.'

Beattie wasn't so certain. 'I don't know...'

McIvor finished his coffee and placed both hands on the table. 'Well I do.'

'I think you should know, it will be more expensive,' I said. 'What the MDU contribute to the legal costs will scarcely look at it.'

McIvor pushed himself to his feet. 'Money isn't a consideration.'

'Perhaps not,' I said. 'Still, I think I should warn you that Caldwell & Clark charge like the Light Brigade.'

'It doesn't matter how much they charge,' McIvor butted in, before Beattie could say a word. 'Whatever the shortfall in funding from the MDU, I'll be more than happy to meet it, personally.'

I took another bite of breakfast and left it at that.

McIvor seemed surprised. Surprised but happy. 'Excellent.' He looked at his watch and nodded to me. 'Mr Munro,' he said, barely glancing in my direction. He unhooked his jacket from the back of the chair. 'Glen, we'll speak later.'

Chris the chauffeur returned and collected his portable hardware. Once they'd gone, I finished my breakfast, pushed the plate aside and poured myself some more coffee.

'Kenny can be a real a bully,' Beattie said. 'He's so used to getting his own way, not many people can stand up to him.'

Including you, I thought. The coffee was nice and strong.

Beattie looked at me apologetically. 'I'm sorry about the way things have turned out...'

There was no need for him to be. I had it all worked out. Client satisfaction is all about perception. Give them what they want. So long as you put on a good show in a trial, shout at the witnesses, argue the toss with the Sheriff, even if you lose the case that client is going to be happy and come back next time he's in bother. McIvor was no different. He wanted a blue-chip, law firm to represent Beattie and so I'd given him what he wanted, before he took matters into his own hands. Glen was too timid to stand up to his prospective father-in-law. If I hadn't suggested Caldwell & Clark, McIvor would have gone off and instructed some other firm, and my client wouldn't have had the bottle to argue.

'A year or so back,' I enlightened him, 'I was a partner with Caldwell & Clark. They stopped doing criminal work – not good for their corporate image, plus there was no money in it. I left on pretty good terms and we have an arrangement whereby they cut-out to me what little crime comes their way.'

'So what does that mean?'

'It means you'll still have me on your side and Kenny will be able to tell his chums down at the row of upturned boats that he's stumping out for a high class law firm for his future son-in-law.' I took another drink of coffee. 'Everyone's a winner.'

Beattie give the muesli and prunes a prod with his spoon. 'I hope so,' he said. 'I really, really hope so.'

Chapter 13

'You seem to be on the mend.'

Late Saturday morning. My dad was standing with his back to me, chipping golf balls into a cardboard box using his favourite pitching wedge. He had a horrible slice off the tee, his approach shots were generally woeful, but around the green or from a bunker he could toss a Titleist in the air and float it down next to the hole like a laser-guided snowflake. That shot, his deadly putting and a flexible handicap had won him many a match.

He turned around when he heard my voice. 'A bit of fresh air works wonders. Here, I'll get one of those.' He let the golf club fall to the divot-pocked lawn and came forward to take one of the carrier bags I was lugging. I fended him off and continued on my way to the back door. The old man had been doing his bit for global warming. The door was wide open letting all the heat escape from the house and tearing chunks out of his winter fuel allowance.

He followed me into the kitchen and sat down on a chair as I unloaded the carrier bags onto the table. Milk, eggs, bread... my dad picked up the loaf and opened one end of the red tartan grease-proof wrapping, grunting with approval when he caught a glimpse of a well-fired crust. 'Don't suppose you picked up a pork pie while you were down the shops?'

There was nothing my dad liked more than a pork

pie, cut into quarters and smothered in Coleman's English mustard. I often wondered how he tasted the pies, which had become over the years a means of transportation for ever-increasing amounts of mustard. The man had to be some kind of masochist.

'No pork pies, but…' I unpacked a small tin of A&B meat roll; another high fat meat product and my dad's favourite sandwich filling, also enjoyed with copious amounts of mustard. Between it and pork pies, I reckoned it was probably the slightly lesser of two high-cholesterol evils. Though I didn't know what either the A or the B stood for in A&B, I did have some theories.

'You bonnie laddie.' He tossed the tin up in the air and caught it again. 'Were they out of the big tins?'

'No,' I replied. 'And you'd better make this wee one last. You know what the doctor said about your diet.'

'Doctor? He's just a laddie. Dr MacGregor was a doctor. And don't think I haven't heard the rumours.'

'Keep them to yourself, then,' I told him. 'I don't want my client thinking I've been telling tales to my dad.'

'You and your clients. I don't know how you can look at yourself in the mirror. Defending perverts.'

The old man was obviously feeling more like himself and warming to one of his favourite subjects: the presumption of guilt. He turned to put away the treasured tin in a wall cupboard, muttering something about quacks that I didn't quite catch.

'What are you mumping about?'

'Doctors. They're hopeless.'

'Is that the entire medical profession or just those under sixty?'

'What do they actually know about anything?' he asked, ignoring my jibe. 'There's wee Vince stuck in the hospital, surrounded by folk moaning and dying and they'll not even let him have a dram. What's the point of living if you can't have a bit pleasure now and again? They'll not even let me in to visit him while I've got the lurgy.' He took a wrinkled strip of toilet paper from his pocket and blew his nose. 'How was he when you went to see him?'

'Fine,' I said.

'Fine? Really?'

I didn't like the sound of hope in my dad's voice. He started to cough. Beads of perspiration stood out on his brow. 'Look at the state of you. Out chipping golf balls in this weather in nothing but a T-shirt and a pair of shorts.'

'I thought it would help cool me down.'

'It'll help you catch a chill. Now go through the room and keep warm.'

He trudged off like a scolded schoolboy. On the worktop I noticed a photograph. In the centre, Vince in his Black Watch uniform, either coming from or going to a tour of duty, my mum and dad either side of him, me, a baby, in my mum's arms and my brother, Malky, in baggy shorts, hair slicked down, reaching up and holding one of my dad's hands. I hadn't seen the picture for years. My dad kept a whole lot of old family photos in a collection of biscuit tins under his bed. He'd obviously dug this one out and found a frame for it. Standing beside the photo was an unopened bottle of whisky. Strange; I thought I had my dad's whisky supply accounted for.

'What's this doing here?' I shouted through to him. No answer. I went through to the living room carrying the dark green bottle by the neck. 'I said, where did this come from?'

He looked around the side of the newspaper he was reading. 'Jill handed it in. The lassie's doing well for herself. She's a pharmacy manager now. Raking it in by all accounts.'

It wasn't exactly breaking news. The success of Vince's daughter was something that my dad regularly brought up in conversation, especially when I was bemoaning my own financial difficulties.

'Vince's is it?'

'Naw, I'm getting Islay malt on prescription now.'

'I see your 'flu has turned into a nasty bout of sarcasm.'

'Of course, it's Vince's.' He tapped the bottle. 'It's his favourite apart from Port Ellen, but that's crazy money these days.'

I picked up the bottle of cask-strength Caol Ila; not so much an Islay malt as a liquid of mass destruction. 'A couple of halfs of that and you could sail to Islay without a boat. I take it you'll be inviting me to the official opening of the bottle.'

'I'm going to keep it.'

That would be a first.

'Till Vince gets back out,' he added.

I didn't mention my recent discussion with Fiona Scott, the chief administrator at St Gideon's.

My dad disappeared behind the newspaper again.

'Do you ever think about death?' I asked, eventually.

He didn't answer my question.

'I said, do ever think about dying?'

He folded the paper in half and turned it about so that I could read a front page headline proclaiming the death toll from the latest roadside bombing in Afghanistan. 'It's hard not to.'

'Dad... you know... Vince is well looked after up at the hospice. It's not easy getting a place there, costs a fortune too. He's lucky —'

My dad snorted. 'Lucky?'

'You know what I mean.'

He laid the newspaper across his knees and held up a hand. 'Enough. It's Saturday morning and I've not had my breakfast yet.'

I set the bottle of whisky down on the arm of the couch and steamed ahead. 'Dad, I think we should talk about Vince.'

'What about him?'

'He's not well.'

'Thank you Doctor Munro.'

'No, Dad. He's really not well. I know you were hoping to see him home for a while, but I was talking to Fiona Scott and she says there's no chance of that happening.'

'Fiona Scott,' he snorted. 'The woman's not medically qualified. I'll have a chat with Jill. She'll be able to sort something out.'

'I don't think so, Dad. Vince is in a lot of pain. You shouldn't put undue pressure on him. The people at the hospice know what they're doing. It's the best place for people in his condition.'

My dad was on his feet now. 'Undue pressure?

What is this? Who do you think you are? Breenging in here, telling me how I'm supposed to treat my friend. A man I've known since we were both in short trousers?'

'Dad, he's not getting home. Vince is going to have to stay where he is – you must know it's for the best.'

He sat down. His eyes filled with tears. I'd never seen him cry. He would have when my mother died, I'm sure, but I was only five years old and my memory of that time was hazy, like a dream. I should have gone over and put an arm around him, tried to console him with some kind words, but we were men. Worse than that we were Scots men.

'D'you mind?' I took the paper from his lap and flipped it to the back page, holding it in front of my face, giving my old man time to get control over his emotions.

'I see Johnny Akbar's back in Scotland. He's thinking about getting into management,' I said after a moment or two. 'Johnny was some player wasn't he?'

But even the introduction of my dad's favourite topic of conversation – football – did not elicit a reply. The springs of the couch sighed with relief. I lowered the newspaper to see him on his feet, the bottle of whisky gripped tightly in his hand.

'Where do you think you're going with that?' I asked.

He walked to the kitchen door.

'Give it to me, Dad.'

'If Vince isn't getting out I might as well crack this open right now,' he said.

'Give me the bottle back and I'll let you go out to the pub for a dram or two when you're feeling a bit more like yourself.'

'You'll let me?' My dad turned and scowled at me, lips set in a grim line. The moustache that was partly camouflaged amidst his unshaven face, bristled. 'You'll *let* me? When did they make you my turn-key?'

'When you pressed the self-destruct button – that's when.' I snatched the whisky bottle from him. 'Now sit down and I'll pour you some cereal. You should be taking it easy.'

'There'll be plenty of time for that when I'm dead.'

'Which will be sooner than you think if you don't start looking after yourself.'

'I can look after myself fine.' He strode through to the kitchen and took the frying pan off a hook on the wall beside the cooker.

I relieved him of it and hung it up again. 'No fry-ups. I said I'd make your breakfast.'

'Ach, do what you like, I'm going to have my shower.'

I lifted the door of a high cupboard. There was nothing inside except a packet of rolled oats.

'And mind I like salt in my porridge,' was his parting shot as he walked out of the room.

Chapter 14

Eventually, it was Vince's next-door neighbour who directed me to Polmont dry ski-slope. It was almost closing time when I parked outside and made my way through the front entrance to the main reception, where sets of skis were laid out on a long wooden counter and a few brave souls sat on benches by the walls, struggling out of boots and changing socks, thick for thin. I marched on, through the back door and outside again, where I almost collided with a group of teenagers, boys and girls, carrying skis, smiling and laughing as they stomped their way back from a session on the plastic piste.

I walked past them to the top of the ski-slope from where there was a panoramic view over the Grangemouth oil refinery, the bright lights of the tall steel structures twinkling like hellish Christmas trees amidst the clouds of steam that spewed from the giant cooling towers and drifted south-west on the prevailing wind. At the foot of the nylon slope, I could just make out a figure clad in multi-coloured ski-wear, gracefully sliding across the criss-cross fabric to the tow. There was a small brick wall. I sat down and waited as Jill was towed slowly up the hill towards me, a hand shielding her eyes from the glare of the arc lights and no doubt wondering why there was a man in a lounge suit waiting at the top.

The weather forecasters had promised an Indian

summer. That evening it felt decidedly Scottish. I stamped my feet, breathed hot air between clasped hands and wished I hadn't left my coat in the back of the car.

I hadn't seen Jill for a while. Usually, we only met at milestone birthday-do's for our respective fathers. Years before, when Jill had come home for the summer after her first year at University, I'd asked her out. It was around the time when my brother, Malky, was edging towards inclusion in the Scotland squad. Although he wasn't actually picked for the team, on the night of my date with Jill, there were VIP tickets going-a-begging for the final friendly before the Euro '96 qualifiers and that sort of trumped the pizza and a trip to the pictures we'd arranged. Basically, she'd been bumped, except I forgot to tell her and she'd stood at the cinema waiting for me. It was something she never let me forget and that wait in the foyer lasted longer each time she reminded me. Scotland won that night; however, any prospects of a romance with Jill were lost. She hadn't changed much over the years; still brunette, petite and pretty.

'Well, well, Robbie Munro, I see the years are taking their toll.'

Still dead nippy.

'How are you Jill? What brings you here?'

I always seemed to say the wrong thing to Jill and she wasn't one to miss an opportunity. She took a step back and looked down at herself from quilted jacket, to salopets, to purple boots each clamped into a ski.

'Yes... okay... skiing, obviously. What I mean is—'

'Why am I skiing when my dad is dying?'

She sat down on a small wall and unclipped her skis. 'I'm an instructor at Hillend in my spare time and because I'm through this way just now, I was asked if I would take a couple of classes. This is where I learned. I used to love coming here when I was at school. Until now I didn't realise how small it actually was.' She stood up, clamped her skis together and hugged them to her chest. 'Let me know if you'd like a lesson. I've been talked into coming back and taking another beginners' class tomorrow evening. Mostly girls, thankfully; they're much quicker learners than boys.'

I couldn't deny it. I owned a chipped tooth that was a permanent reminder of one of my few school trips to Polmont. When the others were doing parallel turns, I was still trying to form a pizza wedge. 'It's easier for women,' I told her. 'You should know that. All to do with the hips. The neck of the femur sticks out further from the hip in a female. That's the reason you lot run funny with your legs doing that windmilly thing.' I noticed an unamused expression form on Jill's face. 'Apparently it's a help for skiing - an anatomical advantage...' I tailed off.

'Is that right? And here's me thinking that girls were quicker learners because they listen and do what they're told. The moment a male straps on a pair of skis he assumes he's a natural and starts looking around for the jumps.' Jill shoved her skis at me and I carried them as she clumped her way up the path to the communal locker room where she stopped to open the door for me 'Now are you going to tell me why you're here?' she asked.

'It's about Vince.'

She spun around. 'Has something happened?' The cold ripped a ribbon of white breath from her mouth. 'I just left the hospice a couple of hours ago.'

'No, everything's okay,' I told her. 'Can we go inside? I'm freezing.'

Once we were in the relative warmth, Jill sat down on a bench to prise her feet out of her boots. 'I heard you were up visiting my dad the other night. That was... it was nice of you.' She whipped off an enormously thick pair of socks and looked up at me with a wry smile. 'If you're trying to get a mention in his will, I wouldn't bother.'

I leaned against the skis I was carrying. 'Jill, I was wondering... what are the chances of Vince getting home?'

She sighed. 'Did Alex send you? I went to see him and he wouldn't let up about Vince's need for dignity.'

'He didn't ask me to try and persuade you, if that's what you think.'

'Good, it wouldn't work.'

'But you're a pharmacist. Couldn't you rig something up?'

'Like what?'

'I don't know. Painkillers, morphine or something.'

Jill tied on a pair of white trainers, pulling the laces tight. 'Tell your dad to leave my dad to the experts.' She sighed. 'Look, I hate saying this, my dad wouldn't like Alex to know, but he prefers being in the hospice. When he was still a day-patient he had pain relief *rigged-up* at home. He was getting morphine via the Hospice pharmacy, supplied via a syringe-driver. I was there as often as I could be and a nurse came into check on him, the full works. It was fine for a while but now he needs constant attention. A nurse can't be there all the time and... well... I can tell you there's not much dignity involved when your daughter has to take you for number two's in the middle of the night. I'd like nothing better than to have him home, but the hospice is so much better. The medical team are experts in palliative care and they don't just provide pain relief, there's counselling and various other treatments. They're experts in the process...' something caught in her throat.

'The process?' I asked.

Jill swallowed. 'Of dying. There's more to it than just pain relief. It's not all physiological. It's psychological too.'

'He seemed quite well when I went to see him.'

'He'd be putting on a brave face. He's come through a really bad spell.'

'I think my dad thought that if Vince was at home he could see him more often and not be limited to visiting hours.'

Jill stood up and looked me in the eye. 'Robbie, your dad has been great—'

'I understand—'

'No, really. His visits mean everything to Vince, but you know what he's like. I shouldn't tell you this, but there isn't really a limit on visits. It was me who asked the hospice to tell Vince and Alex that sessions run for an hour. Your dad means well and yet he can sometimes be a trifle... overwhelming.' There being no disagreement from me she continued. 'Vince tires easily. I know he'd never ask Alex to leave and right now I think your dad's better in small doses.'

'Unlike morphine?'

She gave me a grim smile. 'He says if he knew how good the stuff was he'd have given up whisky and been a junkie years ago.' Tears welled in Jill's eyes. She sniffed. 'Look, I know I sound ungrateful and I don't mean to be. There's no doubt Alex keeps my dad's spirits up.'

I propped Jill's skis against a soft-drink vending machine and risked an arm around her shoulders. 'I hear what you're saying...'

She pulled the hanky from the breast pocket of my suit jacket and blew her nose in it. 'I sense a but.'

'But, on the subject of keeping his spirits up,' I said receiving back the handkerchief. 'Could I make another suggestion?'

Chapter 15

'I just phoned to say thanks.' It was Glen Beattie on the other end of the phone and sounding remarkably chipper for nine o'clock of a Monday morning.

'What for?' I was busy stuffing files into my briefcase. Now that the court had moved, I couldn't just nip across the road at two minutes to ten. I had a half hour drive every morning.

'The police have just been here to give me back my laptop. Your efforts were not in vain.'

My efforts had been non-existent. 'Glad to have been of assistance,' I said.

'The way you were talking, I didn't think I'd have it back so fast.'

Fast? It was unheard of fast. Normally when the High Tech cops removed hardware for investigations, you could say sayonara to it whether you were guilty or innocent.

'It's a good sign, isn't it?' He sounded excited. 'Oh, and by the way, you were right, they did ask about any other laptops I might have and—'

'You told them about Dr MacGregor's?'

'Thought I'd better. Hope you don't mind, I said they could pick it up from you.'

'Do they have a warrant?'

'Does it matter?'

Grace-Mary poked her head around the door. 'There's a police officer here to see you.'

I waved her away and continued my conversation with the doctor. 'And you want me just to hand it over?'

'Don't see why not.'

'With or without a warrant?'

'Mr Munro, I've got a full waiting room. That laptop has nothing to do with me. Hold on a moment.'

The line went dead for a moment and then my eardrums were assailed by Peer Gynt being played on glockenspiel.

'Sorry about that,' the doctor said upon his return from the Halls of the Mountain King. 'One of my patients has taken a funny turn in the waiting room. I've got to go.' It sounded to me like the *something urgent's just cropped up and I have to leave immediately for court* excuse that I used to get rid of time-waster calls from people who phoned-up to 'pick my brains' or as I called it, 'get free legal advice'.

The door to my office opened again and in came a short, stocky man with longish hair and a short beard that jutted out from his chin. He was smartly dressed in dark suit, white shirt, dark tie.

Grace-Mary came into the room after him. 'The officer's in a bit of a hurry.'

I replaced the receiver.

'Sorry for barging in like this, sir,' said the man in the beard. 'I've just had a call to return to HQ. That the laptop there?' He pointed to where Dr MacGregor's ancient device lay on a corner of my desk.

I'm suspicious by nature, but mainly from experience. Section 52A of the Civic Government (Scotland) Act makes it an offence for a person to have

in their possession any indecent images of a child. I
didn't know if there were any such images on the hard
disk of Dr MacGregor's ancient laptop, but, if there
were, I was technically in possession. Of course, if I
could prove I had a legitimate reason for having the
laptop, and, therefore, any illegal images, that would be
a defence. I could imagine Sheriff Brechin mulling that
one over for a nano-second before placing me on the sex
offenders' register. Best to keep a hold of the laptop
until I had Jimmy Garvie's report and knew exactly
what was on it.

'Can I see the warrant?' I asked.

The man's eyes betrayed his attempt at a smile. 'Dr
Beattie assured me you'd co-operate.' He lifted the
laptop from the desk. 'These old things are heavy,
aren't they?' I didn't know exactly what, but there was
something not quite right about the man. I glanced
down the length of him to the toes of his shoes. He was
certainly well turned out and I think that was what
irked me. Every officer from the High Tech Unit that I'd
ever met wore jeans and a T-shirt, not a suit with
scalpel creases. And what was with the shiny black
shoes? Where were the scruffy old trainers? The beard
too was a puzzle. Stubble, yes, but what tecky could
drag himself away from the computer screen long
enough to craft a skilfully manicured Van Dyke?

'You're taking nothing from my office without a
warrant,' I told him. I took back the laptop and replaced
it on my desk. I could see Grace-Mary standing in the
doorway rolling her eyes.

The man in the beard looked out of the window. I
followed his line of vision to a black saloon: a Mercedes

or could have been a Lexus or 7 Series, parked on the opposite side of the High Street and causing something of an obstruction to other road users. He turned to me again, tugging at the point of his sharp little beard. 'Why don't you call your client? Speak to him and he'll confirm he's given me permission to remove the laptop for inspection.'

I'd be speaking to my client all right, just as soon as I had got rid of beardy. Then I'd personally return the laptop to the doctor and let him, if he wanted, hand it over to the cops himself.

'I'm sure Doctor Beattie is busy with his morning surgery.'

'Mr Munro, this is police business and if you do not co-operate I will have to—'

'What? Arrest me? You going to do that without a warrant as well?'

He didn't reply.

'Grace-Mary,' I said, 'show the officer out.'

My secretary came over and stood beside him.

'I'm not leaving without it,' said the beard. I put a hand on top of the laptop. He sighed hugely. 'I must warn you again. If you continue to obstruct me you will leave me with little alternative. Now I'm going to ask you one final time – will you give me the laptop?'

He held out a hand and stepped forward. I moved to the left blocking his access to the laptop with my body.

'Very well. I must caution you, Mr Munro, that you do not have to say anything, but it may harm your defence if you do not mention when questioned something which you later rely on in court. Anything you do say may be given in evidence.' He reached into his pocket and produced a set of handcuffs. Not the usual kind with the fixed bar between the cuffs; these ones had a chain.

Grace-Mary stepped in between us. 'For goodness sake, give him the laptop, Robbie.'

'You're from the High Tech Unit? I asked the man in the beard. That's based at Fettes, right?'

He stared at me for a moment. 'That's right.'

'So when did Lothian & Borders start using the English wording for a police caution? Or did you skip that lecture at Tulliallan and watch an episode of The Bill instead?'

The man shuffled his feet and, I noticed, slipped the handcuffs back in his pocket. A car horn peeped. I looked out of the window. The black car was still there, a queue of cars behind it waiting for a space to overtake on the narrow street.

'Hey!' yelled Grace-Mary. I turned to see the man push my secretary. She fell backwards over one of the many piles of files that were stacked on the floor by my desk. Before I could react, the man had dipped a shoulder and rammed it into my chest, sending me flying to join my secretary on the floor, only on the other side of the room. He grabbed the laptop from the desk and ran out of the door with it. By the time I was on my feet again, I could hear the sound of feet running down the stairs and through the close that led out onto the pavement.

Grace-Mary groaned.

I ran over to her. 'Are you all right?'

'I'm fine,' she said. 'Just a bit winded.'

I helped her into my chair and went over to the window. The man in the beard was waiting to cross the road, Dr MacGregor's museum-piece under one arm. I reached into my pocket for my cell phone to take a photograph. The battery was dead. All I could do was watch. There was a break in the traffic. The man made a dash for the black car. He didn't make it. An impatient white van pulled out from behind the black saloon and clipped one of his knees. The man spun around, trying to keep his balance, still clutching the laptop. He stumbled, tripped and fell. The laptop flew from his hands and skidded along the road. The van hadn't been travelling fast. The man would probably have walked away with a few bumps and bruises and some scuffs to his shiny black shoes. That is, if it hadn't been for the oncoming lorry that first ran over the laptop and then over him.

Chapter 16

'What did you say his name was?' Inspector Dougie Fleming asked me, for the third time. The face that launched a thousand prosecutions couldn't have looked any more bored.

'That's what I'm hoping you'll tell me.'

'And you say he was a police officer?'

'No. I said, he said he was a cop.'

'See any ID?'

'Nope.'

'Oh, I see. You just took his word for it did you?'

'Where's your ID? In all the years I've known you when have you ever flashed your warrant card?'

'And this car – the one that drove away - did you get the registration?'

'It was too far away.'

Fleming closed his notebook. Many of his colleagues used the new electronic versions, but Dougie Fleming preferred pencil and paper for reasons many an accused person had discovered to their cost. He stood up.

'Is that it?' I asked. 'What's going to happen now?'

'Happen?'

'A crime was committed - a theft. The man came into my office and stole a laptop.'

'But not your laptop. You told me that it belonged to Dr MacGregor and as we know he's dead. Can't really have a theft without an owner. Tell you what, why don't you go off and mull over that tricky legal point and I'll get on with some police work?'

'The man assaulted me – and my secretary.'

'And now he's dead. Punishment enough wouldn't you say?'

I thumped the reception counter wishing it were Fleming's smug face. 'I want to know who he was and if he really was a policeman, which I doubt very much, I'd like to register a formal complaint.'

'Put it in writing, you've lodged enough police complaints to know how. Meantime, I've a fatal road accident to investigate.'

'If he was a cop, surely you'd know his name by now.'

'If I did, which I may or may not, that information couldn't be released at the moment. Not until the next-of-kin have been informed.'

He held out an arm, gesturing to the door.

I didn't move. 'Why don't you ask his accomplice?'

'The accomplice to the non-theft? The man you didn't see, who drove off in the car, the number plate of which you failed to note and described by you...' he checked his notebook, 'as, *a big black one*?' He snapped shut his notebook again, came around to the public side of the counter and strode to the door which he then held open as an invitation for me to leave.

'Can I see the laptop at least?'

'Those parts of the laptop not scattered along Linlithgow High Street are in the back of a bin-lorry heading for the dump.'

'And the dead guy - you'll let me know his name when you find out?'

Fleming opened the door wider. 'Any written request for information will be given the Force's full consideration.'

Chapter 17

'*Psst!*'

Vince opened his eyes.

'*Vince!*'

The wee man raised his head from the pillow and fumbled about on the bedside cabinet until he found a pair of horn-rimmed glasses. He pushed them onto his face, peering through the thick lenses, squinting in the half-light. 'Robbie!'

'Wheesht. Keep your voice down and no sudden moves.'

'Why... why are you wearing a white coat?' He blinked several times. 'And that stethoscope - what are you doing?'

'Getting you out of here.'

'Robbie, people don't get out of here. I'm supposed to be dying.'

'Not tonight, you're not. You're going down the pub.'

Vince struggled up onto his elbows. 'Are you crazy? They'll not let me leave the ward.'

A nurse slipped into the room. She disconnected Vince's arm from the line that entered his left arm and coughed loudly, twice, whereupon a figure in a brown knee length coat backed through the double swing doors pulling along a wheelchair which he parked up by the side of Vince's bed. I pressed a ten pound note into each of their hands.

'You never saw us,' I said meaningfully. They each winked at me and Vince in turn before slipping back out of the room, looking shiftily from side to side as they went. Hopefully they'd spend the money on acting lessons. Vince's escape was all arranged – only he didn't know that.

'Put this on,' I chucked him the tartan dressing gown that was hanging over the folded screen partition. 'And climb aboard. I manoeuvred the wheelchair to the edge of the bed so he could slide into it with a little help. In a moment I was pushing him out of the door and into the corridor. 'If anyone asks, you're on the way for a scan.'

'What kind of scan?'

'How should I know? I'm not really a doctor. This isn't my stethoscope.'

'Okay, okay. Just keep pushing.'

I'd cleared the escape with the on-duty consultant earlier that evening. Vince might be feeling better, but his future didn't hold too many chances for a night out down the boozer and, for the wee man who'd served twenty-two years in the Black Watch, the whisky would taste all the sweeter drunk under the wire.

Halfway along the corridor we turned a corner and, front door in sight, were stopped by the ward sister coming towards us, an unusually stern look on her face; someone else wanting in on the act.

'Keep calm,' said Vince.

'Where are you taking this man, doctor?' the Sister asked, standing in our path and causing me to bring the wheelchair to an abrupt halt.

'Urgent scan.'

'A scan?' The nurse scratched the back of her head and pursed her lips at the same time – it was called multi-tasking in the NHS. 'Strange. Are you not headed the wrong way for ultrasound?'

'Oh well,' maybe we'll just go for a breath of fresh air before we about turn,' I said, between my teeth, leaning forward on the handles, trying to get the wheels rolling again.

The nurse wasn't quite finished. 'Outside? I don't know if that's wise.'

It had been nice of the hospital staff to agree to the whole escape from Colditz routine. I appreciated the attempts at making it seem real, but the amateur dramatics were becoming tiresome. There was nothing for it but to play along. I prepared myself for a spot of indignation, ready to pull rank; I was the one with the stethoscope after all. Suddenly, a tartan clad arm shot out. A gnarled, liver-spotted hand seized the nurse by an ankle, lifted the leg up and pulled. You can take the man out of the Black Watch... The nurse gave a startled shriek, toppled and fell to the floor, hands slapping against the polished linoleum floor as she broke her fall.

'PUSH!' Vince yelled, and in a matter of seconds we were outside into the car park and I was heaving the patient into the front seat of my car.

Chapter 18

My dad was waiting for us in the Red Corner Bar, a bottle of whisky, a small jug of water and two shot glasses on the table in front of him. At one end of the room stood The Red River Trio, both of them. One on lead, the other on drums. Helping hands removed Vince from his wheelchair and into a seat. 'Take a look at this will you?' my dad said, proudly tilting the whisky bottle.

Vince put his head close, nose almost touching, lifted his glasses and read the label. 'No way - a twenty-four-year-old Port Ellen? Now I know I'm dying.' He took the cork out and sniffed. 'Or maybe I'm already dead and this is heaven.'

'Aye,' my dad said, 'and I'm keeping that bottle of Caol Ila for when you get out.' He poured them each a measure and topped the glasses up with a drop or two of water. 'Here's tae us…' he said raising his glass. Then he noticed me standing there. 'Brendan!' he yelled over to the bar.

Brendan Patterson, former prize-fighter, now licensee of Linlithgow's dodgiest boozer, the Red Corner Bar, came over drying his hands on a tea-towel that had probably once been white. Grey tufts of wiry hair poked from the open neck of his white nylon shirt. Hard to think this wee, walnut of a man had been in my class at school. The years most certainly had not been kind. Maybe, like Jill, he looked at me and thought the same. He came over. 'What'll it be?' he asked.

'A soda and lime for the laddie,' my dad said. 'Robbie's Vince's getaway driver.'

'Tell me about it,' Vince said. 'The traffic cops chased us on foot.'

All three of them fell-about. As they were wiping away tears of mirth, I noticed a familiar face behind a whisky tumbler at the far side of the bar. Sammy Veitch was a sole practitioner from Bathgate, a town eight or so miles to the south. He specialised in personal injury claims and had made a good living over the years, mainly from car crashes; the easiest type of claim. Whether it was a minor dunt or a multi-vehicle pile-up there was always someone to pin the blame on. Hook up with the least blameworthy driver, or his or her next-of-kin, and you were quids in. Even better, act for the passengers and it was a no lose situation. The important thing was to be first at the scene. Once an injured-party speaks to a solicitor and has a business card pressed firmly into their blood-stained mitt they're usually not inclined to go seeking legal advice elsewhere and are happy to go home, heal-up and let someone like Sammy fight for compensation. Sammy's secret weapon was my office landlord, Jake Turpie, who along with a portfolio of mainly run-down buildings including my own office premises, also owned a scrapyard and recovery service. The police called Jake out whenever there was a road accident and he called Sammy. It was a brown envelope carousel and it meant that Sammy never had to chase ambulances. He was usually at the scene before the paramedics arrived.

'How's business?' I asked, as I sauntered over to

him.

He thought for a moment before replying. 'Nightmare.'

'Too many careful drivers?'

'It's not just them,' Sammy said, failing to detect my sarcasm. 'It's that no-win-no-fee mob and their adverts on daytime TV. How am I meant to compete with them and their jingles?'

'Did you hear about the accident in the High Street?' I said, trying to lighten his mood.

'When?'

'Yesterday. Right outside my window.'

'Continue.'

'A pedestrian was hit by a van. It was overtaking a car and never saw him.'

'Anyone injured? Badly?' he added with an air of faint optimism.

'He died.'

I now had Sammy's undivided attention. He reached into his sporran. 'Same again for Mr Munro,' he called to Brendan. The kilt wasn't formal wear for Sammy, he always wore one, with a little leather sporran, more functional than ornamental.

'Watch and not over-dose on the vitamin C,' the barman said as he set down another soda and lime.

Meantime, Sammy had removed a notebook and pen from the inside of his tweed jacket. 'Let me have the details.' His shoulders sagged. 'Wait a minute. This wasn't a kid was it?'

'Who?'

'That got knocked down?'

It was a sympathetic side of Sammy I had never

experienced before.

'It's just that kids are a waste of time. The most anyone's going to get out of a dead sprog is ten grand tops for the parents' loss of society, maybe the funeral costs as well. My slice of that makes it hardly worth the bother.'

I eased Sammy's concerns on that score. 'He was an adult – a policeman.'

'The polis? You are kidding. There'll be loss of earnings, pension rights; the full bhuna. Who's the next of kin? Please, tell me he's got a widow and kids.'

I had to explain that I didn't even know the dead guy's name.

'But he's definitely dead and he's definitely a cop?'

'He's dead all right and five minutes before he died he was in my office claiming to be a cop.'

'Good enough for me. Where's the body?'

'No idea.'

'Not below ground or burnt yet, though? He wasn't a bud-bud or a four by two?'

'We never discussed religion.'

'If he's just a normal Proddy or Tim, I'll be able to catch up with the family at the graveside.' He was talking to himself now. 'He'll have been taken to St John's, Livingston. Wee Joe at the Co-op will know who's got the funeral.' He made a note in his book, giving me a knowing leer as he tucked it inside his jacket pocket.

The band struck up Kenny Rogers', 'The Gambler', a safe bet in the present company.

'So?' Sammy enquired of me.

'So what?'

'So what's your angle? Expecting some commission?' He grimaced. 'Thanks for the tip-off and all that, but if I'm going to be doing all the work...'

'No angle,' I said, almost truthfully, 'though I'd like to know who he was. Will you let me know when you find out? I think I should send flowers or something, seeing how I was the last person to see him alive.'

Sammy eyed me suspiciously, but seemed happy enough with that explanation. He finished his drink, rattled the base of the glass on the countertop and called out to Brendan. 'Another, Robbie?' he asked, looking at the pale-green fizz-water in my untouched glass with a faint look of disgust. 'Or something stronger?'

'Better not. I'm driving that pair.' I jerked a thumb in the general direction of the table where my dad and Vince were now ensconced and around which a small group of well-wishers had formed.

'Oh, aye, poor wee Vince,' said Sammy. 'Cancer isn't it? Terrible, terrible.' He leaned over and whispered in my ear. 'Soldier wasn't he?'

'Black Watch,' I confirmed.

Sammy's drink arrived. He turned and raised it above his head. 'Here's to you Vince,' he called out. Vince briefly disengaged from the chat to wave back. Sammy scratched the back of his head and thought for a moment. 'Don't suppose he was anywhere near Easter Island back in the fifties?'

Chapter 19

I returned Vince, unscathed but slightly under the influence, to the hospice just after nine o'clock. After an hour or so, reminiscing with his pals down at The Red Corner Bar and a few glasses of extremely good whisky, he'd started to wane. I wasn't feeling that hot myself, though that had more to do with the country music than anything else.

'Just walked out the front door and down to the pub - easy,' he slurred. 'Wish I'd never bothered to start that tunnel under the bed.' He looked up at me and winked. 'Cheers, son. Tell that old man of yours not to visit me the morn. I know him, he'll have a heid like a burst balloon.'

A nurse came into the room and started fussing around. I was about to leave when Vince took my wrist. 'Thanks, Robbie. You're a good lad.'

'Get to sleep,' I said.

'Don't know how you talked the hospice into letting me out, far less Jill.' Vince was ill, not daft. He laughed. 'I'd love to have seen you two get together.'

'Who? Me and Jill? How much have you had to drink?'

'She likes you. Always has. Don't listen to what your dad says.'

'What does my dad say?'

The nurse came over and gently released Vince's grip on my arm.

'Look after your dad when I'm gone,' Vince said. 'He can be right dour at times. Remind him that it's me that's dead not him.' He coughed a laugh. I wondered if this was the last time I'd see him. My thoughts must have registered in my face. 'Don't look like that. It's my time. I'm just standing down, making way for new recruits to the human race.'

This time the nurse wasn't kidding and practically bundled me out of the room. On the way out, the night porter opened the door for me, humming the tune to the Great Escape as I walked by.

'Mr Munro?' A voice from behind and footsteps clicking on the hard floor. It was Fiona Scott. I was in for it now.

'Don't worry, we're back safe and sound and all tucked into bed.'

She looked puzzled. 'Sorry?'

Was the hospice's chief administrator the only person not in on Vince's big night out? 'Vince Green. I was just checking to make sure all was well.'

'As well as can be expected, I'm sure.' She looked at her watch. 'Bit late for a visit isn't it?'

'My dad,' I said. 'He worries.'

She didn't seem the slightest concerned. I expected the hospice was used to friends and relatives arriving at all hours to check on friends and relatives as they neared the end.

'I wonder,' she said. 'Would you mind if I had a quick word?'

I didn't and she took me down the corridor to her bright and airy office. No desiccated umbrella plant or stacks of finished case files anywhere, just one red-lacquered and highly polished filing cabinet and some artistically arranged stainless steel and glass furniture. Grace-Mary would have loved it.

'I hear things are looking up for Dr Beattie,' she said.

Who had she been speaking to?

'It's great news,' she continued over the strains of Nessum Dorma, theme tune of World Cup 1990; Costa Rica one, Scotland nil. I shuddered. She smiled, which was strange because Fiona Scott had always struck me as something of an ice-queen. Heading up one of God's more exclusive waiting rooms couldn't have been an easy task. Holding the purse strings, crunching the numbers and deciding who was admitted and who wasn't: not a job for the faint of heart. Softies need not apply. Whenever I'd met her previously she'd had a fairly austere aura around her, now she was positively beaming. I hated to jump all over her sandcastle.

'I'm afraid he's not out of the woods yet,' I said. 'Still a few loose ends to tie up.'

The smile wilted. 'But you're confident – about the case being slung out?'

'Let's not tempt providence.'

'It'll ruin him. Even if he's found not guilty after a trial, how many patients want a family doctor who was suspected of paedophilia? What have they got on him?'

I'd run out of helpful clichés. 'I think I've probably said enough.'

'If there's anything I can do,' she said. 'I mean it, anything at all that will help.'

It was my job to try and have Glen Beattie acquitted and yet, if he was guilty, then hell mend him. Why was

Fiona Scott so keen to assist?

Pavarotti or whoever, was giving it big licks, finishing off with a never-ending final note.

'Thanks,' I said. 'I'll bear that in mind.'

Chapter 20

Monday morning. I pulled Professor Bradley's provisional autopsy report hot from the fax machine and read it as I walked to my car. Unfortunately, it wasn't everything I'd hoped it might be. The Prof. opined that Tanya had indeed died of a heroin overdose; however, he'd identified some signs of blunt force trauma: a superficial scratch on the left elbow and some minor bruising and abrasions on the arms. It was inconclusive and yet significant enough without further explanation to prevent Prof. B. from ruling out that Tanya Lang had been forced to inject her final fix. Not good. Still, this was criminal law. We didn't deal in maybe's. The Crown needed proof beyond a reasonable doubt. If there was not enough to support forcible injection, then there was a chance that, if I caught the PF early enough, the culpable homicide charge might be reduced to a supply charge in time for the case calling later in the day. That would lower the odds on Brandon Biggam's release on bail to around the one-hundred-to-one mark. If you don't ask you don't get. Before I approached the PF I took a trip to the cells to see my client.

'If it's supply only, I'll sign the section right now,' he said. 'Can you no' get it down to a summary and I'll plead the day?'

Brandon was wanting jam on it. Even if the culp hom charge did disappear we were still talking about the supply of a class A drug, not his first conviction of that type, and this time the supply that had resulted, accidentally perhaps, in a death. If the charge was dropped to a summary complaint, carrying a maximum twelve month sentence, then with a one-third discount for pleading guilty, a further one-half standard remission and the chance of early release on a tag, my drug-dealing client would be back on the streets and up to his knees in smack before the Christmas decorations were back up the loft. I didn't see Hugh Ogilvie, the PF, as the Santa Claus type.

'We can but ask,' I told him, and left as a turnkey arrived bringing breakfast: a polystyrene cup of milky tea and a roll on square sausage.

'You always did have an over-developed sense of humour,' Hugh Ogilvie said. We were in the well of court two, five minutes before Brandon Biggam was due to appear for his full committal hearing. 'And don't think we in the Crown Office and Procurator Fiscal Service don't appreciate a good laugh now and again, but a summary complaint? What? For killing his girlfriend and probably his kid as well?'

The Procurator Fiscal had a smug face folk would pay good money to slap. I spread Prof. Bradley's faxed report out on the table between us, hoping he wouldn't read it too carefully. 'His *junkie* girlfriend,' I said, putting on an air of extreme patience.

'Yes, *your* former junkie client, as I recall. Ever heard of conflict of interest?'

It was true, Tanya Lang had been my client before she died; however, so far as I could see she had no earthly interests left with which I could conflict. I, on the other hand, had bills to pay. 'Let me worry about that,' I told Ogilvie, 'and, no, he wouldn't be going on a summary complaint for killing her. It would be for giving her a tenner bag.'

Ogilvie sighed. 'I take it you're aware of MacAngus –v- HMA and HMA –v- Kane? If the supply is reckless, it's culpable homicide. Bench of five judges said so.'

'What's reckless about giving a fellow junkie heroin?'

'She was a junkie who had been de-toxed and clean for several months – that's what was reckless about it.'

'Come off it. He would have thought he was giving her a present. Like you giving Mrs Ogilvie a box of chocolates. She likes them and yet she knows if she eats them they'll go straight on her hips. It's her decision: an autonomous act of an adult with full capacity. Might be some question of insanity in the case of Mrs Ogilvie, seeing how she married you, but Tanya Lang knew her way around a tenner bag.' Ogilvie rolled his eyes. 'Look,' I said, 'she was a heroin addict. She knew the possible consequences and took the risk. It's very sad, but it wasn't my client's fault she couldn't handle the hit and O.D.'d.'

'Or that your client injected her with it?' Ogilvie said.

'There's nothing substantial to suggest that.' I turned the report around to face him, flicked over the first page and pointed to the summary at the foot of the second.

This report is compiled without reference to toxicological data and on the received information that the deceased had a history of illicit drug-taking including misuse of diamorphine. That being so and as I can find no conclusive evidence of bodily trauma or physical injury to satisfy me that the deceased was forced to inject (unless threatened with a weapon) I would opine that on the balance of probabilities the cause of death was due to a fatal dose of diamorphine self-administered intravenously.

There were the usual disclaimers after that but I skipped them to stab a finger at the signature at the bottom. 'Edward Bradley, emeritus professor of—'

'Yes, I am familiar with Professor Bradley's C.V.,' Ogilvie opened the red folder in which resided the case of Her Majesty's Advocate –v- Brandon Biggam, 'and I'm familiar with your client's too. How long has he been dealing drugs?' He removed a sheath of papers. 'Let me see… first conviction for being concerned in the supply was four years ago and since then he's scarcely looked back. Are you telling me that when he supplies his girlfriend with a lethal dose of smack he doesn't know what he's doing?'

'A tenner bag and she didn't have much out of it.'

'Your client tell you that?'

'No, the forensic report says they found a wrap with heroin weighing point one five six grams.' Tenner bags used to weigh about point one of a gram but the low grade smack that Brandon Biggam and the like supplied was cut so much that weights were creeping up to double that. 'And, most importantly, you can't even prove he was there when she took it.'

'There's a strong circumstantial case. There was no citric acid in the house, no spoon was found, no signs of cooking-up at all.'

'So she smoked it.'

'No tin foil found, no tooter.'

'How was he supposed to know half a bag would kill her?'

Ogilvie smiled. He never smiled. Not unless he had the defence by the short hairs. I suddenly realised he had been toying with me up until now. 'I have a report too.' He slid a crisp sheet of paper across the table at me. It was headed, *Toxicology*. It didn't take long to read. I couldn't believe it and had to read it again.

'That was no fiver's worth,' Ogilvie said. 'Not even a tenner. Young Miss Lang had enough heroin in her blood stream to keep half the junkies in West Lothian from rattling over a holiday weekend.'

He slipped the report back into the folder and removed another sheet of paper. He handed it to me. It was a fresh petition. 'You can tell your client that the Crown will be dropping the culpable homicide charge.' Ogilvie closed the red folder again and stood to attention. For a moment I thought he might click his heels. 'Because now it's murder.'

Chapter 21

'Baa-Baa rainbow sheep have you any wool?' the little girl sang, oblivious to the man in the suit who was standing by her side.

The first batch of disclosure from the Crown in Dr Glen Beattie's case had arrived. As soon as I heard from Maggie Sinclair at Caldwell & Clark, I'd have to formally notify the prosecution of my withdrawal as principal agent, but until then all the correspondence came to me. There was no sign of any forensic reports on any of the computer analyses, only a list of witnesses and a schedule of the various items that had been taken by the police for examination. All but one of the fourteen witnesses on the list was a police officer, each speaking to a link in the chain of evidence: receiving the anonymous tip-off, obtaining a warrant, carrying out the search, signing production labels, passing the equipment on to the High-Tech Unit for analysis etc. Until the results of the computer examination were known, the defence would be no further forward; however, I was intrigued to find out Megan McIvor's take on things. The Crown had provided me with a care of address, south of Edinburgh, in the border town of Jedburgh. It turned out to be a children's day care centre where Megan had found temporary work.

She closed the book of nursery rhymes and lifted the child down from her lap. 'Off you go and play with the others, Jenny, we'll read some more later.' Megan stood. Tall and slim, she led me through the throng of children, dodging flying dods of plasticine and splashes of poster-paint, to her glass-walled office in the corner of the play area.

I took the book from her. 'Rainbow sheep?'

'Yes, and Snow White no longer has seven dwarves, she has seven guardians of the forest, and, you may be interested to learn, all the king's horses and all the king's men *can* put Humpty together again.'

'I take it Robertson's jam is verboten on the playtime pieces.'

Megan looked at me for a moment and then cracked a smile. 'I hate all that political correct crap.' She closed the door. 'The kids here used to have blackboards and chalk. I've not been here a week and they've already chucked them out and replaced them with flipcharts and felt pens.' She filled an electric kettle and switched it on. 'I suppose everyone is just trying to be kind, or, at least, not wanting to cause offence, but, I mean, why do they think I'd find a blackboard offensive?' Megan removed a couple of floral patterned mugs from a shelf. 'Oh, no,' she said in a silly voice, 'I'm black and so is that board – help - it's racial harassment.'

Megan's skin was black all right. It was black the way that the finest pearls are white. She set the mugs on the work top, the back of her slender neck catching the light from the window and taking on a golden sheen. She must have inherited her colour from her mother and, fortunately, her looks too for Megan bore no resemblance to her father.

The was an iPod station on a nearby unit. Megan turned it on, no opera: Aztec camera, *Oblivious*.

'Coffee?' Megan unscrewed the blue lid from a jar. 'Hope you don't mind caffeine-free. I'm covering for one of the girls who's on maternity leave - good to see that she was looking after herself - it's important when you're expecting.' She patted her stomach.

'When are you due?' I asked.

'Early days. I'm only ten weeks.'

'One of the advantages of being a man,' I said, 'no babies.'

'Don't you like children, Mr Munro?'

'I'm not talking about the package, it's the delivery I wouldn't fancy.'

She smiled and heaped a spoonful of instant coffee into one mug and then the other. 'As a mid-wife, before I became a community nurse, I helped a lot of woman bring their children into this world. It's amazing how soon they forget the pain of child-birth.'

A little face appeared at the glass door that separated us from the mayhem beyond. Sticky hands smeared the glass.

'You've got a fan there,' I said.

'Jenny's lovely. I don't think she's seen a black woman before. Not too many of us in this part of the jungle. Do you have any children, Mr Munro?'

'Please, it's Robbie and, no, I've no kids. I've a dad who behaves like one though.'

The kettle boiled.

'Let's keep our fathers out of this,' she said.

'Do you know what you're having?' I asked.

'Call me old fashioned, I've decided to surprise

myself.' Megan looked wistfully out of the window. 'When I worked in ante-natal, the mid-wives used to always tell the mums-to-be they were having a boy and then write 'girl' in the margin of their medical notes. That way they were always right. If the mum came back for a post-natal check-up and said the staff had guessed wrong, they just said the mum must have misheard because the prediction was written right there in the notes.' She laid the teaspoon down, screwed the lid back on the coffee jar and stared hard at me. The smile had disappeared again. 'I take it Glen sent you?' Megan broke off her stare and poured boiling water into the two mugs. 'A bridge over troubled waters?'

She'd better believe it and her ex- boyfriend would be paying the toll.

'Would you like to know how he's doing?' I asked.

'Go on then. How is he?'

'Innocent—'

'Until proven guilty, you mean?'

'It's my job to see that never happens.'

'Why you? Has my father not been able to sort it out for him? Can big Kenny not make all the nasty charges go away?' Megan went over to a small fridge in the corner of the room and took out a carton of milk. She pulled the top of the carton apart and shaped the waxed paper into a spout.

'I thought we were keeping fathers out of this?' I said. Deep breath. 'Don't you think you're being a bit hard on Glen? The case is pretty thin.'

She slammed the carton down. Some milk slopped out of the spout and onto the countertop. 'Oh, please. The police told me he left his credit card details on that scummy web-site.'

'Identity theft is rife. The internet is full of cookies, Trojans, spy-bots...' I wasn't sure if I hadn't made that last one up, but pressed on anyway. 'There is a whole industry out there that exists for the sole purpose of stealing people's identities and bank account details. Along with the dozen emails I get each day there's always one questioning the size or rigidity of my penis and another inviting me to update the password for a savings account I don't have.'

'And the dirty pictures on his PC?'

'A lot depends on their whereabouts on a PC—'

'Right there on the desktop.'

'It's possible to download stuff without even knowing it,' I said, aware of how feeble it all sounded.

'Look, Mr Munro, I don't care if you manage to get him off on some technicality.'

'I'm not talking about technicalities. I'm talking about proof beyond a reasonable doubt.'

'There is no doubt. Not so far as I'm concerned.'

'Was it you who phoned the police?'

Megan didn't answer. Jenny the toddler returned and pressed her happy, shiny face against the other side of the glass partition before waddling off, leaving behind another sticky imprint. Megan wiped the spilt milk with a cloth from the sink and picked up the milk carton again. 'I know what I saw on Glen's computer and I'm going to be a witness. The Procurator Fiscal has told me you have the right to take a statement and I'm trying to make this as pleasant as possible - but if you're here to attempt some sort of mediation, or to make me say something I know isn't true, you can forget it. I'm staying in Scotland only until the trial or until Glen pleads guilty, then I'm off and,' she patted her stomach, 'I'm taking this little fellow with me.'

'Okay,' I said, taking out my notebook and pen, 'let's get started. Tell me - do you know Glen's favourite opera?'

Megan narrowed her eyes at me, sloshed milk into one of the mugs and hovered the milk carton over the other one. 'Black or white?' she asked.

'Without milk,' I said.

Chapter 22

The I.T. revolution that swept through the business firmament sometime in the mid-nineties had somehow, in all the excitement, managed to by-pass the world of criminal defence. Every other branch of the law had succumbed to the pressures of global marketing, introducing case management systems and integrated data networks; however, the average criminal defence lawyer got along, as always, by word of mouth recommendations, a typist and a lot of paper. At any rate, that's how I'd operated until Grace-Mary had insisted on the firm investing in some hardware, which meant we now had three un-networked PC's, one with email.

I studied the heap of paperwork on my desk. The pile of finished files in the corner was considerably higher and tilting noticeably to the left.

Grace-Mary came in and looked about for a place to put that morning's mail. Somehow, despite diminishing rates of prosecutions, as Procurators Fiscal diverted more and more cases from the courts in a flurry of warning letters and fixed fines, I was wallowing in a rare oasis of work.

I sat back in my chair to let my secretary fully take in the congestion of case files and miscellaneous paperwork that lay strewn across the desk and onto a nearby chair. 'How am I supposed to wade through all of this?'

'Well, you should have kept Andy on.'

'If Andy had wanted to stay he would have. I wasn't offering that bad money.'

'You could have made him a partner.'

'He's a year qualified. And I don't need a partner. I just need a body to occasionally cover court when I'm double-booked. The clients come here looking for Munro, not the Co.'

Grace-Mary placed the wire basket of mail on the highest pile of files. 'I've dealt with the routine stuff,' she said, 'but there are one or two urgent things you'll need to look at.' She went over to the filing cabinet to look out files for the next day's court. 'So I take it you'll be doing your famous being-in-two-places-at-the-same-time trick, tomorrow? Edinburgh and Glasgow. You know you have the makings of a great cabaret act there.'

Juggling courts is just one of the abilities a defence agent needs to master if he's going to make any money. So far as the Scottish Legal Aid Board is concerned, inflation and the need to increase the legal aid rates ceased to exist sometime around nineteen ninety-one. The combination of derisory payments and a prosecution service that preferred not to prosecute but to dish out fixed fines that no-one paid, meant the only way to survive was to never turn away business. It also meant that when cases called at the same time in different courts it took some fancy footwork to keep a step ahead of a finding of contempt, especially when those courts were on opposite sides of the country.

'If Andy was still here, you could have sent him to Edinburgh. He liked going into Edinburgh and it was handy if I needed something taken back to John Lewis. You never have the time.'

'I'll just have to get in there early, do the bail undertaking and then charge through to Glasgow for my trial. Phone the Sheriff Clerk at the back of ten and say I'm held up in traffic, or having car problems, something like that.'

'I thought you were taking the train?'

'It's what we lawyers call lying,' I said. 'Try it. It's easy with a bit of practice.'

The fact was, no-one really cared if you were late for court. It only became a problem if the rest of the court business disappeared and yours was the only case left standing between the Sheriff and an early bath. The most serious crime known to the criminal courts was wasting the judge's time.

'If Andy was still here, you wouldn't have all this bother dodging between courts.'

Grace-Mary tended to go on at length when she found a topic that interested her. Speaking for one minute on a subject, without hesitation, deviation or repetition, wasn't really the challenge it might be to others.

I lifted the first letter from the basket. It was from Brandon Biggam, an untidy scrawl on prison notepaper, A5, with printed lines spaced well apart. From what I could decipher, my client was none too pleased at the Crown's change of tack. I'd have to go and placate him. Unhappy prisoners who thought they were being ignored started to look for new lawyers. It was good having private clients like Glen Beattie, but I couldn't afford clients going elsewhere. Not even pond-life like Brandon Biggam. I logged onto SLAB on-line. The notifications page was mainly red messages demanding to see the pay slips and bank statements of clients who'd applied for legal aid. Right at the top was intimation of a refusal. The applicant had no previous convictions. The Government had fixed a presumption against prison sentences of less than three months; therefore, according to the Daleks at SLAB, there was no likelihood of loss of liberty and so legal representation was not required in the interests of justice. Great, another fee slipping through my fingers.

I realised Grace-Mary was still talking. 'There's a letter in there from Caldwell & Craig.'

'It'll just be my agency instructions in Dr Beattie's case,' I said, raking through the basket. 'Charge like a wounded rhino that lot. They'll be billing him three hundred an hour, paying me two-thirds for actually doing all the work and keeping the other third for fronting the show – all because Kenny McIvor wants his son-in-law to be represented by a posh law firm.' I laughed. Grace-Mary was uncommonly quiet. I found the letter. It was a two-liner simply asking that I send on the case file. There was an enclosure stapled to the back of it. 'A mandate?'

'Maggie Sinclair from C&C thought you might want to give her a call,' Grace-Mary said, but I was already punching the numbers in.

'What's this about you taking on Glen Beattie's case?' I asked, once I'd been put through to the senior partner of my former firm, waving the letter and attached mandate at her as though we were on video phone.

'Sordid stuff, isn't it?' Margaret said.

'To you. All grist to the mill for me. In fact, a private client like this is a God send.'

'You're not pleased then?'

'Pleased?'

'About being out of the case.'

'No, of course I'm not pleased.'

'Then why did you send him?'

'Because of our understanding.'

'But why refer him to us if you had him in the first place?'

'I referred him to you, so you'd refer him back.' I realised how that might sound and so expanded. 'His father-in-law is—'

'Kenneth McIvor. I know.'

'And he wanted a big name law firm to deal with the case.'

'So he said.'

'You've spoken to him?'

'He came along with Beattie. I have to say, I thought it funny that you'd be backing out of a fee-paying case. Thought you'd gone and got yourself a conscience.'

'Well, I haven't, so the plan is that McIvor thinks you lot are dealing with the case but in actual fact I am. I get two-thirds of the fee and you'd get a third for basically doing nothing.'

'That's not happening.'

'What do you mean it's not happening? We've got an agreement.'

'I thought of it as more of a temporary understanding. Sort of pro loco et tempore, as you criminal boys like to say.'

'Yes, that's right - us criminal boys. Caldwell & Clark don't do criminal law. That was my job remember? The one I did before you and the other partners thought my work was economically unviable. Am I ringing any bells?'

Margaret cleared her throat. 'Yes, well, we've revised our policy on that. In the present climate we can't go turning work away, even if it means acting for the occasional pervert...' She qualified that statement with, 'at least those perverts who can pay privately.'

'But, Maggie, you don't know anything about criminal law.'

'I don't need to. We have a new boy. In fact you know him. Andrew Imray.'

'Andy? Andy's just newly qualified,' I managed to splutter after the moment or two required to absorb the news that my former assistant was now working for my old firm; the same firm that had asked me, very nicely, to resign my partnership on the grounds that there was no money in crime.

'But if you trained him he must know his stuff,' Maggie flattered.

'What about crime doesn't pay?'

'I think the actual words were *legal aid* doesn't pay.'

I couldn't believe what I was hearing.

'Come on, Robbie, don't be like that,' she said, in response to my snort down the telephone line. 'You're a man of the people. It's not your fault that you can't sit idly by and see the great unwashed get their just deserts. It's a character flaw I for one always found rather endearing. Impractical, but endearing. Anyway,

Andrew comes relatively cheap – which, as I recall, you didn't and if we have one or two white-collars a year then at the very least we'll wipe our face.'

'But there's the corporate image to consider. Is that not what you and the others told me as I was gently squeezed out of the door?'

'We've decided that Caldwell & Clark should provide a holistic service to its clients, even if it risks sullying the livery occasionally.'

'I'll do it for half,' I said.

'Half what?'

'I do the work, you keep the client's important father-in-law happy and we split the fee down the middle.'

'What about Andrew?'

'Tell him to find his own clients.'

Chapter 23

Next morning, after a cameo appearance at Edinburgh Sheriff Court, followed by a race for the ten forty-five train from Waverley to Queen Street and a taxi to the court, I found neither a trial nor a finding of contempt awaiting me in Glasgow. As planned, Grace-Mary had called ahead to say that I was stuck on the M8 or something, but when half the Crown witnesses failed to trap, the case had been called in my absence and put off to a later date. I returned to the agents' room where I'd left my coat and recognised, at the far end of the room next to the cafe counter, a familiar face eating a roll on sausage. It was Andy. His face was about all I recognised, for the mass of curls had been cutback to a manageable thicket, the black-framed specs exchanged for a set of frameless lenses and the rumpled suit and coffee-stained tie, replaced by bespoke tailoring and a strip of Italian silk. He waved me over. 'How's it going, Robbie?' He held out a hand and we shook.

'I don't need to ask you that,' I said, looking him up and down. 'They're obviously paying you far too much at Caldwell & Clark.'

I let Andy buy me a coffee and we took our polystyrene cups and sat down, our backs to the long row of windows from which there was a fine view of the Clyde.

'Maggie Sinclair and I had a little chat,' I said.

He ripped open a paper sachet of sugar, emptied it

into his cup. 'She told me. I hear you're not too pleased about me taking on Dr Beattie's case?'

'You could say that.' What really annoyed me was that I'd been too smart for my own good. Cutting the case out to Caldwell & Clark so I could get it back again had seemed like a stroke of genius at the time, but had really back-fired.

'To be perfectly honest,' Andy said, tipping in another sachet of sugar, 'I don't really want it. C&C only has two live criminal cases at the moment. One's a Health & Safety contravention by a construction company whose employee drilled a hole, hit an electric cable and fried himself and then there's Beattie's child-porn case. Both are losers so far as I can see. Won't be a great start to my career in the city if my first two clients get done. Before I know it I'll be back...'

'With Munro and Co?'

'I wasn't going to say that.'

'Doesn't matter. I'm glad you got a good move and, anyway, I think you're missing the point.'

'Which is?'

'A big city firm like Caldwell & Clark doesn't care if you get Dr Beattie off or if the company that electrocuted their employee is hit with a huge fine. They just want the fee. Churn the billable hours and you'll be their golden boy.'

He took a pen out of his inside jacket pocket and stirred his coffee with it. 'I never realised Munro & Co. was a charitable organisation.'

'It's not, it's just that I have to earn my reputation and I can only do that by winning. No-one walks up the close to my dingy wee office unless someone else has recommended me to them. C&C are a big name. Their gents' cloakroom is bigger than my entire office and the fact that I've forgotten more criminal law than Maggie Sinclair has ever known won't stop rich clients like Glen Beattie and Kenneth McIvor queuing up at the door and ready to pay for the privilege.'

Andy didn't look so sure. 'Maybe you're right. All the same, I want to get off to a good start. There are hundreds of young lawyers looking for jobs. I think it was telling Maggie that I'd worked for you that swung it. She said you didn't suffer fools gladly.'

If Andy was trying to butter me up with a spot of flattery, he was doing not a bad job.

'She also said that if I could put up with you for eighteen months I must be unusually resilient. Either that or mad,' he added, slightly taking the sheen of things.

'Well, like I say,' I raised my cup to him, 'all the best, and if you ever find the sudden urge for junkie clients and legal aid forms give me a shout.'

He smiled. 'I'll always be grateful to you, Robbie. For giving me a start.'

The coffee was lukewarm. I finished it with my second gulp. A leisurely walk back to the train station and I could be in Linlithgow and setting about a bacon roll and a proper cup of coffee at Sandy's by one o'clock. I stood up. Andy joined me.

'Robbie, what should I do about Dr Beattie?'

'Looks like he's yours now.'

'No, I don't mean that. How can I get him off if I can't see a defence.'

'I'm afraid that's your problem,' I said, trying to

keep the vindictive note out of my voice and failing.

Andy turned to look out of the window.

'What I mean,' I said, 'is that I can't help you. I don't even know what evidence there is against him. I know the cops took away his PC and laptop and other equipment, but I've no idea what, if anything, they found.'

Andy bent over and unlatched the straps on his new black leather briefcase. He removed a bundle of papers. 'Disclosure,' he said. He sat down again and stared up at me. He was a worried young man. 'It's the latest batch for Dr Beattie's case. I downloaded it from the Crown web-site this morning.'

What was Andy doing at Glasgow Sheriff Court anyway, if he was only working on two cases and one of those was based in Linlithgow? 'Our meeting like this,' I said, 'it's not a coincidence is it?'

'Do you mean it was fate?'

'No I mean it was Grace-Mary, wasn't it?'

'She phoned this morning to see how I was settling in and happened to mention that you were coming through.' He screwed up his face. 'Do you think you could take a quick look?'

Thrown in at the deep end, I could understand why he wanted to make a good first impression. I just wished it wasn't with a case that was rightfully mine. Bad enough to lose the brief, without having to do work on it for free for the Firm that had taken it from me. From twenty-five miles away I could almost hear the sizzling of bacon and gurgling of pure Arabica. 'Andy, this case has nothing to do with me anymore. You've got to deal with it yourself. Look at the evidence and find a defence.'

'I can't,' he said. 'I've tried and there isn't one.'

'Then plead guilty.'

'Were you going to plead him guilty?'

'If he's a paedo, I'd be happy to string him up by his nuts.'

'But you were going to try and find a defence if you could?'

'That was my job. Now it's yours.'

He slumped in his chair and started to shove the papers back into his briefcase.

Was I being too hard? 'Give me them,' I said.

'What?' Andy looked up, a faint glimmer of hope in his eye.

'I'll read the papers on the train and let you know what I think. I got the other laptop forensically-examined. Who knows? There may be an angle somewhere.'

'What laptop are you talking about? There's nothing in here about any laptop. It says the indecent images are on the hard-drive of a home computer.'

So, despite Beattie's declarations to the contrary, there were images on his PC. Megan McIvor had found them. No wonder she'd decided to break-up with him. 'Beattie has a couple of laptops,' I told Andy. 'An old one and a new one. They used to belong to Dr MacGregor and he inherited them. The police took one away and it turned out to be clean. They didn't know about the old one and so I had it looked at by Jimmy Garvie, the I.T. guy I use, just in case there was some sort of mix-up.'

He smiled. 'You mean in case you could *create* some

sort of mix-up?'

I took the bundle of papers. 'I'll let you know what I find. And by the way you owe me one.'

Chapter 24

'How's Andy?' Grace-Mary asked as I walked through the door.

'In a mild state of panic,' I said, emptying my briefcase. There had been a train delay, I was due at Polmont YOI to see Brandon Biggam in forty minutes and there was still a bacon roll waiting for me at Sandy's.

'It's a shame. He's too young to be working all by himself through in Glasgow. The place is full of nutters.' Grace-Mary made it sound like my former assistant was working from the boot of his car in a slum area of Glasgow. She was clearly oblivious to Andy's palatial surroundings in the city centre and the team of secretaries and paralegals he no doubt had at beckon call.

'Oh, I'm sure he'll muddle through,' I said. I'd learned from bitter experience never to disagree with my secretary unless absolutely necessary. 'After all he had a good grounding here.'

Grace-Mary grunted. 'He phoned just before you came back and said he'd bumped into you in Glasgow.'

'Oh, yes, he bumped into me all right.'

'That must have been nice. I think you're helping him with the Beattie case?'

'Apparently so. Now can *you* help *me* with a few cases? I've got a stack of files here with no disclosure yet. Get onto the Fiscal and ask what's happening.' I rummaged around on my desk for Brandon Biggam's file. It took me a minute or so to realise that my secretary hadn't moved. 'Please?'

Grace-Mary left the room momentarily. 'There was a lot of disclosure sent from the PF this morning,' she said upon her return. 'I downloaded it for you.'

No longer did Crown & Procurator Fiscal Service send me documents by post. Someone, somewhere, had decided that even though Her Majesty's Advocate was prosecuting my clients, Her Majesty's Royal Mail couldn't be trusted to deliver the paperwork. It had either to be collected on a pen-drive from the Fiscal's office, something I usually did while I was at court, or downloaded from the new CPFS web-site, which was where Grace-Mary came in. Either way, I strongly suspected that it had less to do with issues of confidentiality and more to do with the prosecution's paper and printing budget and the added bonus of annoying defence agents.

'Thanks,' I said, 'you must show me how to do that some day.'

She dropped several bundles of paper down in front of me. 'And there's an email in about Dr Beattie's case too. Will I print it off? Wouldn't want you straining your baby-blues and I'll need a copy to put on the file before we send it to Andy.'

I told Grace-Mary it could wait and located the email message. It was from Jimmy Garvie, who'd examined the hard-drive from Dr MacGregor's now obliterated laptop.

Hi Robbie. Find attached report for your doctor client and my fee note. Regards to the old man. Cheers Jimmy.

I opened the attachment and gave it a cursory look-through. I'd say this for him, Jimmy knew how to pad out a report. Not only was there a list of all the document and image files on the hard drive, he'd included each one in an appendix to his report. The whole thing ran to over eighty pages. Jimmy had obviously realised that this was not a legal aid case and if he was going to charge a packet he might as well make it look like the client was getting his money's worth. Expert reports like newspapers are usually best read from back to front. I electronically-flicked past the endless list of Jimmy's qualifications and I.T. definitions, until I came to the end. To summarise the summary, Doc Mac had nothing on his laptop apart from Windows 98, the usual standard programs, some correspondence and absolutely no image files other than Microsoft icons, wallpapers and themes. There was no porn of any kind. Could Jimmy not have told me that over the phone? I closed the report. There was another attachment. Jimmy's fee-note: six hundred pounds! To say there was nothing incriminatory on a laptop that was now in a landfill? That would bite a huge chunk out of the one thousand pound payment to account I'd received from Beattie.

Still fuming gently at the size of Jimmy Garvie's bill, I arrived at Polmont Young Offenders' Institution where there was a slight difficulty at the reception desk when the X-ray machine picked up a suspect item in my briefcase. It turned out to be an apple that I'd threatened myself with a few days before as part of my new health-eating regime and then forgotten about. I was told to eat it or put it in the bucket. Instead, I stored it in one of the mobile phone lockers.

When, eventually, I had cleared security, I came across Paul Sharp sitting in the visitors' waiting room surrounded by mothers and girlfriends ready to go up to the main open-visit room. A squad of toddlers played amongst the sticky-plastic toys scattered beneath a silent flat screen TV that was showing the NASDAQ equity-movers on the Bloomberg channel.

'Here to see someone?' Paul asked. 'Or did you just come to check your stock portfolio?'

I sat down beside him. 'Bit of both. Brandon Biggam is a big part of my pension plan.'

'Any sign of the kid?'

'None.'

'You mean you haven't beaten it out of your client yet?'

'No need. I've already told him I can work him a great deal if he tells me where the baby is. He says he can't help and we all know he'd shop his granny to the Nazi's for a week less in the jail. The baby is either dead or he genuinely doesn't know where it is. One way he definitely won't say: the other he can't.'

Paul had thought of another possibility. 'Biggam would also *sell* his Granny to the Nazi's. Do you think he might have found a buyer for the kid and killed its mum?'

Anything was possible, but it sounded slightly too elaborate for my client. This was a guy who was not twenty-one years old yet and about to do his third sentence for drug-supplying. If he couldn't sell some tenner bags without getting caught, I wasn't convinced he could organise the sale of a baby without somebody finding out.

A side door opened and a female prison officer came in and asked the visitors to follow her upstairs to the open visits room. 'I'll be back in a minute for you two,' she called to us.

Paul tried to put another question to me. 'Do you ever think—'

'I try not to.'

He laughed. 'No, really, do you ever think if you hadn't done such a good job for him the last time he'd have still been in jail and not able to give his girlfriend the drugs that killed her?'

'Might have delayed the inevitable,' I said. 'That's all.'

'You did sort of take advantage of that floater, though, didn't you? Made Brandon Biggam sound like a confused young lad. What was it you said? Youthful experimentation with drugs? That new Sheriff didn't look like she'd seen a real-life junkie before. She was straight out of Edinburgh Uni, ten years at the Bar doing intellectual property rights or something and then, bosh, here's a wig, now listen to what Mr Munro has to say about his poor misunderstood client who's been frightfully inquisitive about drugs.'

What was this all about? Paul had been a defence agent longer than me and knew the score. 'Easy,' I said. 'I realise you've lodged an application to the Judicial Appointment Board, but you're not a Sheriff yet. No need to get all holier than thou. Remember that if there hadn't been an automatic one-half remission on sentences, Brandon would still be inside despite a sugar-coated plea in mitigation.'

The female screw returned and held the door open for us.

'I didn't mean it to sound like that, Robbie,' Paul said, as we walked out of the waiting room. 'It's just that, you do start to think about these things.'

'How is the search for your third referee going?' I asked, while we waited at yet another locked door.

'Don't ask. I'm almost on the verge of going cap in hand to Hugh Ogilvie. He's a Procurator Fiscal and you know how much the JAB like the Prosecution. Being a PF is practically your personal invitation to don a horsehair wig. A reference from him couldn't hurt any.'

It was true; there was an inordinate number of ex-prosecutors on the bench. Not necessarily a bad thing, mind you. Defence agent turned Sheriff, poacher turned gamekeeper, could make for a real dog of a Sheriff. To a prosecutor, accused persons were just names on a file. Get some Sheriff who's spent the last twenty years defending the scum of the earth and the quality of mercy could become very strain'd indeed.

I didn't have any fears about Paul, neither did I want to hurt his feelings, but there was no way I could go grovelling to Hugh Ogilvie for a reference, even if the reward was a six-figure salary and copper-bottomed pension. Nearly as bad as the only guaranteed route to becoming a Sheriff that I knew: doing a stint as prosecutor for the Solicitors Disciplinary Tribunal. It was an unremunerated post, but being such a disloyal, heartless scumbag that you'd prosecute your professional brothers as a hobby, was obviously the sort of quality the Board most looked for in a shrieval candidate.

The door opened at last and we climbed the two flights of stairs. 'I suppose you've got to do what you've got to do,' I said.

'But you wouldn't? Who's being holier than thou now?'

Paul was one of my best pals. I didn't want to fall out with him. I knew he'd make a great Sheriff, no point trying to put him off the idea. 'Don't worry, you'll find someone. You just haven't given it enough thought. Stop thinking local, widen your horizons. You've been around a long time in this business. There must be someone important who owes you one.'

We parted company when we reached the closed-visit rooms, a long L-shaped corridor with glass-walled rooms down the right hand side. Brandon Biggam was waiting for me in the first of the rooms. I didn't expect him to be Mr Happy now that the charge against him, far from being reduced, was raised to murder. He wasn't. 'I'm getting charged with murdering the bitch? All I did was give her a tenner bag. She practically begged me for it. She never even paid for it.'

'The toxicology report—'

'The what?'

When they did a post-mortem on Tanya they took samples of her body fluids and tested them.'

'Like blood and pish and that?'

Not exactly the terminology used, as I recalled. 'The results showed a massive amount of diamorphine. Easily enough to kill her.'

'I gave her a tenner bag. I told you. Geordie Lyons was there – he'll go a witness.'

'If that's right,' I told him, 'then Tanya must have taken it on top of smack she'd had earlier.'

'She was too skint to buy gear.'

'I'll have to have the samples re-tested,' I said. 'There must be a mistake.'

'You better believe it. I'm not going down for life for that wee cow.' He smashed his fist down on the table, swung back on his chair and booted the underneath. The table was bolted to the floor and didn't budge. The screw in the booth at the end of the corridor lowered his newspaper a fraction and then carried on reading.

My client pointed his finger at me. 'I'm telling you right now you'd better get this sorted or —'

I'm not sure what he was going to say after that because his next words were more of a yelp of pain than anything intelligible. He stood up, eyes screwed in pain, as I twisted his finger in my hand. The average garage mechanic is paid more than a legal aid lawyer – even on a murder case - a plumber would balk. I rose to my feet, his finger still gripped tightly in my hand. 'I'll do what I can,' I said, 'and I'll be back when I have more news.' I let go. He was nursing his injured finger as I left. 'Until then - don't go anywhere.'

Chapter 25

Six hundred quid for a negative report? I was still trying to come to terms with Jimmy Garvie's fee when I returned from court, around noon the next day, and was on the verge of giving him a call when I remembered my promise to Andy. I hadn't looked through the new evidence on my way back from Glasgow the other day, because I'd found a newspaper and spent the forty-minute journey trying to answer a question in the Herald crossword. Eventually, I'd just entered some random words so that the other train passengers wouldn't realise how hopeless I was.

I found the bundle of papers. Maggie had put them in the case file along with the earlier batch. I now had all the evidence in Glen Beattie's case. Andy might be a high-flyer, but he was far too trusting. Just because I'd agreed to peruse the documentation didn't mean I was ready to wave good-bye to HMA –v- Beattie. After all, why should I do work for an employee who'd jumped ship, on behalf of a client for whom I no longer acted?

I phoned the surgery, using Jimmy Garvie's laptop report and the new disclosure evidence as an excuse to set up a meeting.

Morning surgery was still ongoing and there was no way the receptionist would give me an appointment any time soon, so I decided to nip down to Sandy's and look at the papers over the top of a bacon roll. That would let the doctor finish what he was doing, grab a bite to eat and I could drop in on him shortly before his two o'clock surgery. With a little gentle persuasion and a lot of criticism of Andy's forensic abilities, I reckoned I would be back on the case in no time.

'Your usual tea and toast?' Sandy laughed when I came in and sat down at a corner table. 'How come you no finda that wean?'

'You mean bambino?'

He shrugged. 'Whatever. Everybody in Linlithgow wants to know where it is. I had the telly people in here yesterday. Asked a lot of questions but never bought any food. Last time I help the media. Next time—'

'Bacon roll, extra-crispy, brown sauce and an Americano.' I tapped my wrist where I didn't have a watch. 'I'm in a hurry.'

'Yeah, a hurry to go see your child-killer.' Was Sandy's parting shot.

The bundle of disclosure papers was only about half an inch thick and mainly related to the police search which had centred almost entirely on Dr Beattie's study. There was a copy of the search warrant and of a search log, giving details of which police officer had found what, where and when, right down to the exact minute. There was also a final schedule summarising all the items seized. So far as I could see, every piece of hardware had been removed: P.C., printer, scanner, digital camera as well as numerous CD's and DVD's. It didn't take me long to flick through it all and my bacon roll and coffee arrived as I was moving on to the important stuff; the forensic examination report. I took a bite of roll, turned to the summary at the back and there it was: twelve video clips had been found on the hard-drive of Dr Beattie's PC, all containing indecent images of children. The legal definition of a child for pornography purposes was increased from sixteen to eighteen years of age in around two thousand and three. I'd once heard a lawyer addressing a jury and asking if they'd ever bought a copy of the Sunday People or The Sun back in the early eighties, when Samantha Fox appeared as a topless sixteen-year-old. His argument had been that, if they had, they'd now be considered paedophiles. It was a good idea... Well, it had been an idea, though not one that endeared him to the jury or that did his client any good, as I recalled. I turned to the middle pages of the report and realised how much trouble Beattie was in. The children in the videos were a lot younger than the teenage Miss Fox, and the clips were assessed as ranging from level one: images of erotic posing, with no sexual activity, right up to level five, which I didn't even want to think about. No wonder Andy was having trouble finding a defence: there wasn't one. Beattie had painted himself into a corner by telling the cops his PC was only used by him, password-protected no less, and now here was a report saying that some extremely bad images had been downloaded onto it. Just when I thought things couldn't get any worse for Beattie, I turned to the next item in the bundle. It was a credit card statement in the name of Dr G. D. Beattie. Someone, presumably Andy, had highlighted an entry dated the week before the young doctor's arrest. It was a payment made to a web-site. The suffix was TH. I was guessing: Thailand. Did I really want this stinker of a case?

I was still wondering that as I crossed the street to the medical centre where I was almost knocked down by a familiar yellow sports-hatchback pulling out of the car park. Fiona Scott seemed to be looking straight at me. I waved, but she turned her head and drove on.

Inside the doctor's waiting room a number of the living dead had already gathered. I didn't quite catch what the receptionist said as I walked briskly through the already partially full waiting room, with a smile and a nod in her direction, and was down the corridor to Beattie's office before she could move out of her seat.

When I walked in, the doctor was sitting behind his desk, face flushed, tying a knot in his tie. I looked around the room. The strip of paper on the examination bed was rumpled and torn.

Beattie smoothed his ruffled hair. 'Mr Munro?' Not Robbie. 'What are you doing here?'

'Just thought I'd drop in with the results of the analysis on Dr MacGregor's laptop,' I said, pretending I didn't notice anything out of the ordinary. What the doctor did during his lunch break was nothing to do with me - even if he wanted to have a say about what I ate in mine.

'So that's it?' Beattie asked when I'd summarised Jimmy Garvie's findings without mentioning the cost involved. 'Just a few word-processor documents. Anything else?'

'Nope. Clean as a whistle.'

'Waste of time then?'

In hindsight that was a fair summing up.

'Well, then,' he said, rising to his feet, 'thanks for popping in.'

He held out a hand. I ignored it and leaned against the examination bed. 'Glen, you know how I recommended you to Caldwell & Craig?'

'Yes, thanks for that. Very impressive. I met with the senior partner, Mrs Sinclair. She speaks highly of you.'

'I think I made a mistake.'

'About what?'

'About thinking they'd instruct me to act as their agent.'

'Yes, I did wonder. Maggie, Mrs Sinclair that is, said she'd be dealing with my case personally.'

'She won't be—'

'Well supervising it. She introduced me to her assistant. Seemed quite young, but very much on the ball.'

'He's a baby.' Not the best choice of word in the circumstances.

Beattie shrugged. 'You know what they say. Always best to have an old doctor and a young lawyer.'

Did they really say that? 'Well, you can decide whether you think that's sound advice when you're dubbed up with the beasts in Peterhead prison.'

The young doctor's features shrivelled. 'What am I supposed to do? I can't keep changing lawyers. It was you who told me to go to Caldwell & Clark.'

'I know—'

'And you also told me that the case against me was weak.'

'That was before.'

'Before what?'

'Before I met your ex-girlfriend and she told me

155

that there was child-porn on your home computer. Before I saw a forensic report confirming that fact, and before I read your credit card statement showing a transaction for twenty-nine dollars to some paedophile web-site in Thailand.'

The young doctor looked liked someone was giving him a surprise prostate examination. If one of his patients had gone as pale as he had at that moment, he'd have called for an ambulance. Beattie kneaded his brow between thumb and forefinger. 'I don't understand.' He grabbed the copy credit card statement. 'This can't be right.'

I took another look at the rumpled white sheet on the examination couch. 'What is the extent of your friendship with Fiona Scott?'

He hesitated, then looked up at me. 'It's…'

'Complicated?'

'A professional relationship…'

I've never been able to raise only one eyebrow but right at that moment I came close.

'And we share certain interests: opera, rugby, the outdoors… look I don't have to explain myself to you – you're not even my lawyer any more. Just leave the report. I'll see Maggie Sinclair gets it.'

'You're not going back to Caldwell & Clark,' I said.

'I'll do—'

'You'll do what I advise you—'

'How dare you!' The pallor had left Beattie's features and his face was now ablaze with anger.

I took my foot off the emotional accelerator pedal. 'Okay. Calm down and listen to me.' He didn't. He jumped to his feet, marched to the door and held it open for me. I went over and closed it again.

'Is everything all right?' came a voice from the other side of the door, the receptionist. 'Dr Beattie, it's five past two.'

'Tell her you'll be another ten minutes,' I said.

'I will do no such—'

I opened the door and gave the receptionist a smile. 'Dr Beattie will be free by quarter past.' I shut the door before she could protest. 'Sit down,' I told the doctor. He did but he picked up the phone. 'Nancy, if Mr Munro has not left the building in the next two minutes I want you to call the police.'

'You're making a big mistake,' I said. 'Your new lawyer doesn't have a clue. Stick with me and —'

'That's thirty seconds.'

'Don't do this,' I said. 'I'm trying to tell you that—'

The phone buzzed and Beattie took the call.

'That was Fiona Scott. A *professional* call,' he said, replacing the receiver. 'One of my patients has died at the hospice. I think you knew him.'

Chapter 26

After work I took a body-swerve into The Red Corner Bar, looking for my dad. I hadn't managed to get hold of him since the sad news of Vince's death. All I knew was that he was on the loose and, of course, being the only human on the planet with no mobile phone, completely off-radar.

Sammy Veitch shouldered in beside me at the bar. 'Grouse - double,' the ambulance-chaser called to Brendan. He bumped against me. 'And Robbie's paying.'

'What's wrong with you?' I asked.

'What's wrong? Oh, nothing. Except I've been rushing around like a blue-arsed fly trying to track down your dead cop.'

'No luck?'

The whisky arrived. Sammy sconed it in one deft, flowing movement and rattled the base of his glass on the countertop. 'Luck? The man's a ghost.' By the grumpy look on his face, the pun was not intended. 'I've phoned every dirt-shoveller in West Lothian - even been up to the mortuary at St John's. Nobody knows nothing. I need a body, Robbie. With a body there'll be a widow and with a policeman's widow there's bound to be a stoater of a claim.'

'It was in the Gazette,' Brendan said, setting Sammy up with another double. He reached under his side of the counter, pulled out the local rag and started flicking through it. 'There you are. Page five. Man killed in road accident... pronounced dead at the scene... tragedy on Linlithgow High Street... the man's name has not been released as the next-of-kin have still to be notified.'

Sammy snatched the paper from under Brendan's nose. 'Let me see that. Pronounced dead? Who by?'

'A doctor?' Brendan ventured.

'Cheers, Einstein.'

Brendan's left eye-lid lowered a fraction.

'Brendan's right,' I said. 'Had to be one of the local doctors. Maybe Dr Beattie. The surgery is nearby and the dead guy had been in to see him before he came to see me.'

'What else do you know?' Sammy demanded of me. 'Who've they got for it?'

'For knocking him down? No-one's been to see me. I don't even know if anyone will actually be charged.'

'And why wouldn't they be?'

'Well, the guy did run out onto the road.'

'I thought you said that the van that hit him was overtaking.'

'A parked car.'

'There you are then.'

'But it was parked on double-yellows. The ones right across from my office.'

Sammy shook his head. 'Won't make much difference. First rule of driving – don't squash pedestrians and, anyway, I can live with a degree of contributory negligence.' He knocked back his drink and rattled the glass on the counter top. Brendan leaned over and put his squashed boxer's nose in Sammy's face. 'Rattle your glass at me again and I'll be happy to arrange a meeting with you and this dead guy.'

Sammy held up his hands. 'Sorry, Brendan. No offence. Got a bit preoccupied there. Who'd think finding a stiff could be this hard?' He wrestled a ten pound note from his sporran. 'Same again for me. Robbie's fine. Have one yourself, though.'

Brendan grunted, took the tenner along with Sammy's empty glass and turned to the optics.

'And, of course, it was the lorry coming in the opposite direction that actually killed him.' I said. 'The van only knocked him down.'

'Don't muddy the waters, Robbie,' Sammy said, receiving his third double in quick succession. 'White-van-man's to blame, the lorry driver's in the clear. It's a case of *sine qua non causans*.' He folded the newspaper and gave it back to Brendan. That's Latin, by the way, champ.' Brendan's knuckles whitened as the newspaper crumpled in his hand. 'Too bad about wee Vince, though,' Sammy said.

Brendan shoved an empty whisky glass at me. 'That reminds me. I kept you a drop back from the other night. Actually it was Vince's idea. Said wasting good whisky was a crime and even you couldn't defend that.' He pulled the cork from the bottle of Port Ellen. There was only half-an-inch in the bottom.

Sammy was about to rattle his glass but stopped himself just in time. 'Don't mind if I do.'

'Vince left it for Robbie,' Brendan said.

'I only want a taste,' Sammy replied. 'Are you not going to let me toast the wee man?'

I shrugged at Brendan.

The barman brought another glass and halved what

was left in the bottle between us. 'Water?'

It was a twenty-four year old, cask strength, two hundred quid a bottle, work of distilling art. I wasn't going to risk drowning it. I raised my glass to Vince and drank. I was savouring the last of Islay's finest when the door opened and my dad rolled in like a buckled wheel.

'Where have you been?' I asked.

He ignored me and approached the bar where he immediately spotted the empty bottle of Port Ellen on the counter. He picked up my glass and sniffed it.

'Take him home, Robbie,' Brendan said.

'He's taking me nowhere,' my dad growled back at him.

'Yes he is. You've had enough, Alex.'

'Come on now, Dad.' I took him by the arm but he pulled away.

'I want a drink!'

Brendan sighed. 'One drink and then you're gone, understood?'

My old man nodded. 'Right you are, son. No bother.' A number of the former occupants had vacated those barstools nearest to us. He pulled one over and sat down.

Brendan waved a hand at the row of optics behind him, well stocked with the usual blended suspects. 'What'll you have?' He put a glass under an optic. 'Bell's okay?'

A loud snort parted my dad's bushy moustache.

Brendan moved the glass along one. 'Or there's Grouse—'

'Port Ellen.'

Brendan sighed. 'I've a bottle of Laphroaig

somewhere - same thing.'

My dad picked up the empty Port Ellen bottle and pointed at the label. 'I want Port Ellen. It's me and Vince's favourite.'

Brendan tried to prise the empty bottle free from my dad's grip but failed. 'Come on now, Alex. You know I had to get that in special. I've a bottle of Laphroaig. You can have a wee-half of that on the house and then Robbie will take you up the road.'

My dad gave him a look that would have stunned a crow. Those regulars who had not retreated far enough, reeled backwards as the hand holding the bottle sent it smashing to the floor. The other hand shot out and grabbed the barman's shirt front, pulling him forward.

Brendan was about the same age as me, an ex-prize-fighter, fit and sober. If my dad had been thirty-years younger it might have been a different story. If he was thirty years younger, they could have sold tickets. But he wasn't. He was sixty-odd with a dodgy heart-valve. I dived in, breaking my old man's grip.

'Right! That's it!' Brendan threw up the flap at the end of the counter and marched to the other side of the bar. 'You're out of here!' He seized my dad by the shoulder and pulled, but couldn't budge him an inch off the stool.

Some regulars came over to try and talk sense to my dad and thought better of it when he turned his head at them and snarled. I'd never seen him like that. He liked his whisky but it never seemed to have that much effect on him. How much had he had to drink? I wondered.

Brendan let go of him and turned to me. 'Take him

away, Robbie or so help me...'

'Let's go,' I said, sounding more confident than I felt. To my surprise he stood, but made no move towards the door. He looked around the bar, hands out by his side; an unspoken challenge to every man present. Brendan planted his feet, tensed his body. I stepped between them. 'What do you think you're doing? How do you think Vince would like to see you acting like this?'

A light tap on my shoulder. It was Sammy. He held out a glass with a measure of whisky. The last drop of Port Ellen in Linlithgow. Without a word I took it from him and handed it to my dad. My old man sniffed it suspiciously. With the amount he must have consumed that night, how he could possibly distinguish a rare Islay malt from a glass of red diesel I did not know. He drank the whisky in a oner and then started to cry. I felt a tap on my shoulder as I led him to the door. It was Sammy.

'Talk to the doctor,' he whispered in my ear. 'Find me the body and leave the widow to me.'

Chapter 27

The following Wednesday morning they burned Vince and put him in an urn.

Jill, his daughter, laid on a spread back at his house and afterwards I found myself in the company of a few of the other mourners in the Red Corner Bar. My dad hadn't spoken about the events of the other evening and imbibed nothing stronger than ginger beer all day. Although I'd had some concern over how Brendan would take to my old man's appearance, fortunately, the publican was acting as though nothing had happened and so, after a quick drink in remembrance, I left the other black ties and went back to the office.

Grace-Mary must have heard me climbing up the stairs because when I walked into reception she was holding the telephone out to me. I read her lips. It was Jimmy Garvie.

'Hi, Jimmy. Is there a problem?' I asked.

'It's about my fee. You know - for that old laptop? I was just wondering, seeing how it's a private case, if there was any chance of you paying it kind of soonish? I'm strapped for cash and I need to fork out on some new equipment. All my other outstanding fees are in legal aid cases and I'm not holding my breath.' I grunted non-committally. 'What's happening with the case, anyway?' Jimmy asked. 'You going to need me as a witness?'

'Unlikely.'

'Not surprised, if that old laptop's all they have for evidence. You still got it?'

'The laptop?'

'Yeah.'

'No—'

'Where is it?'

'Gone.'

'That's a shame. Any of it left? Sometimes you can recover the hard disk. Those old machines can be pretty tough.'

'You know it's damaged then?' He didn't answer. 'I'll see what I can do about your bill,' I said.

'And the laptop?'

'What about it?'

'I'm interested. I'll buy it, even if it is damaged. You could take it off my fee.'

'Are you serious?'

'Yeah. Those old computers are very collectable. You'd be surprised how much—'

'Jimmy, I don't have it. It's completely destroyed.'

Jimmy paused. 'I meant to ask, how's your dad?'

'A very good friend of his has died. I'm just back from the funeral.'

'Sorry to hear that, Robbie. Give him my best will you? Speak later, cheers.'

The line went dead. Talk about optimistic? There was no chance of me paying Jimmy's fee any time soon. Beattie had only given me a grand up front and I wasn't about to part with more than half the cash on an outlay for a useless report. Jimmy would just have to wait until I'd squeezed some more money out of my former client. Why had he seemed so keen for me to give him the laptop? A collector's item? I couldn't imagine anyone on the Antiques Road Show getting all worked-up over a Windows 98 laptop. I was still mulling things over when Grace-Mary put through another call. Jimmy Garvie again.

'Sorry to be a pest, Robbie, but, my report—'

'You'll get paid just as soon as I do, Jimmy.'

'It's not that... I was thinking... If you're not needing me as a witness... I don't suppose you'll really be needing the report? I mean it was negative for any dirty pictures and if the laptop's destroyed...'

'Yes?'

'Well you might as well just delete it.'

'I could, but then how would I justify charging my client six hundred notes for a non-existent report?'

It was nearly three o'clock, other than dropping into the office first thing, I'd done nothing all day because of the funeral and I had a Kilimanjaro of paperwork to scale. I took the opportunity of another long pause from Jimmy to try and wind up the conversation. 'So, thanks again, Jimmy, and as soon as my client pays up, you'll have your money. Okay? See you later then—'

'Forget it.'

'What?'

'My fee.'

'But—'

'After all, the whole examination was a damp squib at the end of the day. Just delete my report and we'll pretend it never happened. How's that?' He laughed. 'And don't say I'm not good to you.'

'Jimmy, it's kind of you, but it really doesn't make

any difference to me. I'm not paying you, my client is. I'm going to ask him for more money to cover it.'

'But he's not your client any more is he?'

'Jimmy, what's this all about? Who have you been talking to about the case?'

'Sorry, I'm only trying to help.'

'Then let me get back to work. I'll speak to you later.'

'Robbie—'

'Bye, Jimmy.'

Top of the pile of mail was a letter from Professor Bradley apologising for the delay and enclosing his final report on the post-mortem examination of Tanya Lang. I didn't expect it to be different in any important way from the draft he'd faxed to me earlier and it wasn't; just a lot more detailed. I flicked through the first few pages containing the usual blurb about the time and place of the examination and setting out the Professor's remit and his impressive C.V.

The autopsy had been performed before the results of the toxicology were known and the report mentioned this, concluding that the cause of death was consistent with respiratory failure due to heroin overdose. There was passing reference to tachyphylaxis, the tolerance to a drug and its contaminants which users develop and promptly lose after a period of abstinence. It was a familiar enough story: junkies came off smack for a while and then, thinking they'd won the battle, relapsed. What harm could one little hit do? They could handle it. Trouble was they couldn't. The tenner bag that had made for an evening's entertainment three months before had become a death sentence.

But that scenario no longer fitted the circumstances surrounding the death of Tanya Lang. Hugh Ogilvie had already taken great pleasure in explaining the contents of the Crown's toxicology report. Tanya had not made a mistake about how much smack she could handle. She'd received a massive overdose that would have killed even the most veteran junkie. The original question I'd asked of Professor Bradley was whether it was more likely she'd injected herself or that the fix had been given by force. I read again his findings on the signs of trauma that had been sufficiently superficial to allow him to opine that, on the balance of probabilities, there had been voluntary self-administration of the fatal dose. Given the level of toxicity, the most likely inferences to be drawn now were that either Tanya had committed suicide or someone had given her a massive over-dose knowing the result was certain death. I knew which of those two scenario the Crown preferred.

Prof. Bradley's fee note was attached to the back of his report. Suddenly, I had a terrible thought that sent me scrambling for Brandon Biggam's file where my worst fears were realised; I'd forgotten to obtain legal aid sanction for Tanya Lang's autopsy. There was no way SLAB would sanction a retrospective request. It meant I'd have to cover the cost myself – or...

Professor Bradley's secretary patched me through to her boss on his mobile.

'That you, Robbie?' he shouted at me. 'I'm on my way to Galashiels. Farming accident.'

'I can hear you fine,' I told him. 'No need to shout.'

'What's that?' he bellowed.

'Tanya Lang. I forgot to get sanction from SLAB for

your fee,' I yelled back at him.

'Sorry. Once it's through the books, that's it. The fee's shared with the University and there's no way that lot will let you off the hook - not with all the cut-backs.'

Great. Three hundred and eighty pounds down the drain.

'I'll give you a call later about it,' he roared. 'The hands-free is knackered. If I don't get off this thing there'll be an accident.'

Accident? That reminded me. 'Before you go, I don't suppose you were called in for that road accident on Linlithgow High Street, last week?'

'What's it to you?'

'I heard he was a policeman. You know what my dad is like – he'll be wondering if it was anyone he knew.'

'Don't think so. Youngish bloke, sub-forty, Renton, I think was his name. Bill Renton? Not sure if he was a cop, but I doubt if he'd have been around when your dad was in uniform. Robbie, I'll really have to go, this road is a nightmare. Sorry about your mix-up over the fee.'

He rang off. I'd not held out much hope of having Prof. Bradley waive his fee. I had to face it - anyone who had to cut up dead people on my request deserved to be paid for it. I reviewed my limited options. One: bump Professor Bradley's fee and look elsewhere for opinions on matters medically Forensic from now on – drastic. Two: pay the three hundred odd quid out of my own pocket – crazy-talk. Three: I picked up the phone and called a certain free-phone number for use by those who'd been involved in an accident.

'Sammy? Robbie. I think I've found that dead cop. His details? Before we come to that, I wonder, could we discuss the possibility of a finder's fee?'

Chapter 28

I had arranged to meet Kenneth McIvor at one o'clock at the Scottish National Portrait Gallery. The grand-old, red-sandstone building had recently re-opened following a major refurbishment and was handily situated for me, a short walk from Waverley Station.

I strolled down Queen Street, gazing up at the poets, monarchs and statesmen carved into the neo-gothic façade while, from the battlements of Edinburgh Castle, the one o'clock gun sounded in confirmation of my punctuality.

I was met at the entrance by a couple of men in sombre suits. One of them I recognised from my breakfast meeting, Chris the chauffeur. He waved a metal-detecting device over my body and then allowed me to pass under the statues of William Wallace and Robert the Bruce and through to the main hall.

It seemed McIvor was killing two birds with the one stone by fitting me in after a photo-opportunity, for a small crowd had gathered amongst the usual throng of art-lovers and sightseers and there were a number of cameras and journalists in evidence. I hovered on the fringes of the ever-growing group that had assembled in the centre of the hall. From that distance I was still well able to see McIvor standing head and shoulders above the crowd, staring up at a pageant frieze depicting famous Scots, starting with Thomas Carlyle, who championed the building of a Scottish portrait gallery, and including figures such as David Livingstone, James Watt, Robert Burns, Adam Smith, David Hume, the Stuart monarchs, Robert the Bruce and Saint Ninian.

McIvor gestured to a large wooden easel on which a cloth of purple velvet obscured the Gallery's latest addition. '...and joining this great ensemble,' he announced to the crowd, 'another of Scotland's heroes, or, am I still allowed to say *heroines* in these politically correct times?' After a murmur of polite laughter, he nodded to the woman by his side. It was the first time I'd set eyes on Mrs McIvor. She was small and elegant. Megan's height had come from her father, but, as I'd suspected, the attractive genes were all thanks to her mother. She stepped forward and gripped a golden cord hanging down one side of the easel. A gentle tug and the purple cloth fell elegantly to the floor revealing the portrait of a silver-haired woman, wearing horn-rimmed spectacles. It was a splendid piece of work and I joined in with the smattering of applause, though I had no idea who the subject was until McIvor continued.

'Dame Agnes Pitcaithly was a leading light in the hospice movement north of the border. Following in the famous footsteps of that other great lady, Dame Cicely Saunders, she devoted her life to ensuring that terminally ill people could die with dignity. She died in the very hospice which she founded in nineteen seventy-five.' He bowed his head for a moment. 'The same hospice where not so many years later my own parents would spend their last days. Ladies and gentlemen, they say only two things are certain in this life: death and taxes. Well, we all pay our taxes and, yet, for those terminally ill we have only fifteen hospices serving the whole of Scotland and most of those depend on the goodwill and generosity of local businesses and individuals to fund their work.' McIvor was turning up the volume. The man could talk; I'd say that for him. 'Ladies and gentlemen, it's high time we stopped relying on car boot sales, coffee mornings and sponsored walks to support our terminally-ill citizens.' I sensed the imminent arrival of a party political broadcast. 'When I am First Minister, I intend to drive through the Bill I first mooted as a junior health minister many years ago. A Bill that the previous Government tried to kill at birth. A Bill to establish Hospice Care Scotland.'

'Do we need another Government quango?' someone at the back of the crowd shouted out.

'Call it what you will,' McIvor thundered at the heckler, 'but, in tandem with the Care Commission, HCS will see the founding of another five hospices: four for adults, one for children, and oversee a rise in Government funding from twenty-eight to fifty-five per cent!'

The same heckler again. 'What about the comments of your opponent Angus Pike? I thought he said it was an expense the country couldn't bear at this time of recession?'

'Firstly,' McIvor replied, 'Angus is not my opponent. He is my colleague and friend.'

'Like Tony Blair and Gordon Brown were friends?' I couldn't work out if the heckler was for real or there to feed McIvor his lines.

Some of the small crowd laughed, even McIvor cracked a grin. 'It's true Angus and I haven't always seen eye to eye on everything, but let me tell you this: recession or no, if we can afford to look after our criminals in state of the art prisons, then we can afford to look after our dying.'

It was an excellent sound-bite. My verdict on the heckler was stooge.

McIvor waited for the applause to fade away. 'I hope my other colleagues in the Party will agree with me just how important my plans are when it comes time to vote at the leadership election.' He lowered his voice, put an arm around his wife and turned to the portrait again. 'If she were still with us today, I know I could count on Dame Agnes's vote.'

It was another half hour before the crowd, cameras and journalists dissipated. Mrs McIvor left in a car with the sombre suit I didn't know, leaving Chris the chauffeur by McIvor's side.

McIvor looked at his watch. 'You said this was very important, Mr Munro.'

'It is,' I said. 'Very.'

He nodded to his aide, who led the way to the cafe where there was a table reserved for us in a corner under a cubist portrait of someone whose own mother wouldn't have recognised him - or her.

I sat down opposite McIvor. Chris remained standing.

'Would you like something to drink, Mr Munro?' McIvor asked, after Chris had dismantled my mobile phone and set his handy bug-detector on the table next to a pink carnation in a small white vase.

'Coffee would be nice, thanks. Black.'

'Make that two,' McIvor said

'And one of those date-slices,' I added. I hadn't had any lunch and from where I was sitting they seemed like the largest of the baked items on offer.

'Two coffees, two date-slices,' McIvor told his aide, before turning to me and then down at his watch again. 'I've a sub-committee meeting to chair at two o'clock. You have my undivided attention for the next ten minutes.'

I reckoned that would give me about five minutes to drink my coffee and eat my date slice because what I had to tell McIvor wouldn't take long. 'Your future son-in-law is having an affair.'

McIvor glanced around quickly in case anyone had overheard. 'Keep your voice down. I really hope you haven't come here to spread some local gossip. You told me you had news of importance to do with Glen's prosecution—'

'Is your daughter the jealous type?' I asked, interrupting his rant and deciding it best to give him the short version.

'You think Glen has been unfaithful and what?' McIvor scoffed. 'That Megan exacted her revenge by trying to destroy Glen with allegations of child-porn? Hell hath no fury?' I had to hand it to him: he was pretty quick on the uptake, even if he was prone to misquoting William Congreve.

The coffees arrived. Chris set them down, went away and came back with two saucers, each with a square of shortbread.

'If that's the best defence you can come up with, I

think Glen was wise moving to Caldwell & Clark,' McIvor said.

My previous good mood was rapidly deteriorating and the substitution of shortbread for date-slice wasn't helping. Grudgingly, I bit a corner off. 'You don't like that idea? I have others,' I said, trying not to spray crumbs into my coffee. 'Here's one: your daughter's boyfriend is actually a paedophile who's idea of a night at the movies is watching video clips of children being sexually abused or, wait, here's another: it's all a conspiracy by the Lord Advocate to see that you don't become First Minister.' I pushed my shortbread saucer aside and spread out a photocopy of Beattie's credit card statement on the table. 'See here?' I pointed to the web-site payment. 'Now look at this, the week before.'

'The Royal Opera House, four hundred and fifty two pounds?'

'A last minute booking of Il Trittico - that's a Puccini Opera,' I enlightened him, having earlier Googled. I drew my finger down a couple of entries. 'Flight tickets and a hotel.'

'What about it? Glen's an opera buff.'

'And Megan isn't... but Fiona Scott is.'

'Are you saying Glen...' he lowered his voice. 'Are you saying that Glen is having an affair with Fiona Scott?'

'I take it you know her?'

He nodded.

I told him about the rumpled sheet on Beattie's examination bed and Fiona's expressed concern at the charges against him. A concern not shared by his fiancée.

'It's all extremely circumstantial. I can't be as certain as you that Megan is behind this.'

'She's a woman scorned – of course she's behind it. Who else would know Beattie's computer password, his credit card number? It would be easy to plant the porn on his PC and tip-off the cops. Why do you think she's left him? If she had nothing to do with it, surely she would have stayed around. He says he's innocent, they're engaged to be married. Why doesn't she believe him? I'll tell you why, because she knows he's guilty, but not of child-porn: of infidelity and this is her revenge.'

McIvor took a sip of coffee. 'Firstly, I don't believe Glen would be so stupid and Megan – she'd never do something like that.' He didn't sound all that convinced of his own argument.

'There's an easy way to find out,' I said. 'She's your daughter. Ask her.'

We sat for a while in silence. Finally, McIvor took another sip of coffee and shook his head. 'No, Megan's not contactable at the moment. She can be a very stubborn girl at times. In any event I think it might be more appropriate if I were to ask Glen in the first instance.'

I finished my coffee, lifted the rest of the shortbread and got up from the table. 'You do that.'

Chapter 29

I went round to see my dad after work. There was a white box van parked outside the house and when I walked in through the back door to the kitchen I found him lying on the floor, rummaging under the sink.

'I was wondering when you'd show,' he greeted me, head appearing from amidst the pipe-work and bottles of bleach. Slowly he rose to his feet, toolbox in hand. He was wearing a pair of faded blue overalls. 'We're going to Vince's to help Jill clear the place. I've borrowed a van.' He chucked me a set of keys. 'You're driving.'

Jill was waiting for us. She showed us into the small furnished flat that was so familiar, yet now seemed so empty without its former occupier bouncing about, laughing and joking.

The plan, I'd been told by my dad on the way over, was to take everything that was in reasonable nick and unwanted by Jill to the St Michael's Hospice charity shop in the High Street. Everything else was to go to the recycling centre in Bo'ness three miles away.

The furniture in the main room consisted of a couple of armchairs, a small two-seater couch, an ancient telly, what seemed to be a prototype DVD-player, a bookcase and an immense oak dresser, the top half of which had formerly and proudly displayed an array of single malts and whisky tumblers.

Jill had obviously made a start, for there were

several cardboard boxes of crockery, kitchen utensils, pots and pans and books already full and stacked in a corner.

I went over to the couch and pulled it away from the wall. It was more unwieldy than anything, but I didn't want my dad doing any heavy lifting.

'I'll take this. How about you make a start on the boxes?' I suggested. But my dad seemed unable to move.

Jill pointed to the top box. It was small and held mainly papers. The corner of a picture frame stuck out of one side and on top balanced a Black Watch Glengarry. 'I'm keeping what's in here,' she said. 'Everything else can go.'

She picked up the Glengarry, brushed the ribbon on the side, twiddled the toorie on top and stroked the ribbons on the back. I'd seen the boat-shaped cap many times before. There was hardly an occasion of any note when Vince hadn't worn it, and it was always on the wee man's head during Scotland football matches either at the game or watching on T.V. 'Stops me pulling my hair out,' had been his usual line.

Jill wrapped the tartan bonnet in a carrier bag and handed it to my dad. 'I think you should keep this, Alex,' she said. My old man couldn't speak. He took the parcel and gripped it tightly. His face creased.

'What's happening to this beast?' I asked, Jill, slapping the side of the oak dresser. It was a muckle big thing and I doubted if it would fit in the van.

'It's a shame,' Jill said. 'Belonged to my grandmother. The wood's beautiful. I hate to think of it being junked, but it's just so damn big and ugly.'

'I'd take it if I had the room,' my dad said. 'Come on Robbie, don't just stand there, let's get her into the van.'

I hadn't realised it, but the dresser came in two parts. The top housed a series of shelves with ornate framing around the edge and two long drawers along the bottom. The base was a big cupboard with two doors that opened outwards. There was enough storage space inside to pack most of my earthly belongings – or, I thought, a lot of closed legal files.

One set of livingroom furniture and a pulled muscle in my shoulder later, I went into the bedroom where Jill had been filling yet more cardboard boxes with clothes. I founded her kneeling on the floor, head on the bed, crying.

'Away you go home, Jill,' I said. 'Dad and I can clear the rest away and lock up.'

'I'm being silly,' she said. 'Dad wouldn't want me to be like this. I don't know how often he told me in the last few weeks that I wasn't to cry when he was gone. He was always so positive about everything. Never mind glass half full, his was always brimming over.'

'To be fair, usually, with a fine, Islay malt,' I said, and was relieved when Jill managed to laugh at my joke. I held out a hand and pulled her to her feet. We were close. I stepped back.

'You know, Robbie, you should watch out for Alex. He's going to take my dad's death very hard. The two of them were inseparable. You and Malky need to rally round. Do something nice, as a family.'

I promised I would arrange something.

'Soon,' she said, and I helped her carry some boxes

to the van where my dad was taking a breather. She went over, reached up and hugged him. 'Thanks for everything, Alex.' She opened her handbag and took out her car keys. 'I can't stay any longer. It's too soon and I have too many memories.'

'I understand.' My dad put his arm around Jill's shoulder and walked with her to her car.

I was pulling down the roller door at the back of the van and securing the clasp when my dad came back. The brake-lights of Jill's car lit up at the end of the street, a yellow indicator blinked in the darkness and she was gone.

'I'll just take a final look around,' my dad said, and came back a few minutes later with the carrier bag containing Vince's Glengarry and a small white cardboard box. 'Some of Vince's medicine from when he was being cared for at home,' he said. 'I'll need to mind and hand it in at the doctor's.'

I climbed into the van and put the box on the dashboard. Once my dad had lowered himself into the seat next to me, I started the engine and in a moment or two we were on our way; my dad leaving behind him the wee flat that had been home to his best pal, with nothing to show for that friendship other than a lot of memories, a tartan bonnet and a box full of morphine vials.

Chapter 30

After my finger-twisting last meeting with Brandon Biggam, I had half-expected the sack; however, when I went to see him on Monday afternoon there seemed to be no hard feelings, even after I'd explained that the findings of the Crown's toxicology report on Tanya's body fluids had been independently checked and the results were the same.

'So what do we do?' he asked.

I was going to carry on with my life, but it looked likely that he'd be spending the rest of his, or at least a very large chunk of it, in prison. 'The big problem with your case is that it's clear you gave Tanya heroin the day she died. The heroin in the wrap you gave her matches exactly the stuff found in your stash.' We'd been over the weakness in the defence case before.

'A tenner bag would never have killed her.'

'I know. That's why you're charged with murder. Someone, the Crown says you, must have injected her with a much bigger dose.'

'Why me?'

'Who else? You're the drug dealer. You're the person who gave her a habit in the first place.'

My client went on the defensive. 'Who says?'

His schedule of previous convictions said, except the jury wouldn't see that. 'Everyone says. Her whole family for a start.'

'How do they know? How can they prove it was

me? She could have been into smack ages before she met me.'

I really wished he'd try and concentrate on the things that might actually help his case. I tried to explain. 'Okay, Brandon. Let's say that Tanya's mum, dad, granddad, all fine upstanding citizens, go into the witness box and testify that until Tanya started going out with you she was clean. What are you going to say about that?'

'She could have got her habit from somebody else,' he insisted.

'Who?'

'I dunno, there's plenty of dealers about the place.'

'And who do you think the jury is going to believe? You or the Lang family?' My client said nothing, just stared at me. 'We don't even want to go there. We have to roll with the punches. We can't take issue with you and Tanya being boyfriend/girlfriend or that you used to take heroin together – socially. Least said, soonest forgotten by the jury.'

'So what's your big idea? Wait a minute – you think I done it, don't you?'

There comes a moment in just about every serious case where the client asks that question.

'I'm not paid to believe *anything*. You say you're innocent, that's fine by me. My job is to try and get you off – that's how it works.'

Brandon leaned against his chair and dangled his head backwards, staring at the ceiling.

'So, if you say you're not responsible for Tanya's overdose, somebody else is.'

'Who?'

'I'm asking you to speculate.'

'Eh?'

'Guess. If you didn't give her the smack that killed her - who did? Give me some names.'

He looked blank.

'Of dealers.'

'Grass?'

We lawyers normally said incriminate or even impeach. 'Yeah, grass. Put someone else in the frame, create a doubt.'

He seemed unconvinced.

'Geordie Lyon? You mentioned him. You said he was with you the last time you saw Tanya alive.'

'Aye.'

'Maybe he gave her some extra.'

'Why would he do that? Tanya never had any money. Geordie wouldnae be giving kit away for free.'

I took a deep breath. 'Maybe it wasn't for nothing.'

He took a moment to process that information then jumped to his feet. 'You saying Geordie was shagging Tanya?'

'Sit down.' He didn't. 'How long were you inside the last time and where was Geordie? Outside, that's where. Same as Tanya.'

He planted both hands on the table. 'You're talking shite,' he snarled.

'The kid. Are you sure he was yours?' He stabbed a finger at my face. I swatted it away. 'Remember what happened the last time you did that?' He lowered his hand. 'You want me to believe you? Okay so here I am – believing you. You never gave Tanya an overdose, therefore, someone else did.' I took his silence as agreement. 'I don't know who else could have supplied Tanya. You say there are plenty dealers out there and yet you don't give me a name. I need something to work on. Right now all we have is you giving Tanya smack and her dying. I don't think they'll be booking the jury into a hotel to mull that one over do you?'

Brandon dropped back into the chair and mumbled something I didn't quite catch. I asked him to repeat it.

'I telt Geordie to look after Tanya when I was inside. Give her some money and that. See her all right.'

'Just money?'

'Naw.'

So Geordie was supplying Tanya. Half the theory I'd plucked out of the air was more or less correct.

'But it couldn't have been for long cos her family sent her to rehab.'

'But,' I summarised, 'for a wee while, when you were dubbed up in here, Geordie was seeing a lot of her? Giving her drugs?'

He knew what I was saying. People did all sorts of things for heroin. Brandon's eyes narrowed, his nostrils flared. He pressed a clenched fist to the side of his jaw and spoke through gritted teeth. He'd shown no emotion over either the death of his girlfriend or his missing son up until now, but suggest that his pal might have been seeing his burd behind his back and he was about to go mental.

'When I get my hands on that—'

'You'll do nothing.'

'I want that wean dug up and DNA'd,' he shouted.

'Dug up? Why would the baby need dug up?'

'If Geordie killed Tanya, he'd maybe of killed the

wean too so I'd no' find out it was his.'

From my suggestion that he might want to take one small step towards an incrimination, my client was turning into Neil Armstrong.

'Do yourself a favour and calm down,' I told him. 'You've got the makings of a defence, but if you start shouting the odds it's not going to help your chances. If Geordie's involved in Tanya's death in any way, then, as soon as he knows that we're onto him, he'll disappear. Understand?'

He nodded.

'Good. Now tell me, does Geordie ever visit you?'

'Naw.'

'Then get word to him somehow. I want to speak to him. Don't say anything about what we've discussed, leave that to me.'

Chapter 31

'Surprise!' Grace-Mary called out to me on my return to the office. She'd been in a good mood ever since the recent arrival of the bottom half of Vince's old oak dresser which, after a lot of blood, sweat and curses, my dad and I had installed in the far corner of the room. Grace-Mary had already sprung into action. The piles of old files had been tidied away into the cupboard space and legal books were lined up neatly along the top surface with my Notary stamp acting as a bookend.

I sat down at my desk ready to make a start on the day's mail before my afternoon appointments began. The latest edition of the Law Society journal was top of the pile. I ripped open the plastic bag and turned to the second back page. There it was: the advert announcing shrieval vacancies. The deadline date for applications wasn't far off. Paul Sharp would have to get a move on finding his third referee. I tossed the magazine onto the desk.

'Surprise!' Grace-Mary tried again.

I thought I'd better go through to reception and see what she was going on about. As I climbed from my chair, my secretary walked in through the door dragging Andy behind her.

'Hello, Robbie,' he said. 'You haven't responded to the mandate so I've come to collect the first batch of disclosure papers for Dr Beattie's case.' Grace-Mary went off to find the file.

'Oh, and I heard you went to see Dr Beattie to try and get the case back,' Andy said, an edge to his voice. 'Apparently I don't have a clue what I'm doing and just the man to see that he spends the next few years in Peterhead.'

Andy was paraphrasing, though, I had to say, it was a fairly accurate summation.

'How would you like it if I tried to steal your clients?' he was saying as Grace-Mary returned.

'I could give you a list of the one's I'd like to see the back of,' she said, and laughed alone. Grace-Mary cleared her throat. 'Anyway, Robbie, I'll need to take Jimmy Garvie's email off your machine and take it through to mine because you're still too mean to buy yourself a printer.' She rummaged around in my desk drawers for a spare pen-drive. There were plenty lying around. 'I bet you're fully networked at Caldwell & Clark, Andy. As you can see, we're still in the Dark Ages here.'

'Don't bother with the report,' I told Grace-Mary. 'Andy's not taking the file.'

'Yes, I am,' Andy countered.

Grace-Mary copied the email onto the pen-drive. 'I'll leave you boys to talk shop,' she said, sensing things were a tad fraught. 'Pop into reception before you go, Andy.'

Andy smiled and said he would. The smile had left his face when he turned to me again. 'I trusted you. I—'

'Whoa, there, Tiger,' I said. 'First of all, Beattie is my client.'

'Was your client.'

'And, secondly, you *don't* know what you're doing

otherwise you wouldn't have asked me for help.'

Andy reached into an inside jacket pocket and produced a cheque. It was signed but the spaces for the payee and the sum were empty. 'How much?' he asked.

'What? You're in the door five minutes and C&C are entrusting you with the firm's chequebook?'

'It's to pay your fee. I told Mrs. Sinclair that there was no way you would part with the papers if you hadn't been paid, so she gave me this.' He held out the blank cheque. 'It's not me she trusts, it's you'

'Tell her she can keep it.'

'Don't be daft—'

'Andy, listen to me. I'm keeping this case.'

'But Dr Beattie doesn't want you to act.'

'He will when He finds out I can get him off and clear his good name.'

Andy snorted.

'And,' I said, taking the cheque from his hand, ripping it up and letting the pieces flutter down into the waste bucket, 'once he's duly acquitted, I'll be sending Dr Beattie a note of my fee. A fee note of Caldwell & Clark proportions which I am sure he will be only too happy to pay – preferably in cash.'

Andy snorted. 'It's not happening. I'm his lawyer now and even if he wanted to go back to you there is no way Kenneth McIvor would allow it.'

Grace-Mary tip-toed in, laid a file on the edge of my desk and retired from the room.

'I'm offering you a way out, Andy.' You keep this case and you'll lose it. How's that going to look?'

'You said no one would care so long as I racked up a big fee for the firm.'

I was hoping he hadn't remembered that. 'You leave me with this case, I get Beattie off and you can move on and give your electrocuted-driller case the attention it deserves – everyone lives happily ever after. Apart, obviously, from the driller.'

I could see he was tempted. 'No, it's okay. If you can get him off so can I.' He lifted the file that Grace-Mary had left behind.

Andy glanced down at in the journal lying open on my desk at the Judicial Appointments Board advert. 'You're not thinking of applying?'

I wasn't, but why shouldn't I? 'Don't sound so surprised.'

'But you hate Sheriffs.'

'I don't hate them. Well, not all of them.'

'Name one that you like.'

'Larry Dalrymple's all right.'

'You only like Larry the lamb because he dishes out soft sentences to your clients on a Friday so that he can get away early. Is there a Sheriff that you actually respect?'

It was a tough question and yet he seemed to expect an immediate answer.

'See?'

'Whether or not I happen to respect any particular Sheriff isn't the point.'

'What is then? What would make Robbie Munro want to join sides with the enemy?'

'The Sheriff's not the enemy. Not exactly. The PF's the enemy. The Sheriff's supposed to be... I don't know... Switzerland.'

'Vichy France, you mean,' Andy muttered.

Andy was sounding more like me than me. How had I managed to instil such a degree of cynicism in my former assistant in such a short space of time? Give me the legal trainee and I'll give you the embittered, cynical, paranoid solicitor.

He chucked the Journal back down on the desk. 'Anyway you don't have the necessary qualifications.'

'No? What am I lacking?' I was intrigued to know.

'It's not what you're lacking, it's what you have – a Y chromosome.'

'You think my being a man is a disadvantage?'

'Come off it, Robbie. I think we both know that the day of the able-bodied, white male is over.'

If that was right, they'd had a good run for their money.

Andy was in full flow, he's obviously made a study on the subject. 'Look at the last batch of part-time Sheriffs. Out of eight appointed there were four women and two men of Asian descent.'

'And the other two?'

'Ex-PF's and one of them had a bad limp. Anyway, you're too young. You can't be more than thirty-six, thirty-seven—'

'Thirty-five.'

'There you are then. You need to be kicking on well into your forties or later for a shrieval post.'

'What about Mandy Morrow?' I asked, wheeling out the example Paul Sharp had given me. 'She was in her thirties when she got the nod.'

'Which,' said Andy, smugly, 'brings me back to the fact that you're... how can I put it?

'Vaginally-challenged?'

Grace-Mary entered and came to an abrupt halt. 'Is this a bad time? It's just that the waiting room is full.'

I took the Journal and lobbed it towards the box in the corner where I kept past issues. It hit the edge of the box and fell on the floor. Grace-Mary picked it up and dropped it along with the others, most of them still in mint condition inside their plastic wrappers.

Andy looked at the file in his hand and then at me.

'Take it,' I said. 'A lot of good it'll do you.'

He opened it. 'The petition, a precognition of Dr Beattie's fiancée...' He removed the print-out of Jimmy Garvie's report on the examination of Dr MacGregor's laptop. 'What's this?'

'Nothing of any importance,' I said, suddenly wishing that I hadn't ripped up the cheque which I could have used to pay Jimmy's fee. 'Look I'm going to have to start seeing some clients. How about I give you a call next time I'm through in Glasgow? Maybe we can grab a coffee - or lunch – I take it they pay you expenses?' I showed him to the door. 'You know, if things don't work out at C&C, you could always come back here. Be like old times.'

Andy smiled politely. I knew what he was thinking. Old times, old salary. He had moved on. 'Thanks, Robbie,' he said, 'but no thanks.'

Chapter 32

Andy had scarcely hit the pavement when Jimmy Garvie
added his presence to my packed waiting room. I still hadn't looked at the day's mail and there was a long list of calls to return.

'Won't keep you a minute,' Jimmy said, jumping out of his seat and following me into my room. 'Just here about that report I did in the Beattie case.'

'Grace-Mary will send you a cheque,' I told him.

'Forget it.'

'Okay, it's forgotten. So why are you here?' He didn't answer so I tried again. 'Jimmy, what's this all about?'

'I want to make sure that you've deleted the report from your PC.'

Grace-Mary poked her head around the door. 'You going to be long? I just caught one of your clients trying to inject himself in the toilet.'

I assured my secretary that I wouldn't be long and then turned to Jimmy. 'I don't want your report, you don't want paid – consider it gone.'

'Do you mind if I check?'

'Jimmy what's this all—'

'It's okay, I know the date I sent it.' He ran around my desk and opened my email application.

I was beginning to wonder what the big problem was. 'Were there dirty pictures on that hard-drive after all?' Jimmy didn't answer. 'You better not have mailed me child-porn!'

Jimmy finished with my computer. 'How many PC's in the office?'

'Three but only mine is set up for email.'

'Great. Any hard copies?'

'One and it just left out of the front door.'

Having managed to get rid of Jimmy, I wheeled in my first client. He'd been charged with assault and released by the police on a bail undertaking to attend court in a week's time. The second had been caught stealing from the local supermarket. I had them in and out within ten minutes. I didn't even bother signing them up for legal aid, though they were both financially eligible. Gone was the old two page Legal Advice and Assistance form, now there was a two page mandate, plus a further one page capital mandate, then a six page electronic form to complete. After I'd spent half an hour doing that, the cases probably wouldn't be prosecuted anyway. Due to public spending cutbacks and the Government's smoke and mirrors routine with crime statistics, offences, unless of the 'zero-tolerance' variety, that is, involving a knife, domestic abuse or racism, were dealt with by warning letters and fixed fines. It meant that, despite the signs in the shops, unless incredibly prolific, shoplifters just didn't get prosecuted and you could punch whoever you wanted so long as it wasn't your wife or a person of another nationality .

Third in the queue was Geordie Lyons, potential, yet unsuspecting, star-witness for the defence in the upcoming case of Her Majesty's Advocate against Brandon Biggam. Turned out it was Geordie who

Grace-Mary had caught trying to shoot-up in the toilet.

He slumped into the chair opposite me. 'Brando, told me to come see you.' Geordie was abnormally fat by junkie standards, like he'd been cutting his smack with mayonnaise. His face was pale and sweaty and he didn't look pleased, probably because he'd been chased by Grace-Mary before he could take a hit.

'You were there the night Tanya died?' I put to him. No point beating about the bush.

'Aye. Me and Brando were there. But it wasnae night, it was about tea time. She wanted money for the wean. He gave her a tenner bag. We left. Next thing I got telt she was deid.'

'Did you give her smack?'

He narrowed his eyes. 'Is that what Brando's saying? Wanting me to take the rap?'

'Take it easy. Tanya had taken a lot more than a tenner bag. She must have got more heroin from somewhere.'

'Not from me she never. I've got enough trouble getting kit for myself.'

'Did you ever supply her?'

'What d'ye mean *supply*? His eyes darted about the room. 'You got this place wired?' He looked at my hand-dictation machine suspiciously. 'Brando said you wanted me to give a statement that I was there and that Tanya only got a tenner bag off him. That's it - I'm saying nothing else.'

'How well did you know Tanya?'

He looked at me suspiciously. 'She was Brando's burd.'

'I know that, but when he was inside doing his last

sentence—'

'Ah've had enough of this.' Geordie jumped to his feet. Face contorted, lips tight revealing a row of teeth like a string of dry-roasted peanuts. Same as his dubbed-up pal he was good at finger-pointing, but he was a bag of blubber. I could have knocked him over with a swing and a miss. 'See you—' There was foam at the corners of his mouth, a fleck spiralled off into orbit and landed on the corner of the desk.

'Shut up and sit down.' He stayed where he was, snarling down at me.

'All right then,' I said. 'Go. And I'll tell *Brando* that you're not wanting to help. I'm sure he'll understand.'

He wiped his nose, catching it between finger and thumb, wiping the snot on his jeans. 'I gave Tanya nothing and when I left the wean was fine, all right?' He growled, taking his seat again. 'You can write that down cos I'm taking the rap for no-one, not even Brando.'

'Brandon was inside for nine months. All I want to know is where Tanya got her gear from when he wasn't around?'

'You were Tanya's lawyer, you saw her. Do you think if she was really needing money she wouldn't be able to get it?'

'You're saying she was on the game?'

'I'm saying she had the equipment to get what she wanted. Anyway most of the time she wasnae using. She was in rehab. Then she had the wean.'

'Before that.'

He sat down. 'When she first got her house, I maybe gave her some kit and a few vallies cause

Brando said I was to watch out for her, but that was only for a few weeks and then she went away.'

'And during that time did you give her anything else?'

'Like what?'

'Like a baby?'

He launched himself out of the chair and across the table with such speed that I hardly had any time to react. He caught a hold of my tie with his right hand, yanking me forward, jerking my neck. He was fat, but a lot faster and stronger than I'd expected. He tried to hook me with his left. I turned my face away just in time and his fist cracked off the top of my head. I felt the blow, but not as much as Geordie did. He yelped. I grabbed his wrist, pinning the hand holding my tie to the desk and wrenched it free from his grip. He tried to hit me again with his left and then right, arms flailing, stretching across the desk. I evaded the wild blows, seized his head in both my hands and slammed it onto the desk where it hit the only surface area not otherwise cluttered with files and notepads. His nose burst. Blood splashed up the front of my white shirt and over my stretched-out tie that by now bore the smallest knot in the world clamped tightly to my throat. I put a hand on his shoulder and shoved him away. He fell to the side of the desk, knocking his head on the corner and taking a pile files and the day's mail with him.

Grace-Mary barged into the room as Geordie was pulling himself off the ground. 'Right. You – out!'

He looked at her, then me, then back to Grace-Mary again. A glob of blood fell from his nose and splatted onto the paperwork at his feet.

'Out or I'm calling the police!' Grace-Mary yelled.

'It's all right. Let's not bother the police,' I said. 'Mr Lyons was just leaving.'

Geordie put a hand over his nose, muttered something I didn't quite hear and shambled past Grace-Mary and out of the door.

'Just look at this place,' Grace-Mary said, staring at the scattered files and papers, some splashed with blood. 'And look at the state of you.' I pulled my red stained shirt out for closer inspection. 'Don't touch it!' Grace-Mary shouted at me. 'He's probably got AIDS or something.'

I transferred my attention to the pool of blood that had formed on the desk top where Geordie's nose had met teak veneer.

'What are we going to do about this mess?' Grace-Mary asked.

I soaked up Geordie's blood with a handful of tissues I kept handy in case of weeping clients, pulled the plastic Law Society Journal wrapper out of the bin and rolled them up inside it. I put the lot in the bottom drawer of my desk.

'What are you going to do with that?' Grace-Mary wanted to know.

'DNA.'

If they did ever found the missing baby, I'd know if Geordie Lyon was his father.

Chapter 33

A job well done is reward enough, isn't, but should be, the motto of the Scottish Legal Aid Board. And yet my paltry fee aside, a majority not proven verdict by the epidermis of the judicial teeth was guaranteed to put a smile on any defence lawyer's face. So it was, at four o'clock that afternoon and pretty pleased with myself, I emerged into the deserted courtyard outside Edinburgh Sheriff Court to be met, not by my newly-liberated client and his friends wishing to carry me shoulder high through the cobbled streets of the Old Town, but by the sting of rain whipped by a gusting north wind. If you expect gratitude or money for a job well done, you're in the wrong game as a criminal defence lawyer.

I waited on Chamber Street long enough to pull on my raincoat, stuff my gown into my briefcase and just in case my freshly freed client had nipped around the corner to Royal Mile Whiskies and at that very moment was rushing back on winged feet with a bottle of something peaty as a token of his gratitude.

I was at the corner of George IV Bridge, opposite the statue of Greyfriar's Bobby, when a black limousine came towards me and pulled up at the kerb. The back door opened onto the pavement in front of me; just like the movies.

'Mr Munro.' I heard the voice before I saw the face peer at me from the gloom of the car. It was a moment or two before I recognised either. 'I thought that was you. Going back to Linlithgow? Me too - constituency surgery.'

As though to encourage me into the car, the rain fell faster and the wind blew stronger. I climbed aboard as, with a broad welcoming smile, McIvor made room for me on the back seat.

'I spoke to Glen and I owe you an apology,' he said, after we'd finished with the small talk, mainly about the weather and the state of the roads. It was approaching rush hour and the streets of Edinburgh were clogging like a Scotsman's arteries.

'When we met with Glen a week or so back I was rude.' He held up the palm of a hand to me as though I might disagree. 'No, I should have listened to you. I just naturally assumed that biggest was best. I thought only a big city centre firm like Caldwell & Clark would have the facilities, the—'

'Respectable lawyers?'

He smiled thinly. 'Quite. Still thanks to your help the whole horrible business is behind us.'

'Is it?'

He leaned forward and tapped the driver on the shoulder. Before he had rested back against the Dakota leather seat, a glass partition had risen silently between the front and rear seats. 'As I've already said, I spoke to Glen. He told me everything. About his affair with Fiona... Hell indeed hath no fury...'

'The woman scorned being your daughter?'

'You can imagine how embarrassing this all is. How Glen thought he could keep it hidden I don't know, and Megan's perfectly entitled to feel... disappointed, but to do what she did to that young man, to almost ruin his career, it's unforgiveable.'

'She's admitted it?'

'We haven't spoken and, frankly, I'm so angry, I think it would be best to let things cool down for a while before we do.'

'Talking about embarrassments, you do appreciate we'll have to cite Megan for the defence?' I said.

'There won't be any need. I've had a meeting with the Lord Advocate this afternoon.'

'And?'

'Case closed. The Crown Office will issue a press release vindicating Glen completely and putting the whole thing down to a computer glitch.'

'And the Lord Advocate is happy with that?'

'Happy? No, but content that the laws on child-pornography are not there to catch women seeking revenge on their cheating partners.'

'And Megan's attempt to pervert the course of justice? All those wasted police hours...?'

McIvor stretched his lips in a thin smile. 'I'll be having a stern word with her when next we meet.'

So that was it. Game over. It would have made a great trial and I could really have milked the publicity.

McIvor took a pack of cigarettes from his jacket pocket. 'Glen will be extremely glad the ordeal is over and very grateful to you, I should imagine.' He rolled down his door window a fraction and lit up. 'I know we got off to a bad start, you and I, but you will send me a note of your fee, won't you?'

He needn't have worried on that score. I fully intended charging a fee that included a sizeable win-bonus. It made no difference how the result was achieved; no-one could deny it was all down to me. I didn't care if Megan McIvor got off with only a row from her dad when anyone else's daughter would be staring at the Wallace Monument and, soon, a row of giant pylons through the bars of Corntonvale Prison. It wasn't like anyone was getting away with murder.

We chatted on. Soon the big black car merged with traffic on the M9 at the Newbridge intersection, slowing down for Scotland's best known speed camera.

'The law has always interested me,' McIvor said. 'Just as well I suppose, my being Justice Secretary and all.' He laughed and nudged me in the ribs with his elbow as though we were great pals. Well we weren't. I was a defence lawyer and for the next ten miles or so he was my prisoner. It was just as well he was buckled in because I was about to go off on a rant on the state of the criminal justice system as seen through the eyes of the defence: the lack of funding, the increase in police powers, the introduction of an unnecessary Public Defender's Office, the erosion of civil rights jealously guarded for hundreds of years and now treated as minor inconveniences en route to headline-grabbing conviction statistics, laws made up on the hoof at the whim of the red top newspapers. Now was my chance and I would have taken it had I not started to feel extremely queasy. I took a deep breath. More used to my Alfa's mythical suspension system, the gliding motion of the limousine, combined with the warmth and the smell of the cigarette smoke was making me feel less like going off on one and more like taking a puke out of the window.

'Must be quite wearing, having to defend all those

guilty people,' McIvor said.

'People like Dr Beattie or like your daughter?'

He let the remark drift out of the window along with the cigarette smoke. 'Have you ever thought what it would be like on the other side of the fence?'

'Work for the Crown - a prosecutor?'

'No, I was thinking of as a Sheriff. You do know there are vacancies?'

'I've a friend who'd like to apply.'

'What's stopping *you*?'

The guy was a comedian. 'Apart from my age, gender, apolitical tendencies, the fact that I've never been a prosecutor and the three referees needed?'

McIvor dragged on his cigarette. 'That's not a chip on your shoulder. That's a full fish supper with a pickled onion on the side.'

The thought of a fish supper, in fact the thought of any food at all at that point, was a most unwelcome one. We turned off onto the slip road for Linlithgow and onto the Blackness Road. I lowered my window a little and sucked in a great gulp of cold air.

'My friend,' I said, 'Paul Sharp, he's an excellent lawyer and would make a great Sheriff.' I'd never have the ear of the Justice Minister again, or him indebted to me. 'He's looking for a third referee. I'm not sure if you know him, but maybe you could put in a word.' I took a few deep breaths to fight off the waves of nausea.

'Not feeling so good?' McIvor asked. 'My fault probably.' He took a last draw on his cigarette and pinged what was left out of the window. That was a seventy-five pound fixed-penalty for littering right there. 'Will I ask Chris to stop the car?'

There wasn't far to go. I shook my head. 'Haven't been car-sick since I was a kid,' I gasped. 'Forgot how quickly it comes on and how bad it is.'

'No need to apologise. I was sea-sick once: Stranraer to Belfast by hydrofoil. It was only the hope of dying that kept me alive.'

I tried a polite laugh with my mouth closed and the result was a silly little snigger. Cold sweat condensed on my brow. I pressed the button to lower my window fully.

'Mr Munro, Robbie, I'm really very grateful to you for all that you've done and I know that you'll be discreet.'

I wanted to speak but couldn't trust myself to open my mouth.

He slapped me on the back. 'Grand.'

I thumped the glass partition.

'Pull over,' McIvor told the driver though the gap as the glass panel slid down, no doubt concerned less about me than for the fine-leather upholstery.

As soon as the car stopped I was out of it and onto the grass verge. A line of traffic quickly formed. I reached in and grabbed my brief case.

'Thanks for the lift,' I just about managed to croak.

'No problem. And if you can find those two other referees, you won't have to look far for a third.'

A car horn honked.

I turned my head and threw up, once, twice. After the third hurl I was aware that the traffic was moving again. I wiped my mouth with my hanky and set off for home, glad of the rain and the cold wind in my face.

Chapter 34

'You look terrible.'

I wasn't entirely sure how my dad had managed to reach this conclusion, accurate though it might have been, because, so far as I could tell, he hadn't looked up from his putt. He pulled the head of his putter back and set the ball rolling across the carpet.

'You been drinking?' he asked. 'Or are you taking drugs now?' The golf ball rolled into the glass tumbler that was lying on its side next to the telly, without touching the rim.

'Car-sick. I'm on my way to the office and thought I'd just drop in and see how you were.'

'Car-sick? I remember when you were wee and we made that trip to Motherwell over the back roads in my Granada. Never got the stink out of the mats. Thought you'd have grown out of all that by now.'

I drank a glass of water to rinse the taste of sick from my mouth. 'I'm okay if I'm driving. I can't handle sitting in the back of the car.'

'Who's been chauffeuring you around?'

'Long story.'

'Not interested. And, as you can see, I'm fine, so you can stop bothering me and get back to your criminals.'

He putted again and once more the ball rolled into the glass without touching the sides.

'You've not lost your touch.'

'Drive for show, putt for dough.'

Five o'clock on a Friday afternoon and he was putting a golf ball at a whisky glass. Normally he'd be down at the Red Corner with Vince or they'd be playing snooker or watching re-runs of classic football games or boxing matches.

'Fancy a game sometime?'

'With you?' he asked incredulously. 'When was the last time you played?'

'Not that long ago.'

'You still using my old sticks?'

'They're fine.'

He lined up another putt. 'You even got a handicap?'

'I'm not trying to get into the Ryder Cup squad. I'm only wanting a bounce game with my dad. What's the big problem?'

He knocked the ball at the glass much too hard, though not too hard to miss the target. The ball ricocheted off the base of the cup and came right back at him. 'The *problem* is that I don't need your sympathy. I've got friends I can play with.'

'Oh, I see, is that it? I'm only wanting to play golf with you because, now that Vince isn't here, I think you're Alex nae mates?'

'Well isn't it?'

'As a matter of fact it's not. I was going to invite Malky up for a game.'

'Really?'

'Yeah,' I said, a little jealous at how much he'd perked up at the mention of my brother, Malky Munro, ex-professional footballer, now a part-time radio pundit; which couldn't be easy since he made loving himself a full-time job. 'I was on the phone to him the other day.'

'You two are still speaking then?'

'We're brothers, dad.' He raised an eyebrow. Ex-detective sergeant Alex Munro was not entirely convinced by my reply. I pressed on regardless. At least the old man was showing some signs of life and if I was going to lie... 'We were talking about arranging a trip to Islay. Malky says they have a good golf course there—'

'Aye, that's right. The Machrie.' The slightest twitch of his moustache might have gone unnoticed to many but I recognised it as sign of immense excitement. 'Supposed to be the best links course in Scotland, so that means the world.'

'Why don't we give it a try,' I said casually, omitting to mention the small matter of the eight distilleries on Islay; a fact which my dad, as a lifelong aficionado of the aqua libre, well knew. He smiled for the first time in ages, picturing himself, no doubt, stranded on a small Scottish Island with nothing to do to pass the time but play his favourite sport surrounded by the very distilleries that produced his favourite malts.

'When?' he demanded.

I took his putter and had a go at the whisky tumbler. 'Let me firm a date up with Malky,' I said, scooping out the errant golf ball from beneath an armchair. 'I take it you're fairly flexible?'

'Elastic.'

'Great. Leave it with me.'

He ruffled my hair like I was twelve again. Now I

was smiling too.

'Before you go.' My dad went to the kitchen and brought back a small, white cardboard box. 'Vince's drugs. Could you drop them off at the surgery?' I exchanged the putter and golf ball for the box and made for the door.

'Oh, and Robbie,' he said, grinning like a small boy who's just been informed that Christmas has been brought forward. He dropped the ball on the floor and with a back-handed swipe of the putter sent it rattling into the glass tumbler. 'We can talk handicaps and prize-money later.'

I'd never seen him so happy. If Malky didn't come through on this I was a dead man.

Chapter 35

It had been several days since my contretemps with Geordie Lyons and yet Grace-Mary was still wiping down the surfaces in my office.

'It's the end of the month next week,' she said, once quite satisfied that not a corpuscle of Geordie Lyon's blood remained on the premises of Munro & Co. 'You're supposed to have done all your CPD for the year by then.'

Grace-Mary and I usually had a chat at the end of the month, almost always with me as the chattee and my secretary as the chatter, on the ever-sensitive issue of office finances and, in particular, the size of the overdraft. For that reason, a discussion on any other topic should have made for a pleasant change, but it didn't. Continuing Professional Development was an annual pain in the backside. Twenty hours of training to do or someone from the Law Society ripped up your practising certificate.

'How much have you done?' she asked.

'Five hours.'

'Would that be the five hours personal study that do not require to be verified?'

I took her question as rhetorical and proceeded to sift through the bundle of publicity leaflets she had dropped onto my desk. Law Society Update seminar on Mergers and Acquisitions, Planning Law – Winning

Strategies, Estate Planning and Tax Management; nothing suitable for my line of work. I picked up another. If you could afford the four hundred and ninety-five pounds to attend the Profitability in an Age of Austerity Seminar, you probably didn't need to be there.

'You don't have to just do legal subjects, there's other stuff too,' Grace-Mary said, as I floated another advertising flyer into the bucket.

'Anything about how to defend yourself against mad ginger-junkies?' I asked.

'I think that's a wee bit too niche,' Grace-Mary replied. 'Look,' she held up a piece of glossy white paper promoting *Assertiveness Training* in bold red print.

I thumped the table with my fist. 'No!'

'Ha-ha.' Grace-Mary threw another leaflet at me.

'Cross-examination techniques? How about something I actually need to develop?'

We flicked through the rest of the advertising-flyers, the more glossier the paper, the more expensive the seminar fee, until one caught my eye. It was typed in grey-scale on a piece of A4 copy paper. The West Lothian Faculty of Solicitors: *Recent Cases on The Misuse of Drugs Act 1971.* At last; something I could actually use. The seminar was set to take place on Thursday evening, more importantly, it was before the end of the month and so ideal for those requiring last-minute CPD. It was only three hours, but at least it was something.

'Fifteen pounds,' Grace-Mary said. 'There goes the training budget.'

The seminar was to be held at Threemile Town Rugby Club. CPD and I'd probably get a really cheap pint there after the seminar. Excellent. I stuffed the piece of paper in my pocket and returned to more pressing matters such as the pile of unanswered mail.

'Three hours? That it?' Grace-Mary asked. 'What about the other twelve?'

'I'll just have to get creative about those when filling in my training sheet.'

The phone rang. Grace-Mary filed the rest of the leaflets into a folder before going through to reception and taking the call. For the next five minutes all I could hear was giggling and laughing. It had to be Malky. I'd been trying to phone him about the Islay golf trip before my dad did and eventually had to make do with leaving an urgent voicemail message.

'What do you mean you're too busy?' I asked, after Grace-Mary had patched me through to my brother.

'I've got a radio show to do,' he said, like it would be impossible for Radio Brighton to draft someone in to talk crap about football for a couple of days while he played golf with his family.

'Dad's looking forward to this. You can't let him down. He's really upset because of Vince. They give you holidays don't they?'

'Not in the middle of the season they don't. It's the fourth round of the F.A. cup next—'

'English football,' I said. 'Who cares? Bunch of over-paid sand-dancers.'

'You know, you're sounding more like him every day.'

'Come on, Malky. Think how happy it would make

him. Just him and his two boys, playing golf and drinking the water of life.'

A long hard sigh travelled down the phone line from Brighton to Linlithgow. 'It's not that easy. Leave the show even for a day or so and they bring someone in and when I come back it's *who are you again*? There are old pro's queuing up for this type of work.'

'It's a weekend away. You're the famous Malky Munro. Ex-Rangers, ex-Scotland centre-back. Everyone's favourite footballer. The man with the golden tongue. How could they find someone to replace you?'

'Well... I suppose...'

'It's not like you're going to be away for a whole week.'

It took my big brother a few moments before he realised I was winding him up. 'Very funny. It's okay for you milking the legal aid dry with all your crazy clients. Some of us have to earn an honest crust.'

Malky probably got paid more for an evening's radio punditry than I made in a week of legal aid fixed fees, the rate of which had just been cut again.

'Are you coming or not?' I asked.

'I'll think about it.'

Why? It wasn't as though Malky gave a great deal of thought to anything else in his life. 'It's a long weekend. So you miss the Seagulls crashing out of the cup?' In Malky's world of sports journalism, teams never just lost in the cup, they *crashed* or *tumbled* out. 'That is if they've made it as far as round four.' I sensed his defences were starting to crumble. 'Anyway, I've told him you're going. If you refuse now, he'll think you're backing out and you know how much Dad hates a quitter.'

'I hate you.'

'We're flying out two weeks this Friday. You can stay here Thursday night. Give me a call when you land and I'll pick you up at the airport.'

Chapter 36

I opened the back door to find my dad sitting at the kitchen table, doing a newspaper crossword, giant teacup at his elbow.

'Do you know any cops called Bill Renton?' I asked.

He took a slurp of tea and studied the strip-lighting for a moment or two. 'No – why?'

'Doesn't matter.'

'It must matter or you wouldn't be asking.'

'Okay - he's the guy who was knocked down on the High Street.'

'Oh, aye, him. The one whose relatives you've got Sammy Veitch hunting for? The one you chased out of your office to his death?'

I checked the teapot and found it empty apart from a couple of sodden teabags in the bottom. 'I never chased him, he ran out and I ran after him.'

'Same difference,' he said, returning to his crossword.

'Not really,' I said, emptying the teabags in the bucket. 'Actually, I never even managed to run after him. He was too quick.'

'See? Now you're changing your story. You'd never hold up under questioning.'

'I'm a lawyer, Dad. I don't answer questions, I ask them.'

He filled in some squares on the crossword. 'Did I tell you, your brother's gone fungal,' he said, folding the paper and placing it on the table.

'What?'

'He's got a video out. It's all over the internet.'

'What do you know about the internet?' I asked. The kettle was still hot and half full of water. I switched it on and as I returned to the table again, noticed my dad re-arranging the newspaper, though not quickly enough to prevent me from catching a glimpse of shiny red and gold striped paper. I lifted it to reveal a packet of Tunnock's Caramel Wafers. 'And where did these come from?'

'I found them.'

'Oh, yeah? Where?'

'Safeway's,' he said defiantly. 'They were right next to the teacakes.'

I reached out for a chocolate biscuit, but he snatched the packet from me.

'Oh, no. If I'm not supposed to have these, how can you expect me to let you have one?'

It was too early in the morning to compete with my dad's own brand of logic. I took a mug down from the cupboard and dropped a new teabag in. 'What were you saying about Malky?'

'It was on the telly. Remember his cup final goal?'

It was difficult to forget, seeing how either Malky or my dad reminded me about it on a frequent basis. Scottish Cup, injury time, everyone is up for the corner. It's taken short, knocked to the corner of the box and met first time by a full-back better known for kicking the ball into touch than at the goals. His shot is ferociously struck but going well wide until Malky sticks his head in the way and diverts the ball into the net from twelve yards. The brain cell loss must have been in the millions.

'Which goal was that again?'

My dad ignored the sarcasm. 'Someone's made a wee video of it, it jumps about all over the place and there's a song in the background. The boy's making a fortune.'

'Malky is?'

'No the boy who made the video. He's got pop-stars everywhere wanting him to do their videos.'

The kettle boiled. 'I'll check it out on YouTube,' I said, pouring hot water into the mug and stabbing the teabag with a spoon.

'Eh?'

'I'll look at it on the internet.'

'Can you tape it for me?'

My dad had only recently been dragged kicking and screaming from his comfortable world of magnetic tape and VCR's into the digital age. Explaining DVD's had been difficult enough without trying to explain downloading from the internet.

'Actually, don't bother,' he said. 'I'll ask Malky to bring me a copy when he comes up for the golf.'

'You'll need a computer to watch it on,' I said.

'Watch what?'

'Malky's video clip. The one that's gone viral.'

'Viral? Oh, aye, right. Ach, well, I can always go down to the library. Have you spoken to your brother recently?'

That's what he really wanted to know. This conversation wasn't about Malky's YouTube video. My dad was checking that the golf trip was still on and that

Malky was going to be there. I took the mug of tea and sat down at the table across from my dad. 'I was speaking to Malky just the other day. He's coming up a week on Thursday and staying at my place. We'll be picking you up Friday, bright and early. We're flying from Glasgow.'

'What? No boat trip?'

After my recent motion-sickness experience in the back of McIvor's limo, I had no wish for a bout of sea sickness crossing a chunk of the North Atlantic in a ferry. 'The plane is quicker.'

He grunted. I could tell he was happy.

'We're all taking clubs so that means only one suitcase per passenger - one *reasonably-sized* suitcase per passenger,' I added, for the avoidance of doubt. 'You're only going for three nights, so go easy – okay?'

I took a couple of sips from the mug. 'Quite wet, this tea.'

He didn't say anything, just ruffled his moustache between thumb and fore-finger, took a long drink of tea, smacked his lips with an air of satisfaction and pushed the packet of caramel wafers across the table towards me.

Chapter 37

Threemile Town was not far from Linlithgow; three miles, in fact. It was situated on the B9080, in pre-motorway days the main road to Edinburgh, and, apart from a few houses, a small primary school and an old red telephone box there wasn't a lot going on. Or, at least, there hadn't been until a vast, new private-housing scheme sprang up. On the back of that development some of the new residents had the idea to build a rugby club. The Three-Milers had no delusions of grandeur, they played in the lowest division of the Scottish rugby leagues and, I suspected, knew that they always would.

I drove a few hundred yards up a narrow, winding road and parked in an already busy car park next to the clubhouse; a small timber-framed structure set a drop-kick away from the pitch itself. It seemed that I was last to arrive, because the door was closing as I stepped through. On the other side stood Paul Sharp who had, by a unanimous vote taken in his absence at the last Faculty AGM, been appointed the Faculty's CPD convenor. His duties entailed laying on a series of legal seminars throughout the year at as low a cost as was possible. Paul was waiting inside the door for late-comers, dressed, conservatively for him, in a black suit, white round-collared shirt and skinny black tie. 'Would you look at this,' he said, as I squeezed in through the door. 'Another CPD desperado. If I'd known so many folk were behind on their hours I'd have booked the Town Hall.'

He introduced me to a client of his, Keith Haggerty, former Scotland B loose-head prop, now Club Chairman of Threemile Town RFC, whose huge frame, squashed nose and one cauliflower ear testified to his familiarity with the egg-shaped ball. Unfortunately, he hadn't been as familiar with the road traffic laws, which was how he'd come to meet Paul. Haggerty had agreed to the use of the rugby club for a nominal payment and, as I discovered, to help plug an upcoming event.

'You're not a rugby man, are you Robbie?' Paul asked. 'Never mind. Even if you're not, the Club's holding a memorial match, Sunday afternoon. It's for the family of one of their players who died in an accident. Isn't that right, Keith?' Cro-Magnon man nodded.

'Here you are.' Paul held out a single A5 size flyer, printed on one side on glossy paper. 'Come along if you can.' I nodded in as enthusiastic a non-committal way as I could and politely stuffed the flyer into the pocket of my suit jacket just as the meeting was being called to order. The room was heaving with solicitors topping up their CPD hours. The world of criminal defence is a small one and I recognised faces from all over central Scotland who, like me, had left things late. I scanned around for a space in the rows of bright red, plastic bucket seats and, as I did, noticed Jill sitting centre of the front row. What was she doing here?

There were some vacant lots in the second back row. Paul shimmied himself into one of them.

'Not done your CPD yet?' I said, after I'd edged my

way along the row, trampled on someone's foot, nearly tripped over a handbag and eventually squeezed in next to him. 'Let's hope the Judicial Appointments Board never hears of such procrastination from a prospective Sheriff, and on that subject may I say that my silence can be bought?'

'I did my twenty hours yonks ago,' Paul said, as we both stood up to let a female solicitor sidle along the row to a seat in the middle that someone had been keeping for her.

'The onerous responsibilities of a CPD convenor fulfilled,' I said, 'there's nothing to keep you here then. I can do the vote of thanks if you want to get away.'

'No, everything's worked out fine,' Paul said. 'I'm staying for other reasons.'

I was trying to think what other reasons there could be for wasting an evening listening to a law lecture, when Paul expanded on his statement.

'See who the main speaker is tonight?' he said.

'Freddy Lamont Q.C.? So what?'

'So, I instructed him a while back in a rape case and I have here...' he tapped the slim black, leather-briefcase at his feet, 'the brief in a cheeky wee cocaine importation.'

'Why didn't you just send it to his clerk?'

Paul smiled.

'Your third referee?' I asked.

'Precisely. I'll dangle the drugs brief from a strip of red tape in front of him, metaphorically speaking, while simultaneously asking his permission to add him as a referee.' He tapped the briefcase again. 'We're talking six-week trial here.'

The third of the evening's three speakers was, indeed, Freddy Lamont who summarised recent case law after we'd all been given an introduction to illegal drugs by a representative from the Independent Drugs Monitoring Unit, and a lecture from one of the local cops who was frequently called for the Crown to testify as a drugs expert. There was even a Q and A to finish. For fifteen quid and refreshments to follow, it had to be the CPD bargain of the year.

'Great lecture,' I told the guest speaker from the IDMU after the seminar, as I pumped myself a paper cup of watery coffee from a large vacuum flask. 'I didn't realise I knew so little about drugs.' She was a big woman with long hair, wearing what appeared to be a small woman's clothes and situated inconveniently between me and the tray of chocolate biscuits.

'Thanks,' she said. 'Would you mind?' She held out a paper cup with a drop of milk in the bottom. I was about to take it when she pulled it away. 'Sorry, I forgot I've stopped taking milk in my coffee. On a diet,' she whispered, drank the milk and handed me the cup.

'I liked the way you put the drug expert cop in his place about tenner bags,' I said, working the vacuum flask once more and handing her a cup of black coffee.

She laughed. 'I hope I wasn't too hard on him, but I don't know what they teach them at Tulliallan, or, rather I do. It's the same old stuff on drugs that police cadets have been getting drummed into them since the eighties.'

She was referring to the ongoing dispute between Crown and defence as to the weight of the ubiquitous 'tenner' bag. The cops clung on to the view that a tenner bag weighed 0.1 grams while the defence argued that these days, due to the increase in cutting agents, it was nearer 0.2 grams.

I nodded. 'It might not seem like such a big deal—'

'Pun excused,' she said.

'But if you've got a client in possession of an eighth of an ounce of heroin, the Crown takes the view that it's the equivalent of thirty-five tenner bags with a street value of three hundred and fifty pounds and therefore a supply-quantity. It's a lot easier to persuade the PF to agree simple possession if it's half that amount and your client is a fairly heavy-user.'

A crowd was beginning to gather around the refreshments, the chocolate biscuits were disappearing fast and I was in very real danger of being left with a custard cream. I had my eye on the last Blue Riband; a biscuit I thought they'd stopped making. It looked a lot smaller than I remembered and I was reaching out for it when someone ducked under my arm and snatched it away. It was Jill.

'Of course what you call heroin isn't actually heroin,' she said, tearing open the plastic wrapping with her teeth.

'What are you doing here?' I asked.

'Pharmacists have to do CPD as well. In fact a lot more than lawyers. Once you've left here you can forget everything and just chalk up the hours. I've got to write a summary of everything I've learned.'

'And what have you learned?'

'Not much I didn't know already.' Jill bit off a piece of biscuit. 'No offence,' she said to the lady from the IDMU.

The big woman looked down at the half-eaten biscuit and then at Jill. 'None taken...'

'Jill,' said Jill, holding out the hand not gripping the biscuit.

'Lynn,' the big woman said.

Jill carried on. 'The brown stuff we get over here and in Holland, places like that, is a diamorphine base.'

'What? Like crack?' I asked. The seminar might have finished, but I was counting this conversation towards my CPD hours; every little helped.

'That's right,' Jill said. 'Proper heroin is a salt, diamorphine hydrochloride. Just like crack is cocaine made for smoking, brown is heroin prepared for smoking by removing the hydrochloride part. Problem is when you want to inject it you can't because it isn't water soluble. That's why it has to be dissolved first in some form of acid.'

'Citric acid,' the big woman said, although I knew that already.

'Speaking of diamorphine,' I said. 'My dad gave me a box of dry-amps that were left behind at your dad's house.'

'Diamorphine dry-amps?' Lynn, the drug expert, said. 'Now there's a drug for the discerning junkie. No cooking-up, just a dash of distilled water and you're good to go.'

A shadow loomed over our little group. It was Keith Haggerty. 'Sorry to interrupt,' he said to Lynn, 'but I'm afraid your car is causing havoc in the car park.'

The two of them left leaving me and Jill.

'Heroin,' I said, 'it must have something going for

it. Tanya Lang said it was like being wrapped in warm cotton wool.'

'The girl in the papers who's baby is missing? The girl who died of a drugs over-dose? Yeah, got a lot going for it, heroin.'

Jill made a fair point, still I wasn't losing an argument with her even if it meant defending the indefensible. I recounted my conversation with her when we were clearing her dad's house and how Vince had said that if he'd known how good morphine was he'd have given up whisky and been a junkie years ago.

Jill smiled. 'Only my dad could find the funny side of cancer.' The smile crumbled and her bottom lip trembled a little.

As usual, I'd said the wrong thing. I put an arm around her.

She pulled away, annoyed with herself, cleared her throat. 'I'll pick up the vials from you. Get rid of them safely.'

'Thanks, I wasn't sure what to do. I suppose I should have taken them over to the doctor's surgery, it's just across the road from my office.

'They wouldn't have taken them,' Jill said. 'You're familiar with the work of the late Harold Shipman aren't you? No, the vials will need to be handed into a pharmacy, or back to the Hospice pharmacy where they came from, so that they can be properly recorded and destroyed.'

'Have you and Malky arranged a get together with Alex?'

'We have.'

'Where?'

'Islay. A weekend of golf and whisky, but not necessarily in that order.'

'When?'

'Weekend after next.'

'Really?'

She seemed pleased, but then women usually are if you follow their instructions.

My mobile phone vibrated in my pocket. Like every court lawyer I always kept it in silent mode because I was in and out of court all the time. 'In fact that's Malky now,' I said.

Jill frowned. 'He better not be trying to back out of it.'

'He wouldn't dare.' I put the phone to my ear.

'What you doing Saturday night?' Malky asked, eschewing any small talk.

'This Saturday night?' I asked, as though I might actually be doing something on any particular Saturday night. 'You mean the day after tomorrow?'

'Yeah. Anything planned?'

'You're definitely not talking about a week on Saturday are you? Because you know that's when we're going to Islay with Dad.'

Malky seemed pretty sure on his dates. I gave Jill the thumbs-up sign and her worried expression lifted.

'My social diary's relatively uncluttered,' I said.

'Good. Then get your back-side through to Hampden. Take the train to Queen Street, I'll send a car to pick you up at half seven. Dig out your dinner suit. Got all that? Good. Oh, and bring a date.'

'Like who?'

'Like a member of the opposite sex – look around –

they make up half the population. Catch.' He hung up.

Find a girl to take to a black-tie function at the home of Scottish Football on less than forty-eight hours notice? Desperate times called for desperate measures.

'What mess has he got himself into now?' Jill asked. She knew Malky like I knew Malky.

'Are you doing anything Saturday night?' I asked.

'Why?' she asked, suspiciously.

'Malky's invited me to some kind of do through in Glasgow and—'

'You need a date?'

'Urgently.'

'You asked me out on a date once before—'

'Then don't think of this as a date.'

'I won't.'

'Pick you up at seven?'

Jill stuffed the half-eaten chocolate biscuit in my top pocket. 'Do not be late.'

Friday morning and the first case of the day had resulted in a sound defeat. Sheriff Brechin's views on the credibility and reliability of a witness depended very much on whether that person was called by Crown or defence. A witness whose evidence he could whole-heartedly accept as gospel truth, when called by the Crown in one case, tended to be discounted as a pathological liar if called for the defence in another.

'See your client's girlfriend did the dutiful thing.' The Sheriff had adjourned the court prior to the start of the custody court and Hugh Ogilvie was full of himself after securing a successful conviction.

I tried not to engage in polite conversation with the Procurator Fiscal, especially after he'd won a case and was in full gloating mode, but couldn't help wondering what he was wittering on about.

'Dr Beattie,' he said. 'The word has come down from on high that the case is to be marked No Pro.' Ogilvie placed the back of a hand against his brow and feigned a swoon. 'It wasn't my boyfriend, it was me, poor little Megan, and I mustn't be prosecuted because I'm a little doo-lally down to him being a two-timing rodent.'

'And I'm also the Justice Secretary's daughter and, oh look, the Lord Advocate is keeping his job,' I added.

Ogilvie no longer saw the funny side. 'I never said that,' he snapped, and dropped his file of papers into a green plastic box. His depute Joanna Jordan arrived to take over from him. I hadn't seen her since the racist trial of Maureen Rooney. She had her own plastic box, a red one, filled with papers for those who'd been arrested the night before and were due to appear from custody. One or two of the defence agents who had been waiting for my trial to finish began to drift into court.

'Any sign of the Lang child?' Joanna asked me.

'Don't expect him to help,' Ogilvie said to her. 'Even if he knew, he'd probably claim some client-confidentiality bull-shit.' With that, he took off his gown, folded it and laid it across the green plastic box.

'Wish I could help,' I told Joanna.

'Your client not saying?'

'Without breaching any client-confidentiality *bull-shit*,' I said, watching Ogilvie leave the court room carrying his box of files, 'I've absolutely no idea where the kid is and I'm not sure if my client does either.'

'Bet he might remember if he could use the information to cut a deal on his murder charge,' she said. So discerning, so cynical, the girl would have made an excellent defence agent and replacement for the traitorous Andy.

Other agents began to crowd around wanting to discuss pleas with Joanna, ask about bail conditions and, most importantly, to try and talk her into calling their case first so that they could escape before lunch-time.

'Have you been given Brandon Biggam's case?' I asked.

'Fat chance. I've just been told that I'm leaving at

the end of the month. I was only on a short term contract because of the cut-backs. A lot of junior Fiscals are going to be looking for jobs soon. Foolishly, I thought my contract might be renewed.'

'My offer is still open,' I said. 'You could work on Brandon Biggam's case from the other side of the fence. Put the thumb-screws on him, find the baby, make a name for yourself.'

'It's kind of you to offer, but I don't see myself as a defence agent long-term.'

'I'll match your present salary.'

'Thanks, but I've got an interview lined up for a job back at the Children's Reporter's Office. I did my traineeship there.'

One state job to another: pension, paid sick-leave, guaranteed holidays; Munro & Co. couldn't compete. 'You'll have seen your share of dead junkie babies at the Reporter's office,' I said.

'You bet. Children dying because they'd not been supervised in the bath, swallowing drugs that were left lying around. Nobody cared. I don't think there were any prosecutions. Junkies and their babies: just one of those things. What's the point cluttering up the jails? Give it to the Reporter's Office to deal with. If I had my way, junkies wouldn't be allowed children. I'd be taking the kids off them the moment they were born and sterilising the parents.'

I was thinking that if she didn't find a job she could always lecture on civil liberties and human rights – in China - when Mr swinging-sixties, Paul Sharp, barged in between us, a tan wool suit with short wide lapels under his gown, a paisley pattern tie around the neck of his black shirt. He was at the head of the queue waiting to speak to Joanna. 'Do you mind, Robbie? Quit hogging the Fiscal, some of us are trying to get away before one.'

'Think about my offer, Joanna,' I said, giving Paul a friendly push back. 'I can't offer you all the civil service perks, sick-leave, pension—'

'Holidays,' Paul said.

'I'll give you my number, you can think it over.' I took my phone from my pocket, brought up the number on the screen and set it down on the table, while I hunted about in my suit pockets for a piece of paper to write it on. I found the flyer Paul had given me at the Rugby Club seminar the evening before and was turning it over to the blank side when I saw the photograph of the dead rugby player in whose honour the upcoming match was to be held. It was the bearded man who'd done a runner from my office with Dr. MacGregor's prehistoric laptop under his arm. His name was Phil Renton, not Bill Renton as Professor Bradley had told me. I stuffed the flyer back into my pocket, took the service copy complaint Paul was holding in his hand and ripped a corner off. I wrote down my number and gave it to Joanna. 'Give me a call if you change your mind.'

My mobile phone began to judder, jumping up and down on the table. It was Jimmy Garvie. I left Paul to his discussions with the young Fiscal-depute and took the call.

'Sorry about the other day,' Jimmy said. 'Sometimes I can be a wee bit OCD about things. Just wanted to make sure that all copies of my report were destroyed,' he laughed. 'Don't want any copies lying around and HMRC man asking what happened to my fee. You know what that mob are like if they think you've not been putting everything through the books.'

I chose to say nothing that might incriminate me re. the evasion of income tax. 'Not a problem, Jimmy. I'm just glad I don't have to pay it. I'm a bit strapped for cash right now.'

'As usual eh?' He laughed again. When did Jimmy develop a sense of humour?

'Anyway, case closed,' I said. 'Turned out the report would have been surplus to requirements even if there had been anything of interest on Doc Mac's laptop. Dr Beattie's in the clear.'

'So you never read it – my report?'

'Not all of it. If you remember, it was very long.' I felt I should mitigate my failure to read any more than the summary.

'How much?'

'The last paragraph.'

Jimmy laughed once more. That was three times in one day; in one phone call. 'Good. And there was only one hard copy?'

'Don't worry. I'm sure Andy will be giving it the attention it doesn't deserve.'

'Yes, I'm sure.' Jimmy wasn't laughing now. 'But the case is definitely finished?'

'Totally. Another famous Robbie Munro victory.' My turn to laugh, but the line had gone dead.

I took off my gown and was rolling it up, ready to leave, when Paul came over to me. 'Sheriff's not coming back on until two. Are you going over the road for some lunch?'

Before I could answer, he checked a text message on his phone. 'Oh, that's just great.' Paul rammed the mobile back into his jacket pocket.

'What is?'

'Not what. Who. Freddy, bleeding, Lamont. My application for Sheriff has to be in by the end of the month and I was banking on him as a referee.'

'What's the problem?'

'The problem is that he's now the competition. He's decided to apply for a Sheriff's job too.'

'Lamont's a Q.C. What's he wanting a Sheriff's job for?'

We walked out of court together in the direction of the bakers.

'The criminal Bar is dead,' Paul complained. 'No-one gets sent to the High Court anymore unless it's a rape or a murder. Not since they changed the max sentence to five years in the Sheriff Court. You know what it's like. Try and get sanction from the Legal Aid Board to instruct counsel in the Sheriff Court and you just get laughed at - and that's if you ask for junior counsel never mind senior. There's no work for Q.C.'s. No wonder Freddy Lamont's applying to be a Sheriff. I'll bet it's a while since he made a hundred and thirty K in a year at the Bar.'

'He *is* a bit of a balloon, though,' I said by way of consolation. 'Not much competition.'

'Are you joking? Lamont will be able to call up plenty of references from his chums in the Faculty and if he's a Q.C. he'll have done a stint for the Crown as an Advocate Depute. As far as the Judicial Appointments

Board is concerned you're not really a sound fellow until you've done a spot of prosecuting.'

'You're paranoid.'

'I'm not. I'm seriously thinking of approaching Ogilvie to be my third referee.'

'And if he gives you a reference and you're unsuccessful? Think what it's going to be like working here – owing Hugh Ogilvie a favour.'

Paul shook his head from side to side. 'You're right. What am I thinking of? Wait.'

He'd obviously had a great idea.

'Malky.'

'What about him?'

'Why don't I ask him to go as a referee?'

'Because he doesn't know anything about the law. Apart from the road traffic laws and that's only because he's broken all of them.'

'No, it might work. It shows a bit of diversity. Bound to pique the interest of someone on the Board, after all, no-one else is going to have a former Rangers and Scotland legend down as a referee. All I need is a foot in the door. Once I'm through to the interview stages, I know I can have them eating out of my hand.'

He probably would too. Talk about silver-tongued lawyers? Paul's should have been hallmarked.

'Malky's old hat,' I said. 'Yesterday's hero. Only a few Rangers' die-hards remember him and, anyway, what if the Appointment Board's full of Celtic supporters?'

'Not a problem. Everyone liked Malky when he played, even Celtic supporters. I should know, I am one. The Huddleboard voted him *Hun you would have least minded wearing the hoops,* and now that he's an internet sensation, the timing couldn't be better. Will you ask him for me?'

Paul seemed so keen. Maybe he was destined for the shrieval bench right enough; his discernment and decision making processes were already highly questionable.

'I mentioned your name to Kenny McIvor,' I said.

'You what? The Justice Secretary?'

'Did you not hear my conversation with Ogilvie just now? I saved his possible-future-son-in-law's career. McIvor owes me big time. I told him that you needed another referee and that you came highly recommended - by me.'

'What did he say?'

I didn't want to spoil things by admitting that the discussion had ended prematurely with me bailing out of the car and throwing-up over the road-side verge, not so near lunch-time and Paul hardly in a position to refuse to pay for our baked goods. 'I reckon he'll be amenable. I'll speak to him again.'

Paul took my cheeks between his fingers and pinched. 'You're a total diamond.'

'What about?' I asked. 'I'm seeing him tonight.'

'Don't bother.' Paul let go my cheeks and slapped me on the back. 'Though you could see if there's any chance of him scoring me a couple of tickets?'

'What for?'

'For the charity match a week on Sunday.'

Was Paul talking about *Islay weekend* Sunday?

'Scotland Legends against an Old Firm Old Boys select. Your brother's captaining Scotland.'

Chapter 39

I was dead on time for Jill. We took the train to Queen Street and were met at the ticket barrier by a mini-cab driver who took us south of the river to Hampden Park.

On arrival we were escorted to an opulent function suite where easily two hundred guests were milling around, chatting, eating canapés and drinking champagne from proper twenties-style champagne glasses, none of your flute-glass nonsense. There were a lot of round tables scattered about, groaning with gleaming cutlery and bright crystal glasses, and on a stage in a corner of the room a jazz band was knocking out a superb rendition of 'Fly Me to the Moon'.

Two members of the cast of a TV soap, I never admitted to watching, walked by. I smiled. They smiled back.

Jill elbowed me in the ribs. 'All right, I'll admit it: this is a lot better than pictures and a pizza.'

Malky hoved into sight, a young woman in a tight cocktail dress on his arm.

'Well, what do you think?' he said.

What I was thinking was that if they gave to charity what they were shelling out on this do, they wouldn't need to host a charity match, but that would have sounded churlish.

'Just another Saturday night, really,' I said. Malky put his fist on my jaw, pushed gently and turned his boyish smile on Jill. He kissed her on the cheek. 'Great to see you again, Jill.' Standing behind her, I caught my brother's eye, made a face and drew a finger across my throat. He seemed to get the message. 'Oh, and sorry about your dad,' Malky said. 'I tried to make the funeral, just couldn't get away.'

A waiter sailed by carrying a tray and I whisked off a couple of glasses of champagne.

'You've got to try the canapés,' said the girl in the tight cocktail dress. She waved a hand above her head and a waitress came over bearing a length of slate on which was a selection of unusual and highly appetising snacks. 'Let me see... we have goose liver and caramelised apples on crisp-bread, duck breast with an apricot, prune and pistachio topping on wholemeal toast, smoked trout, cucumber and trout eggs on brown bread and a chiffonnade of smoked salmon with a lemon and chive cream cheese on rye bread.'

'This is Ciara,' Malky said. 'She's helped her dad to arrange this whole thing.'

I'd guessed it wasn't an SFA event; for one thing there was a distinct lack of pies and I couldn't smell any Bovril. I helped myself to one of the chiffonnade things.

'Ciara...?' Jill enquired.

'Akbar.'

'Johnny Akbar's your dad?' I said, almost choking. 'Is he here?'

In his youth, Johnny Akbar had played two glorious seasons for Celtic before moving to the continent where he'd won a hat-trick of Champions League medals with three different teams. Despite the fact he hadn't played at Parkhead for twenty-odd years, every Celtic fan still regarded him as their property and someone they'd been kind enough to loan to the rest of the world.

'He's over there,' Ciara said, pointing to a cluster of people on the far side of the room, 'somewhere. He's asked me to keep an eye on Malky – apparently he takes some watching.'

Jill and I were part of a table of ten that included Malky and Ciara, two members of boy band 'Prize-Guys' and their girlfriends and another player of yesteryear whose promising career as a striker had, like Malky's, been ended by injury at much too young an age. If he was upset at his lot he seemed to be letting his wife drown his sorrows for him. He removed her from our company just as Johnny joined our table and as I was digging into hot marmalade pudding with Drambuie custard.

'Ciara taking good care of you all?' Johnny asked. 'Watch out for this guy,' he told his daughter, slapping Malky on the back at the same time. 'Last time I saw Malky,' he joked, 'I was running past him to celebrate a hat-trick at Ibrox.' And so it went on. All the old stories that I'd heard Malky tell dozens of times before tumbled out: how he'd once gone round to Johnny's house the night before a game and kicked him, just in case he was unable to catch him the next day; that Rangers had never made a bid to sign Johnny because they couldn't decide if he was a Catholic Muslim or a Protestant Muslim. It should have been tedious but it wasn't; it was terrific and the chat continued long into the night as we took full advantage of the free bar, courtesy of Johnny who himself drank nothing but iced-water with a slice of lime.

When the girls had gone off on another sortie to the ladies, I took the opportunity to confront Malky. 'You've got to try and get out of this,' I said. 'Dad's heart is totally set on Islay. It's all booked up, flights, B&B, the lot, and if you don't go it's me who'll get the blame.'

Malky slung a drunken arm around my shoulders and laid his head against mine. 'Is this Islay thing really all that important?' He waved an arm around wildly. 'Compared to all this? This is for charity. Bring Dad to the match. He'll love it.'

I wasn't so sure if he would; not when he could be golfing with his sons on the Queen of the Hebrides.

'Charity begins at home,' I said. 'Dad needs this trip to give him a lift. You've not seen him lately. He's hardly been out since Vince died and he's drinking more than ever.'

Malky shouted us up another round of eighteen-year-old Macallans.

'Nice to see you and Jill out together on a date - at last,' he said, when almost instantaneously two bubble-tumblers of the precious Highland malt appeared.

'It's not really a date and what do you mean – at last?'

'I shouldn't really tell you this.' Malky put a drop or two of water into his whisky and shook his head. 'No, really, I can't, he'd kill me.'

'I'll kill you, if you don't tell me what you're going on about.'

'You and Jill. Remember that date you had when you were at the school?'

'University,' I corrected him.

'Remember how you stood her up?'

I glanced around, there was no sign of Jill and the other females returning from their tour of the plumbing. 'Go on.'

'That was Dad's idea.'

The man had clearly consumed too many expensive malt whiskies, if that were possible. 'How was it Dad's idea? I went to the football. You got those great tickets...' I tailed off as through the clouds of alcohol I began to see clearly.

Malky smiled as the penny dropped.

'You never got those tickets did you?'

'Nope.'

'Dad bought them, so that I...'

He nodded. 'You're getting there.'

'So that I wouldn't go out with Jill?'

Malky raised his glass to me. The dark-amber liquid had been newly distilled alcohol around the time I'd attended the final friendly match before Scotland's Euro '96 qualifying campaign began in earnest. The night I'd bumped Jill.

Malky swallowed his drink in a oner. 'Dad and this Islay thing - I'll see what I can do. It won't be easy. Johnny is a very persuasive guy, he always gets his man and, thanks to YouTube, I'm the man everybody wants right now.'

I heard the chatter of female voices behind us. Malky called out for more drinks. Around one in the morning, Johnny, who had been busy working the room, advised those remaining that he was calling it a night. He came over again to our table to say a farewell to Malky who'd been yelling 'party-pooper' at him.

'It's okay for you Malky,' he winked at the rest of the table. 'Us old guys need our beauty sleep. It's an early start tomorrow. This match isn't organising itself.' He raised his mobile phone. 'Had a call-off already. Anyone know the number of a famous clapped-out old footballer?' He ruffled Malky's hair. 'It's okay, I've got your number already.'

'Robbie used to play football,' Malky said.

Johnny was interested. He turned to look at me. 'You any good?'

I was hardly in a position to give an unbiased account of my several seasons spent churning up the mud at amateur-level.

'Hopeless,' Malky answered for me, 'but he knows which end of a football to kick.'

It was my turn to have my back slapped by the legend that was Johnny Akbar. 'Excellent.' He took a menu off the table and pen from a waitress who'd come over for a drinks order. 'I'll add you to the Scotland squad. Robbie Munro – celebrity lawyer – how's that sound?'

It sounded totally brilliant.

As soon as Johnny had left, making sure Ciara went with him, Jill took me aside. 'You can't play,' she said.

'Everyone's a critic.'

'No, I mean apart from your lack of ability—'

'It's the only thing that stopped me from being a superstar.' The quips were coming fast and furious and it wasn't just the expensive scotch, it was the thought of me, Robbie Munro, fulfilling every Scotsman's ambition; to run out onto the hallowed Hampden turf. As part of a twenty-two man squad, I knew I'd be lucky to get a few minutes: I didn't care. One minute, one kick of the ball, it would be enough to say I'd played for Scotland.

'You're not playing,' Jill said, rather too firmly for a woman with whom I was not in a relationship. She didn't even think this was a date.

My reply was equally as firm. 'Unless you've got a team of wild horses stabled nearby, I think you'll find that I am very much playing.'

Jill stood and raised herself to her full five feet six; she was wearing heels. 'And the Islay trip?'

'Is it really that important?' I asked.

Evidently it was, because Jill lifted her silver clutch-bag from the table, thrust it under one arm like a colour sergeant's swagger-stick, about-turned and quick-marched from the room.

Chapter **40**

Despite the excesses of the night before, thanks to a bed-time pint of water and Diarolyte sachet, I was hanging on in there and, late Sunday afternoon, was ready for a bite to eat. My dad was sitting at the table reading a golf magazine when I arrived unannounced and looking to cadge a snack.

'You know...' My dad lowered the magazine. 'I don't believe in all that big-bang nonsense.'

By this time I had my head in the fridge looking for cheese. I'd put several hours between myself and the hot marmalade pudding, much of which time had been spent lying in front of the telly with a damp towel wrapped around my head. I emerged with a block of mature Cheddar. My dad would eat nothing else. 'Are we talking here about the beginnings of the universe or the latest driver from Callaway?'

As I rummaged around for a couple of slices of bread, my dad, on automatic pilot and clearly deep in thought, got up and turned on the grill. 'I saw this thing on telly last night all about the universe,' he said. 'You know that wee Eye-tie star-gazer—'

'He's the Astronomer Royal and he's English. I think his parents may have come from Iraq or Iran.'

'He was saying,' my dad said, retaking his seat, while I carved chunks of cheese, 'that there are one hundred thousand million stars in our galaxy and, you won't believe this, one hundred, billion galaxies in the universe.'

I began to geometrically arrange the cheese on two slices of bread. 'Are those not the same numbers? One hundred thousand million *is* one hundred billion isn't it?'

He sighed. 'Does it matter? It's a hell of a lot of stars. In fact, apparently, there are more stars up there,' he pointed at the polystyrene ceiling tiles, 'than there are grains of sand if you added up every single beach in the world.'

'Yeah, that is very interesting,' I said, wondering if there was a point to it all.

'And, according to this Italian guy, everything in the entire universe was once squashed down to the size of an atom and then exploded.'

'What about it?' I asked, thinking that the old man had more or less summarised the big-bang theory as I understood it.

'What about it? It's a load of crap. That's what about it.'

I bunged the bread and cheese under the grill. 'Will you break the news to Steven Hawking or shall I?' But my sarcasm was lost on him.

'How could everything in the world, far less the universe, have once all fitted into the size of a single atom? You've seen the size of St Andrew's beach, there's tons of sand on it. Imagine every grain of sand is a star the size of the sun.'

I didn't want to imagine. I was already fighting off a headache. 'There were enormous gravitational forces at work,' I said.

My dad wasn't listening. He picked up his

magazine with a disgusted look on his face. 'Must have been a bloody big atom,' he muttered, turning his attention to the crossword in his magazine. 'Mind your toast.'

I turned to find the surface of the cheese bubbling and turning black in places.

After I'd manoeuvred the food onto a plate, dropping a splash of molten cheddar on my hand in the process, I sat at the table opposite my dad. 'See there's a big charity match on at Hampden this weekend,' I casually remarked. If he suspected anything he showed no discernible sign, not even to my trained eye. 'Scotland Legends against an Old Firm Old-Boys team,' I continued cautiously.

He jotted an answer down and then scored it out, mumbling into his moustache something about Lee Trevino.

'Should be a good game.'

'Doubt it,' he said, re-writing the answer. 'Friendlies are bad enough without some ancient footballers and a bunch of...' he made a quotation mark with two fingers, '*celebrities*, making a fool of themselves.'

'It's for charity,' I said, feeling myself losing ground in the discussion.

'Then they should all give one week's wages and stop putting on a publicity stunt to make themselves look good.'

Okay, perhaps now was not a good time. I still had a few days left to break the news. Toasted cheese duly scoffed, I was ready to say good-bye. He scarcely looked up from his crossword. He'd probably sit there by himself all afternoon doing it. I thought back to his big-bang rant. 'You should get out more,' I said. 'And I don't mean to the pub. It doesn't do you any good sitting here pondering on the universe. Get out and have a game of golf instead of reading about it.'

'I'm saving myself for the big weekend,' he said, a cheerful note threatening to break through his usual gruffness. 'And, on that subject, take a look at this will you?' He led me through to the livingroom where there was an opened suitcase on the floor, stuffed with clothes. 'Islay in the autumn – it's bound to be a bit chilly and wet. And no doubt you and your brother will be taking me out for a nice meal, after we've seen round a few of the distilleries. I'll be needing a few changes of clothes and waterproofs. How am I supposed to get all my gear into one suitcase?'

He went over and kneeled on the lid of his suitcase. 'I'll tell you - there'd need to be some enormous gravitational forces at work to get this thing to close. Now if we were going by ferry—'

'I was thinking, Dad...'

He looked up at me, eyes narrowing.

'What if we postponed? Waited for the spring. That way,' I attempted a laugh and managed only to emit a dry choking sound, 'you wouldn't need to take so many clothes. Or we could take the ferry when the weather was better.'

He stood. His moustache twitched. The Hampden floodlights in my mind began to dim.

'We're going Friday,' he said. 'And we're taking Vince with us. We'll scatter his ashes at Port Ellen. It's what he'd have wanted, so I hope you can book another seat on the plane...'

At one hundred and fifty quid a ticket, I thought Vince might be prepared to travel as hand luggage.

'Because Jill's coming too.'

'When did you arrange this?' I asked.

'A couple of days ago.'

'And you didn't think of telling me?'

'I'm telling you now, am I not? Have you spoken to the lassie recently?' I couldn't tell him about Jill's walk-out at the Hampden-do without explaining the reason why it happened. 'She'll pay her own way if that's what you're worried about. I didn't think you'd object.'

'And it's okay with you is it?' I asked. 'Me being in such close proximity to Jill.'

He bent over and hauled a thick woolly jumper out of the bottom of his suitcase. He studied it carefully. 'I suppose I could leave this behind. I've got that wind-cheater Malky bought me for Christmas. It's a lot thinner.'

'I mean, I wouldn't want to contaminate her in any way.'

My dad stared at me. 'It's been years – let it go.'

'Let it go? I've only just found out. What was the problem?'

'There was no *problem*, it's just that... it's just that Jill's a nice girl and your record with women... well it isn't really all that good is it?'

'I was eighteen, I didn't have a record.'

'But you do now and look at it.'

'Vince wouldn't have minded,' I said. 'The last time I saw him he told me he'd always hoped me and Jill might get together.'

At the mention of his old friend's name, my dad's shoulders slumped. 'I know he did. Vince was my best friend, but he didn't know you like I do. Let's face it you'd have only made a mess of things.'

It was an argument I wasn't going to win, but I'd have my revenge.

'Put your shoes on,' I said.

'Why?'

'We're going.'

'Where?'

'Out.' I picked up the woolly jumper and threw it at him 'And you'd better bring that - you'll be needing it.'

Chapter 41

It had not long stopped raining and the wind was blowing west to east from one end of the rugby pitch to the other.

We found a space along the touch-line between the twenty-two and half-way, on the less populated side, opposite a recently erected temporary stand. While my dad was away checking out the refreshment stall, I spied Sammy Veitch striding through the mire towards me, kilt flapping in the stiff breeze.

'Great minds think alike,' he said.

The teams were lined up in the centre. The Club Chairman, Keith Haggerty, announced one minute's applause through a feedback-shrieking microphone.

'Took you long enough to find him,' I said, as the hand-clapping died away. 'You must be losing your touch.'

The whistle blew and the Threemilers kicked off into wind.

Sammy rubbed his jaw. 'Can't believe it. I've been all over the place looking for him and here he was right under my nose. The family was the problem. His wife took the body back to Ayrshire.' He looked around the couple of hundred or so spectators who'd gathered to watch the match between the home team and neighbouring Linlithgow RFC. 'Cheeky, if you ask me. Renton separated from his wife a year ago and came to live in Livingston.' Sammy nodded across the width of the pitch to where a woman and little girl, both wrapped up warmly, sat one side of man mountain, Keith Haggerty, in the front centre seats of the stand. On Haggerty's west-face, I was surprised to see Fiona Scott. I remembered Glen Beattie mentioning that she was a rugby fan and I'd assumed he meant corporate hospitality at Murrayfield, not a lower-league clash between two teams killing time until the pubs opened. 'Now that hubby's dead,' Sammy chuntered on, 'she's back on the scene and milking the grieving widow role for all it's worth.'

There had been no admission price, just some people with white plastic buckets collecting donations. It wasn't much of a widow's pension.

Sammy slapped his hands together. 'Still, mustn't grumble. I like the cold, grasping type. My kind of gal. Come the final whistle I'll be right in there.'

My dad arrived back with two paper cups of tea. 'Sorry, Sammy,' he said, 'Didn't know you were here or I'd have brought you one back.'

A gust of window caught the cups and some tea spilled out onto the grass.

'Some weather, eh, Alex?' Sammy said. 'Tail end of the hurricane that hit New York. They say it's been down-graded to a Scottish summer.'

My dad handed me a cup. How he'd carried it that far without burning his hands I didn't know. I had to pull the cuff of my pullover down over my hand to serve as a glove.

'Sammy's got designs on the widow,' I said.

My dad raised his eyebrows. 'The man died weeks ago. You chasing ambulance's on foot these days?'

'I had a spot of bother tracking this one down,' Sammy said. 'Done my homework, though. Seems like the dead guy was crossing the road and some impatient driver pulled out from behind a parked car and hit him.'

'Overtook a car that was parked on yellow lines,' I reminded him.

A drop-kick attempt sailed through the air, hit an upright and the ensuing scramble resulted in a scrum on the five-metre line.

'Makes no difference. Shouldn't go overtaking if the road ahead is not clear.'

'What if the person you knock down is being chased?' my dad asked.

The ball emerged from the rear of the scrum where it was quickly gathered by the Threemilers' scrum-half and whisked away again before the opposing team's wing-forward could intercept.

'He wasn't being chased,' I said.

The home team had been under pressure but were now on the charge. The ball switched quickly from stand-off to centre, in seconds it was in the hands of the winger and he raced towards us spurred on by loud shouts of support. Just as he reached the half-way line his run was halted by a desperate challenge. The ball broke free, bobbling along the rutted pitch. Linlithgow's fullback, aware of the lack of defensive support, raced across to fly-hack it into touch, knocking the paper cup clean out of my hand, splashing Sammy with hot tea.

'If I don't have any luck with the cop's wife, I'm going to sue that egg-chaser,' he said, glowering at the full-back and wiping tea from his kilt.

'What cop is this?' my dad asked.

Sammy opened his sporran. He pulled out one of the flyers advertising the benefit match, unfolded it and pointed to the picture of the man with the beard.

'My dad doesn't think Renton was a cop,' I said.

'He wasn't,' my dad said, firmly.

From my coat pocket I felt a call coming through on my mobile phone. It was Maggie Sinclair.

'Robbie,' she said, 'I was wondering if you knew what was happening with Andy. Has he been in touch?'

I had no idea what Maggie was talking about.

'Andy was assaulted a week ago, right outside the office. I thought you'd have known.'

I stepped back a few paces to make room for the winger as he delivered the ball for the line-out. 'What happened. How is he?'

'He was mugged. The exact details aren't clear yet. I spoke to his dad the day after it happened and know he spent a night in hospital. He's at his parents' home now, recuperating, but no-one's been in touch and I just thought you might have some information.'

I didn't and we left it at that. My dad and Sammy were still discussing the occupation of the deceased rugby player when the call ended. Sammy re-folded the flyer and slipped it back into his sporran, next to a small silver hip-flask. 'Aye, well, Alex, you say he wasn't a cop, but you don't know every cop in Scotland.'

'True,' my dad said. 'But, I recognise the face on that piece of paper and he wasn't a cop.' He took a sip of tea. My dad loved it when he was a step ahead. 'He was a security guard at St Gideon's.'

Chapter 42

For someone who'd long proclaimed a dislike for the oval ball, my dad seemed actually to be enjoying his rugby experience and so at the half-time whistle I left him in the company of Sammy and the ambulance-chaser's hip-flask, and headed for my car which was abandoned on a nearby road-verge. Fifteen minutes later I was crossing the Forth Road Bridge, forty-five and I was in the centre of Perth, crossing the Tay on the A93 and in another half an hour I was parking my car outside the red sandstone home of Andy's parents.

Andy's father was a minister and I'd visited the manse once before, when Andy had been working for me and invited me to his Dad's fiftieth birthday party. He'd caught me at a bad moment with excuses in short supply which, given that they were my stock in-trade, was unusual enough, but the party had not been at all what I'd imagined. I had expected women in hats, a lot of hymn-singing, orange-juice flowing like water and, instead, I'd been wheeched around all night by some attractive young ladies at a Ceildh in the Reverend's honour at which the produce of nearby Eradour, Scotland's smallest distillery, was liberally available. I'd gone uncertain of, and, indeed, indifferent to, any distinction between a Gay Gordon and a Dashing White Sergeant and returned proficient in the Military Two-Step and Orcadian Strip-the Willow.

'Mr Munro,' said the Reverend Ian Imray, meeting

me half way down the garden path, 'Andrew's had a bit of a rough night and he's not long dropped off to sleep. He should really have stayed in hospital longer, but you know what the NHS is like these days.'

'Won't let your bum warm the bed-sheets will they?'

'Quite.' He marched past me out of the gate and obviously intended for me to follow.

The manse was situated adjacent to the Church. We exited one gate and entered another further down the street that served a small, manicured graveyard.

'I come here when I want to meditate,' the Reverend Imray said. 'Many is the sermon I've cobbled-together while walking between the gravestones.'

'How is Andy?' I asked, trying to steer us onto the reason why I'd driven fifty-five miles on a Sunday afternoon.

'He has a nasty bump on his head and some badly bruised ribs.'

'Do you know what happened?'

'I'm tempted to say Glasgow happened, but it's no worse or better than any big city, I'm sure. We don't get a lot of muggings in Blairgowrie.'

More chance in Blairgowrie than outside the offices of one of Scotland's premier law firms, I couldn't help but think.

'He's young, he'll get over it soon enough,' I said. 'The physical side of things anyway. It can be a knock to the confidence, though – being mugged. It's the unexpectedness of those type of unpremeditated attacks. Andy was just in the wrong place at the wrong time I suppose.'

The strong wind I'd left in Linlithgow was only a light breeze in Perthshire. It ruffled the Reverend's greying hair. 'Andy's not so sure,' he said, patting the top of his head with the palm of his hand. 'About it being unpremeditated. That's what I'd really like to talk to you about.'

We continued our leisurely stroll through the graveyard, here and there a fresh bunch of cut flowers arranged at the side of a headstone, the grass mown bowling-green close, shrubbery and ornamental trees pruned to perfection. 'I'd always hoped Andrew might enter the ministry,' the Reverend said. 'I suppose clergymen are no different than other fathers in that they'd like to see their sons follow in their footsteps.'

'Not sure about the priests,' I said with a laugh, but the man in the back to front collar didn't see the funny side, if, indeed, there was one; nonetheless, something was definitely wrong. This wasn't the happy, care-free man I'd seen cavorting around in an eight-some reel just a few months ago.

'You don't have any children do you Mr Munro?'

'It's Robbie,' I said, 'and I have my hands full looking after my dad.'

He stared at me through a set of lenses housed in the sort of thick, black-rimmed frames until recently favoured by his son. 'I think you know that when Andy went to work with you, Andy's mother and I weren't really all that keen. Not about him working with you, specifically, although one does hear the rumours, but about the area of law he was interested in. I mean, crime, it takes a certain sort of person. I can't believe it's a wise career move for a young man, no matter how much money he makes.'

He seemed to be looking at me when he said that. Had he never heard of legal aid rates?

'Must be hard not to be contaminated, coming into close contact with criminals, day in, day out,' the Reverend continued.

It was hard to shake off the feeling that I was being given a row. Talk about being savaged by a dead sheep? 'As I recall, Jesus came into regular contact with criminals, crooked tax-collectors, prostitutes, thieves. Wasn't it the religious people who had him killed?' What was I doing debating the life of Christ, not my specialist subject, with the clergy?

The Reverend took a deep breath. 'Down the road from here is a much bigger graveyard,' he said, apparently giving my comment no heed. I was glad. I had only come to see how his son was, not engage in a theological argument. 'It's called the Kirkyaird. There are gravestones dating back to the mid-seventeenth century. About twenty years ago they found a highly-ornate stone depicting Abraham preparing to kill Isaac, his son. I'm sure you get asked particular legal questions a lot of the time.'

'If I had a fiver for every time I've been asked how I can bring myself to act for people I must know are guilty, I'd probably be able to clear my over-draft.'

'Well, one of the questions I'm asked the most is: why, if God is love, did he ask Abraham to kill his son, even if he later changed his mind?'

It did seem a bit strange to me too. Not quite as strange as the fact that I'd come to see the Reverend's injured son and had somehow ended up in a cemetery on the receiving end of an uninvited sermon.

'I'm sure you tell those who quiz you about your clients that everything is relative, that a person's actions must be viewed in context. Well the Bible is the same. With Abraham, we're dealing with events that took place over four thousand years ago. We can't judge through twenty-first century eyes.'

'I would have thought that asking someone to kill their son was just as socially unacceptable back then as it is now.'

'Then you'd be wrong. You see, back then in the middle-east, there were no Jews, no Palestinians, only wandering tribes of which Abraham was the leader of one. They all worshipped their own gods: Ba'al, Moloch, Dagon to name a few and none enjoyed anything better than a child-sacrifice. So when Jehovah asked Abraham to kill his child, it wasn't the least unusual compared to the surrounding cultures and their gods. What was different was that Abraham's god was only testing Abraham's faith. He didn't change his mind. He had no intention for Abraham to kill his son, for He was not a god like the others.'

I was glad he'd cleared that up for me. 'So, should I wait and see if Andy wakes up or, maybe, come back later?' I asked as we reached the cemetery wall, turned and started to walk back towards the gate down another avenue of tombstones.

'I'd rather, Mr Munro, if you did neither. You see, I've looked at matters in what I consider is the correct context, and all I can see is your hand in this.'

'What are you talking about?'

'Andrew told me that you might not like that he'd

taken your old job.'

'He didn't. I was a partner at Caldwell & Clark before I left—'

'Asked to leave, surely?'

'And while I wish him nothing but the best—'

'Andrew also told me how unhappy you were that one of your private clients had ditched you and gone to him.'

Was this what Andy had really told him? Or was it the Reverend's own take on matters? Whatever, I was not about to start telling the complicated tale of my failed referral to C&C. 'Andy asked for my help.'

'And you reacted to that cry for aid by trying to steal his client, did you not?'

I was angry, though unaware of the fist clenching at my side until the Reverend mentioned it.

'Violence – is that your answer, Mr Munro?'

I quickly relaxed my hand. 'I suppose you'd turn the other cheek.'

'There you go again, taking things out of context. Jesus wasn't telling his followers to be punch-bags. In the ancient Middle East the left hand was reserved for toilet purposes. Back in year dot, if you hit someone, you hit them with your right hand. If you were chastising a slave, a child or, I suppose, a wife, you would strike them with the back of the right hand. To strike someone of equal status one would use the palm or fist.'

The man was a walking sermon machine and was beginning to bug me. All of a sudden, the thought of watching some over-weight men rolling around in the mud at Threemile Town Park seemed enticing.

'Our Lord was a splendid orator. You don't follow a man for miles and up a mountainside in the blazing heat for a dull lecture. The people who listened came from the lowest strata of society. They would have been batted about with the back of the hand countless times by their masters, religious leaders, Roman soldiers. Jesus was saying: if that happens again, turn your cheek. Let your attacker know that if he wants to hit you again, he'll have to use the other side of his hand, treat you as he would an equal. It might not sound it nowadays, but it was revolutionary stuff - every man was equal in the sight of God.'

At the cemetery gate again, we turned right and when we reached my car the Reverend stopped. It was clear he didn't intend me to go any further. 'Here is the context in which I place the attack on Andrew,' he said. 'He left your office, Mr Munro, with a file of papers for the very case you did not want to relinquish. He arrived at his office and was mugged. His attackers didn't take his wallet or his watch. They didn't even take the new leather briefcase I'd given him when he started his new job. They took what was inside it. They took the file. The file you didn't want Andrew to have.' He held up a hand to stifle my protests. 'You're a criminal lawyer. I'm sure you can present an excellent defence and will no doubt have an airtight alibi; however, I think you'll agree how it all looks – in context.'

Right at that moment, man of the cloth or not, I'd have happily slapped him with either hand, but without another word he turned, walked through his garden gate and left me with a long drive home and a lot of thinking to do.

Chapter 43

I tried phoning Jimmy Garvie on the way back down the road from Blairgowrie. I'd thought long and hard. Why would anyone mug Andy for Dr Beattie's case file? What was in it that could not be obtained by legitimate means? The petition, containing the now abandoned charges, was a public document that could be acquired, albeit for an exorbitant photo-copying fee, from the Sheriff Clerk. Then there was the list of witnesses; all cops with one exception: Megan McIvor, and her contact address wasn't even on the list. She was down as c/o Lothian & Borders Police. The only piece of confidential information on the file was Jimmy Garvie's report. I recalled the I.T. man's obsession with making sure all traces of his email were removed from my computer equipment, to the extent that he'd actually waived his fee.

No answer from Jimmy. A gadget freak like him would no doubt have caller-recognition. If, as I now suspected, he was in some way involved, he wouldn't want to take my calls. I'd have to meet him face to face. Unfortunately, I didn't know Jimmy's address. His details were at the foot of his emails and would be gone now that he'd wiped my PC clear of his report and he never committed anything to paper, not when there were electronic means available. I thought I might have to call on the investigatory skills of my dad or leave it to Grace-Mary to track him down the next morning, when

I remembered SLAB.

The Scottish Legal Aid Board had all the records I needed and they were right there on-line. I drove to my office and switched on my PC. I logged-in and searched for an old case where I'd instructed Jimmy to examine the mobile phone of one of my drug-dealing clients who had been, it was alleged, accurately as things turned out, brokering a lot of his transactions by text message. In a legal aid case you didn't do anything without first obtaining sanction from the Board; retrospective permission was not happening, no matter how important the work was or how urgently required. In every case where an expert was instructed an application giving full details of who, why and how much had to be completed in advance. I knew who I was looking for. In under a minute I'd found where he was.

Infirmary Street in Edinburgh's Old Town. Just off The Royal Mile. I parked outside a coffee shop. Flat 4/3 was directly opposite over an Indian restaurant serving tapas curries. There was a security buzzer at the side of the large green entrance door. I pressed the button against which there was a smudged label stating 'Garvie'. No answer. Not sure what to do next, I was still standing there when a young man arrived, hair falling over his face and with an enthusiastic, if premature, attempt at facial hair. He was pushing a bike while carrying a heavy holdall and a couple of other smaller bags. He dropped the bags on the pavement and pulled a key out of his jerkin pocket.

'I'll take that for you,' I said, and held his bike while he opened the door and we both entered. He chained the front wheel and propped the bike up against the wall behind the door and was still climbing the stairs after I'd stopped on the second floor landing. So this was Jimmy Garvie's home/office. It looked like Mrs Garvie had instructed the better lawyer in the divorce. I hammered on the door: no answer. There was no window, just a strip of frosted glass at the very top showing that there was a light on somewhere inside the flat. I hammered again: still no response. I was turning away, when out of the corner of my eye I thought I caught a flicker, an almost imperceptible darkening of the lit-up strip of glass, as though someone inside the property had walked in front of a light source. I banged again. 'Jimmy! I know you're in there!' Still nothing. 'Jimmy!' I yelled. 'If you don't open up I'm going to assume that you're dead and phone the police to break down this door before you start smelling and annoying the neighbours.'

I was stepping away from the door when it opened an inch or two on a chain and Jimmy's face poked out through the gap, swivelling from side to side, checking who was there. The door closed again and then opened wide.

'Get in here,' Jimmy said, shutting and locking the door after me. He showed me to the left, down a small hallway into a spacious livingroom with two large picture windows looking out onto the coffee shop across the street and my beat up Alfa, more miles on the clock than Sputnik, parked outside. Further up to the right: the floodlit corner of Old College, Edinburgh School of Law, where I'd dreamt of a career in the law. Perhaps if I'd spent less time reading Clarence

Darrow's interesting, if unimaginatively titled, autobiography, *The Story of My Life,* and more studying books on acquisitions and mergers or corporate tax law, I wouldn't have to spend Sunday evenings tracking down the missing report in a child-porn case and, instead, be left to ponder mysteries such as, what am I going to do with all this money I'm making?

I sat down on the well-worn, brown-leather couch that had coffee-cup circles branded into the arms. Jimmy sat in a similar armchair. This seemed to be where it all happened. There was computer equipment lined-up neatly along two of the walls. On a workbench a PC tower case was lying open on its side, electronic entrails spilling out, illuminated by an angle-poised lamp which at that time, apart from the television, was the only point of light in the room. The Antiques Roadshow: one of my dad's favourite programmes. He would be back from the rugby by now and watching it.

'What was so important about the report that my friend was mugged for it?'

'What report is that?' Jimmy asked innocently, wafting an arm in the direction of his workbench.

I'm a calm, collected kind of a guy. I find that the loss of one's temper loses more battles than it wins. Count to ten. I turned my eyes to the glowing box in the corner where an elderly man in a yellow bow-tie was telling a young woman, with mounting excitement, that her second edition of Tolkien's The Hobbit was even more valuable than the first, because the first was such a publishing flop that J.R. had made some illustrations and added them to the next run. A second edition was worth between ten to twelve thousand pounds. 'I take it you've kept the dust-jacket somewhere safe?' the bow-tie asked. The young woman hadn't. Excitement turned to doubt, doubt to dejection. Even the bow-tie seemed to droop. As us viewers were soon to learn, the value of a second edition Hobbit with no dust-jacket was five hundred tops and that was further reduced by other factors such as dog-eared pages and a tea-cup ring on the hardback cover. The young woman failed to put on a brave face. 'I'm sure you wouldn't have wanted to sell it anyway,' said the rather embarrassed face above the yellow bow-tie. My dad would probably be finding the whole thing hilarious. I'd counted way past ten and yet I wasn't laughing.

I sprang to my feet and grabbed Jimmy by the front of his T-shirt. 'You know what report I'm talking about, and you'll tell me what's in it and give me a copy or I'm going to do to you what somebody did to Andy Imray.'

Jimmy wrenched himself free, toppling the armchair and scrambling to what he seemed to think was a safe distance. He picked up a coffee mug by the handle and held it like a large pottery knuckle-duster. 'Get out!'

'Calm down,' I said.

'*Me* calm down?'

'Okay, okay so I lost it for a moment there. That's what happens when people try to treat me like an idiot. Now why don't we both sit down? And if you tell me all about the report then I won't have to come over, take that mug off you and stick it somewhere it probably won't fit all that well.'

Jimmy thought over the offer for a moment and then put the mug back on the work bench. Cautiously, he resumed his seat. 'I'll tell you what I know then you'll leave, understand?'

Seemed fair enough.

'After that you tell nobody about this conversation.'

'Will you stop being so Secret Squirrel and tell me what was in the report?'

'I thought you'd read it.'

'Just the summary and the enormous accompanying fee note.'

'Which, as you'll recall, I am no longer charging you.'

'Jimmy...'

'Okay, I really can't remember what's in the report. I know you asked me to check that old laptop for porno-pictures and it took me about five seconds to find out there weren't any. Even after noting my findings and the usual bumph about my qualifications and a glossary of technical terms, the report was only two or three pages long and so...'

'You padded it out?'

'A little.'

As I recalled there had been more words than The Hobbit, first or second edition.

Jimmy shrugged. 'All that was on the laptop was some word-processor files and so I added them as a sort of appendix.'

'Let me see it.'

'Can't - it's gone.'

'Why were you so keen to get rid of it?'

'It's like this.' Jimmy shifted uncomfortable in his seat. The closing theme music from the Antiques Roadshow began to play. 'A few weeks ago, I had a visit from a couple of guys.'

'Did one have a beard?'

'Yeah.'

I wished I still had the flyer from Phil Renton's testimonial match. 'Did they say they were cops?'

'No, but they did say that if I didn't erase everything from Dr MacGregor's laptop, they would come back here, open the window and give me a free flying lesson.'

'So why didn't you phone the cops? You used to be a cop.'

He sighed. 'Not all the work I do is for law firms. Other people employ me too; serious people who wouldn't like to think I let the cops in here to nose about their stuff. I didn't want any fuss. It was a lot easier to go to your office and scrub that email than involve the police.'

That explained a lot; not everything. 'What about Andy?'

'I don't know anything about that.'

'He had the only hard copy of your report. You knew that didn't you?'

Jimmy clasped his hands at the back of his neck and looked at the ceiling rose.

'When I came to your office last week, I tried to catch Andy at the train station, but I was too late.'

'So you made a call?'

I took his silence as agreement and stood. Jimmy followed me to the door.

'Don't be expecting too many more instructions from Munro & Co.' I said on my way out. The door closed behind me. I had some more thinking to do. I walked down the two flights of stone steps to the front door and opened it. It wasn't the first time in my life I'd been punched in the face, but it was definitely the hardest. I didn't remember falling over, only lying on the cold floor, a bicycle on top of me and the figure of a very large man in the doorway, silhouetted against the street lighting. 'That's just a warning,' he said. 'Case closed.'

'I'm not even going to ask,' Grace-Mary said, walking into my room next morning to find me pressing an ice-cold can of Jamaican ginger beer against my severely-bruised left eye. As usual, she was carrying the morning's mail in a yellow wire-basket. She waited, presumably for me to explain my injury. I didn't. She put the basket on the desk and left the room. I pulled it over for a quick sift through before I left for court. Grace-Mary was back a few minutes later with a bulging A4 manila envelope. 'What are we going to do with all these pen-drives now that we're downloading disclosure straight from the Crown web-site?' I was tempted to tell her to scrub them and put them on eBay; several dozen four-gig USB memory sticks had to be worth something.

'We better give them back,' I said. 'The PF probably keeps a list so that he can try and do some defence lawyer for theft of Crown property if any go missing.'

She closed the envelope, stuck the flap down with tape and laid it on my desk. 'Drop it off next time you're at the PF's then,' she said.

From the basket I selected a letter and started to read. Grace-Mary hadn't moved. Her nose was bothering her. I winced to wind her up a bit more and dabbed my eye with the can of ginger beer.

'Okay,' she said. 'What happened?'

I'd have to tell her something. If not, she'd harp on

about it for days or give me the silent treatment; either way it wasn't worth the hassle.

'I—'

She held up a hand. 'The truth. I'm not your dad.'

'Andy was mugged.'

Grace-Mary sat down in the chair on the other side of the desk where my clients sat. She stood again, flicked the seat a few times with the back of her hand and sat down once more. 'When?'

'Last week.'

'Why didn't you tell me?'

'I didn't know.'

'Is he all right?'

I told her what little I knew and gave her the abbreviated version of the Reverend Imray's sermon.

'So, Andy's dad thinks you were responsible?'

I shrugged. 'Looks like it.'

Grace-Mary shook her head in astonishment and then stopped. 'You weren't, were you?' I didn't reply and she seemed to take that as a no. 'Good.' She climbed out of the seat. 'I think I'll just nip over the road and buy Andy a get well card...' she walked to the door, 'and maybe order some flower—' She reversed back into the room, green-cardiganed arms folded, scowling down at me. 'What's Andy getting mugged got to do with your black-eye?'

'His dad was right about one thing,' I said. 'The person who assaulted Andy was after Beattie's file.' I could see the next question start to form on Grace-Mary's wrinkled lips. 'Because whoever it was assaulted me too.'

'Why?'

'To stop me making anymore enquiries about what's on Jimmy Garvie's report.'

'What is on it?'

'That's the problem - I don't know.'

'Then read it.'

'I don't have it.'

'Yes, you do.' Grace-Mary unfolded her arms, lifted the brown envelope and ripped open the top. 'I put Mr Garvie's email onto one of these the other day, so I could print it off from my PC for Andy. Remember?' She tipped the envelope, scattering dozens of pen-drives across the desk in front of me. 'And you've got court in half an hour,' Grace-Mary reminded me.

I phoned Paul Sharp and asked him to do me a favour by covering my court cases. I had only a few intermediate diets to knock onto trial and he was happy to oblige. That done, I settled down to scan through the pile of pen-drives. I didn't want to enlist Grace-Mary's help. If people were being hurt for their connection with Jimmy Garvie's report, no point having her added to the list. I plugged the first one into the USB slot on my PC. The processor unit was on the floor between my desk and the wall and awkward to reach. It wasn't going to be much fun doing that a hundred or so times, still, the odds on me striking it lucky shortened with each passing pen-drive. They were down to around a thirty-three to one shot when I eventually found what I was looking for. I printed off the report. By this time it was well after five because I'd still had to deal with the day's usual phone calls and clients.

I printed off the report and put all but the one pen-drive back in the big envelope. The important pen-drive

I put in an empty crisp packet and buried it in the roots of my dead but not forgotten umbrella plant. I was settling down to read the report, having already skimmed through Jimmy's C.V. and the glossary, when the phone rang.

It was my dad. 'What's this about a football match? Is the Islay trip still on?'

'Dad, I'm really busy right now. Something important has cropped up.'

'More important than me? Oh, well that wouldn't need to be *too* important.'

'There's a bit of a problem with one of my cases.'

'There always is.'

'Don't be like—'

The line went dead. I could have phoned back, but I really wanted to know what the big deal was with Jimmy Garvie's report and I still hadn't quite worked out what to tell my dad about Johnny Akbar's charity match; or my injured face. Who'd told him about the game? Malky wouldn't have the nerve. It had to have been Jill. I'd need to go round and see my dad sooner or later.

Later, I decided.

Chapter 45

The life of a Member of the Scottish Parliament is a busy one. There are committee meetings, debates, votes and, of course, surgeries where the MSP has the chance to come face to face with his constituents; get to know them better. Kenny McIvor, it appeared, had become rather too well-acquainted with one of his young female constituents.

Dr. MacGregor's old laptop was a gold-mine of gossip. A catalogue of Linlithgow's great and good whose embarrassing secrets could simply not be entrusted to the general medical records of a small town G.P. practice. Confidentiality was all very well, but staff came and went, and if the secrets held on Doc Mac's laptop had gone with any of them there would have been a series of scandals, followed by a number of lost careers and broken relationships. Doc Mac would normally have handwritten his records, I was sure, and, yet, even his clinically-illegible writing would not have been safe from prying eyes. His laptop, kept locked in the surgery safe, was a great deal more secure and I could imagine him bashing out these notes with two fingers, including those medical records relating to the Justice Secretary which I thumbed through, pacing the office as I read.

From the first entry I discerned that Kenny McIvor had contracted a rare and potentially drug-resistant STD. Later entries referred to his placement on a list for the clinical testing of a new pharmaceutical. There were more notes as the treatment progressed and a final entry indicating that the signs were extremely good and setting up a review in a couple of month's time. Doc Mac had never made it that long. I flipped over to the next page. A copy of a letter addressed to McIvor at his constituency office and marked Highly Confidential. It was dated not long after the STD diagnosis had been made. There was only one female in the area with the same ailment; a young woman with a heroin habit, a young woman who would do anything for her next fix, a young woman called Tanya Lang. Doc Mac thought McIvor should know that the girl was going to have a child. The tone of the letter was friendly enough, as befitted correspondence between two men who'd been friends for many years, but it was clear that Doc Mac wasn't happy. They both knew the girl's grand-father. The girl was in a bad way, homeless and in need of drug rehabilitation. Even if McIvor wasn't the father of the unborn child, Doc Mac expected him to do something about it.

And that was it. The next of the appendices to Jimmy's report concerned a local Justice of the Peace with an addiction to painkillers. Each patient, and there were several of them, received a preferential and totally private service from Doc Mac on their individual ailment. It was interesting stuff, yet it would mean nothing to an Edinburgh I.T. expert who'd used it simply to pad out computer report on child-porn.

I wandered over to the window. I could see why Kenny McIvor wouldn't want his medical records made public and why, after Dr MacGregor's death, it would seem like a good idea to recover them. Was there a link between McIvor and the dead rugby player? What about the person who'd mugged Andy and given me the black-eye of a lifetime? My deliberations were broken by the doorbell ringing. I went downstairs, through the close to the front door. Malky was standing on the pavement outside. He poked me in the stomach with a finger. 'When was the last time you took any exercise?' He noticed my eye. 'Who did that to you? Are you going to be able to play on Sunday?'

'You could saw my legs off and I'd be playing on Sunday.'

'Don't suppose there would be any noticeable difference in the standard of your play,' Malky said as he pushed by. 'Come on. Grab your jacket and we'll go get something to eat.'

A few minutes later and we were further down the High Street, tucking large white napkins into the collars of our shirts. September was the best month, no, the only month, to be eating mussels, according to Malky.

'So how did Dad take it?' he asked. Using, like a pair of tongs, two empty shells that were still attached at the narrow end. He extracted a mussel and dropped it into his mouth.

'He didn't. I haven't told him yet.'

Malky almost choked on the poached bi-valve, coughing and covering his mouth with the corner of a napkin. 'Just great,' he croaked. 'I'm supposed to be going round to see him on Thursday night. I thought you'd have broken the news to him by now.'

'He knows about the game,' I said, slapping his back. 'I think Jill must have mentioned it. I just haven't had time to talk it over with him, he was too angry. I thought I'd give him time to cool off. He'll be all right if I explain... actually, it would probably be a lot better coming from you. I take it tickets won't be a problem. Then all we do is buy him a bottle of something and take him to Islay the following weekend, I'll try and re-book the B&B. We might lose the money on the flights but it will be worth it.'

Malky was digging into the mussels again, dipping hunks of crusty bread into the shallot, cream and white wine sauce. 'There's no chance of me going to Islay the weekend after next. I've no holidays left to take and I've already told the Station I'm up here for urgent family reasons. I'm due back behind a microphone Monday night and that's me until after Christmas. We'll need to go next year.'

I was so surprised that Malky posed no objection to the idea of breaking the news to our dad that I agreed. 'Okay, we'll go in the Spring.'

The waiter came over. 'Robbie, there's a guy at the front the door wants to speak to you.'

'Tell him I'm eating and he can catch me at the office in the morning.'

'Can you not go and see him?' the waiter said. 'He says it's important. And he's very big. And he gave me a tenner to pass on the message.'

I walked down to the front of the restaurant. JayJay, Tanya Lang's father, was waiting for me outside where some of the restaurant's clientele had gathered for a smoke. He raised his hands and showed me his palms. 'I'm sorry about what happened back at Tam's house.'

I was prepared to give the big man the benefit of

the doubt. 'What can I do for you?'

He glanced around. 'Not here.' He walked a few steps away from the smokers and, when I'd caught up with him, pushed something at me. It was an envelope. 'There's three grand there,' he said.

'Thanks. Why are you giving it to me?'

'I want to know.'

'You want to know what?'

'Where my grandson is.'

I held out the envelope to him. 'I don't know. Really, I've no idea.'

He wouldn't take the envelope, not even look at it.

'Then you talk to him. You talk to Biggam. Tell him he either says where Logan is or the day he steps out of prison is the day he steps into his own grave.'

'Mr Lang, I know how —'

'I feel? No, you don't.'

'Maybe not, but I'm doing my best to find out what happened to the baby. I don't want your money.' I took his arm and tried to press the envelope into his hand.

He pulled away. 'If it's not enough I can get more.'

'It won't do any good.'

Lang turned. The envelope fell to the ground. By the time I'd picked it up he was striding on down the High Street.

Back at my plate of cold mussels I told Malky what had happened.

'It's understandable,' he said.

'I suppose. Can you imagine what Dad would have been like if one of us went missing way back when?'

Malky nodded in agreement. 'But, then again, strange men used to give you sweeties to get *out* of the car.' He fished the last stray mussel from the creamy sauce and sat back in his chair. 'JayJay Lang's all right, though. He used to be a not bad footballer. Do you not remember I replaced him at the Rose?'

Malky had joined Linlithgow Rose at the tender age of seventeen. As I understood it, JayJay Lang had not been at all amused about losing his place at the heart of the Rose defence to a boy just out of school, but Malky had been such a stand-out that he barely lasted a season before being signed by Rangers where he quickly attained cult status. He won the Cup with his famous injury time header and had just broken into the national side when his footballing career had been shredded, along with most of his knee ligaments, during a European tie in Dortmund. Our dad, who had never held the Germanic nations in particularly high-esteem, had never bought a bottle of lager since.

'There's a Rose game on tonight,' Malky said, as the waiter cleared away our dishes. 'I'm surprised JayJay isn't there.'

I was surprised Malky wasn't there, soaking up the adulation.

'I'll bet he's away off down the Black Bitch,' Malky said.

Black Bitch was the name given to someone, like myself, born and bred in Linlithgow. The animal was on the town's coat of arms and there was a pub of the same name, one of Scotland's oldest, at the West Port. Say it aloud in the wrong place and like my 'racist' client Maureen Rooney you'd probably be prosecuted.

We ordered coffee.

Malky reminisced. 'When I first joined the Rose I

used to go down to the Black Bitch with JayJay and his father-in-law after all the home games. Tam wouldn't let me have anything stronger than a shandy. Now there was a real player. Tam Fairbairn - don't make them like that anymore.'

Our coffee arrived. Malky was still chuntering on about mid-field battlers of yore and I was zoning him out and trying to remember what it was Maureen Rooney had said to me about Tanya, or, as she put it, her *wee black neighbour*. She'd been talking about junkies and Tanya in particular. How they got everything given to them on a plate. *Even gave her a darkie health visitor.* Megan McIvor.

'Fancy going down to the Black Bitch for a pint after this?' Malky asked, as I tuned back into his chat. 'Yonks since I've been in there.'

'Maybe one.'

'Don't worry.' He poured a sachet of sugar into his cup. 'One's all you'll be having. I wouldn't want you sleeping in for your five mile run tomorrow. I'll draw you a route. It's the same circuit I used to do when I was training.'

Chapter 46

A mile was a lot longer than I remembered. Through the windscreen on the motorway, a mile flew past like the Red Arrows. Slapping one out in a pair of worn-out Adidas Samba's (the thinking five-a-side player's choice of footwear) was a different story; five in a row was madness. Anyway, what difference would it make? With only a few days to go before my Hampden Park debut, there was no chance of achieving peak fitness and why would I need to? I was there to make up the numbers. I'd be lucky if I were allowed on the pitch for the last five minutes, by which time the other players, most of whom would be 'legends' or 'old boys', that is clapped-out footballers like Malky, would be blowing out of their collective backsides.

So persuasive were my thoughts, that after a fraction of Malky's route, I laid a little route of my own; one that led me, tired and sweaty, through the door of Sandy's Cafe at around six-thirty a.m.

'First customer of the day,' he said, as I collapsed onto a chair, head resting on my arms folded on the table in front of me. 'What are you having?' It was too early and there were too few customers around for an Italian accent. He didn't wait for a reply and, anyway, I was too busy panting to give one.

Ten minutes later, I was tackling a well-fired roll on crispy bacon with lashings of brown sauce.

'You do know that the guy who invented jogging

died doing it,' Sandy said, setting a double Americano in front of me.

I took a reviving sip of coffee. 'Yeah, but he was really old wasn't he?'

'That famous squash player wasn't. Dropped dead right in the middle of a tournament.' Sandy returned to the counter and was filling his cake stand and I was munching shards of best Ayrshire, when the bell above the door tinkled to announce the cafe's second customer of the day.

Glen Beattie approached the counter and ordered a skinny latte. He glanced around, saw me and did a double-take. I mumbled a good morning through a bite of roll. He came across. I was foolish enough to think he was going to thank me for sorting out his child-pornography difficulties, but the magnanimous expression I was trying to adopt, while swallowing a mouthful of bread and bacon, was unnecessary.

'I see your eating habits haven't improved,' Beattie said.

In mitigation, I gestured to my sweat-soaked sports gear: a baggy T-shirt and pair of trackies.

'I thought I should let you know that I didn't appreciate you going behind my back to Kenny,' he said.

'But I take it you are happy at no longer being labelled a paedophile?'

Beattie checked around to make sure no-one else had come into the cafe. He sat down.

Sandy came over with Beattie's latte in a tall cardboard cup. 'I'll put that on your tab, Doctor.'

I pointed to my food. 'This too.'

Sandy looked to the doctor for his consent. Beattie nodded. 'Yes, I am pleased that the charges have been dropped,' he said, when Sandy had moved on. 'I just don't like the way you went about it. You're not even my lawyer.'

'But, as an interested member of the public what was I supposed to do? Sit back and watch you being struck off for something you were innocent of?'

'I still don't believe Megan would be so vindictive.'

'She's not going to be charged with anything. Her father's seen to that.'

Beattie took the lid of his cup and blew on the coffee. 'Megan sent me a letter. She's not coming back.'

'Are you surprised?' I polished off my bacon roll. 'Would *you* have acted any differently if *she'd* had an affair?'

'Fiona threw herself at me.'

'Well maybe you should have ducked.'

'You know something? I think Megan could have forgiven me my fling with Fiona. I'm sure it's the images on the PC; she still thinks I downloaded them.'

'I'm sorry, that simply doesn't make sense.' I checked the clock on the wall above the door and wiped my hands on a paper napkin. I still had to get home and shower before work.

'It does to me. I know Megan. I know what she's like. Walking out on me is exactly what she would do. Trying to ruin me, send me to jail, that's definitely not.'

'It's called revenge,' I said. 'You can't put anything past a woman scorned. I mean there she is, hormones on the rampage, and while she's busy decorating the nursery, you're off on the ran-dan with another woman.'

'Hormones?'

'Naturally produced chemicals in the blood stream.' What did they teach them at medical school these days?

'Leave Megan's hormones out of this. You don't know what you're talking about.'

I had gone too far. The man was really suffering and I was making light of it. It must have been all my own recently produced hormones; endorphins, the by-product of my morning's exertions. I'd heard it said their feel-good sensation could make exercise addictive. I felt sure I'd be able to fight off the effects. 'You're quite right, it's none of my business. Just be glad the case against you is closed, which, like it or not, was entirely down to me. I appreciate that you're left with some relationship problems and if you'd like me to give you the name of a good family lawyer I'd be happy to do that. I certainly wouldn't recommend Caldwell & Craig, not unless Kenny McIvor is footing the bill.'

Beattie drank some coffee. His dejected expression reminded me of our first meeting in the cells at Livingston. He looked at his watch. It seemed he was in a hurry too. I wondered if I had time for a second bacon roll after he'd left. I tried to plan my movements for the rest of the day: shower, office, check the mail, go to court and then try to make it to Polmont YOI in time for my late afternoon appointment with Brandon Biggam. The only snag with the last item on my agendum was that, under the Scottish Legal Aid Board's block fees, I was only paid for two prison consultations. I'd already had them and the indictment hadn't even been served yet. I'd have to fill in some more forms. I seemed to spend my life writing begging letters to SLAB.

Beattie put the lid back on his coffee. 'I might take you up on that referral,' he said. 'Shouldn't be a difficult job. Megan says she's not coming back. I'll take on her share of the house and after that there are just a few belongings to divide up. We could probably manage without lawyers.'

'Not where there's a child involved, you couldn't.'

He laughed, dryly. 'There's no child involved Mr Munro.'

'No,' I agreed. 'Not yet.'

'Not ever.'

'What's happened?'

He screwed up his face in puzzlement. 'What do you mean? Nothing's happened. We don't have any children. We can't... that is, Megan can't have any children.'

'I'm sorry, I—'

'It's quite all right.'

Megan must have had a miscarriage. Me and my big mouth.

Dr Beattie stood. 'I suppose I should thank you. It's been, still is, a very difficult time for me, but I know that during the court case you had my best interests at heart.' We shook hands. 'Don't take it personally when I say I hope I don't see you again.' He was about to leave, when he turned and patted my stomach. 'And don't over-do the exercise, will you?'

Chapter 47

I spent part of Tuesday afternoon perusing the latest evidence in the case against Brandon Biggam, as usual drip-fed via the Crown web-site. The most interesting item was a forensic report from the drug lab. In every case it was normal practice to send all drugs and associated paraphernalia for analysis; however, what made this report out of the ordinary was that it contained only a single entry. All that had been found in Tanya's flat was a wrap of heroin weighing 0.156 grams. The police would say that a tenner bag weighed 0.1g and that therefore this must have been a twenty bag with some of it used. In fact, it was more likely to be an untouched tenner bag. It supported what Brandon Biggam had told me; that he'd given Tanya a tenner bag to sell so she could buy nappies. All the signs were that Tanya was clean. There was no cigarette lighter, no foil, no tooter, no citric acid, no spoon not even a syringe. How could she have accidentally overdosed if there was no evidence that she'd taken any drugs? And yet according to the toxicologists there was a vast quantity in her bloodstream. It was bad news for Brandon. If there was no syringe on the premises, someone must have not only supplied the heroin but taken the syringe away.

It was time for me to take more instructions from Brandon Biggam. The rest of Tuesday was spent on the phone with SLAB seeking permission to visit my murder client. Eventually, a Team Leader told me that I could go, but if I wanted paid – which I said would be nice - I'd have to justify the consultation in my final account. Basically, I'd have to do the work and then, when the case was finished, a bean-counter would decide whether to pay me or not because, obviously, some pen-pushing, unqualified clerk knew a lot better than me how to run the defence in a murder case.

I'd wasted so much time with SLAB that it was too late to go out to Polmont and when I called to book for the next day, the only available appointment was a half hour slot at quarter to four.

'What's going on?' is what Brandon said to me, minus the expletives, as I walked into the visit room the following day.

Given that consultations would be few and far between now that I was either not going to be paid or have to roll about on the floor and have my tummy tickled by SLAB's accounts division at a later stage, I gave my client the colouring-in version of my deliberations to date. They hadn't changed much since the last time we'd met. 'Tanya didn't O.D. accidentally - somebody killed her.'

'She could have killed herself.'

'No she couldn't. She'd had a barrow-load of heroin and there wasn't so much as a needle in her flat. Which means that either you killed her—'

'I never.'

'Or somebody else did. Let's assume it wasn't you. Who else would have a motive?'

He grunted. We'd been here before.

'What if the baby isn't yours?' I asked.

'Are you going on about Geordie again?'

'The baby was born two or three weeks after you got out from your last sentence. You got eighteen months and did nine.'

'So?'

'The baby was either over-due or it's someone else's.'

'It's not Geordie's. He knows I'd kill him.'

'Exactly,' I said. 'So he killed Tanya to stop her telling you and got rid of the baby at the same time.' A ginger-headed, black baby? Not many of them in Linlithgow. No need for a DNA test.

Brandon shook his head. 'Geordie telt me what happened at your office and I'm telling you that he's my mate. Tanya was my burd. The wean's mine.'

Should I tell him about Kenny McIvor? About the drug-resistant STD? Now there would be a corker of an incrimination. Tanya's death had occurred around about the same time as the bogus cop Phil Renton was trying to get hold of Doc Mac's laptop. The laptop that contained confidential information linking McIvor to Tanya. It was almost too much to take in.

'You all right?' my client asked.

'Brandon, I need to know everyone who went to Tanya's house the day she died. I don't care if you were there and folk were coming round to get smack off you, I need names.'

He hesitated.

'If you don't help me now you're going to have a life sentence to wish you had.'

'Geordie came with me. We got there about four o'clock, maybe later. Tanya had phoned, wanting money as usual. I gave her a tenner bag and told her to sell it.' He put his elbows on the table, the heels of his hands against his forehead. 'Tanya texted a couple of folk to tell them she had gear. They never showed when I was there.' He struck the front of his head with a fist which seemed to dislodge another memory. 'That old woman from down the street came in to see the wean.'

I recalled my conversation with Maureen Rooney. She'd already been questioned by the police in their door-to-door enquiries. In fact, they'd started at her house and worked their way up and down the street. Maureen had gone to see Tanya and the baby, but left when Brandon and, as she described Geordie, *the other junkie with the ginger hair*, arrived sometime late afternoon. She hadn't seen Brandon and Geordie leave because she'd been busy doing housework and hanging the washing out.

'That's all I can remember,' Brandon said. 'We weren't there that long. What about her, though?'

'Who?'

'The wifey. She loved the wean. She was always in and out to see it. She could have killed Tanya and stolen him.'

'Her name's Mrs Rooney. She was only in Tanya's place for ten minutes that day. She went away when you arrived and stayed home until she left to go round to her pal's and then off the Bingo at the back of six.'

'Aye, but she could have come back later.'

'The police searched her house. They searched the whole street—'

'That was the next day. She could have... ach, I don't know.'

'Keep thinking,' I said.

'What do you think I do in here? I'm dubbed up twenty-three hours a day. I don't know why anyone would kill Tanya, but you hear of folk stealing weans all the time. Mad women go into hospitals and do it. Women who can't have their own weans and that, and I just thought that Mrs Rooney...'

Women who can't have their own weans. Megan McIvor.

'Where are you going?' the prisoner asked, when I stood up and walked to the door with still five minutes of visit time left.

'To find the baby,' I said.

Chapter 48

As soon as I returned from Polmont YOI, I phoned Jill at her work. She wasn't in and they didn't expect her back that day. Jill's mobile was switched off and so I called St Gideon's to speak to Fiona Scott. I wanted to know how easy it would be for a health visitor, like Megan McIvor, to acquire diamorphine. Who kept the records of the amount of diamorphine being used by patients being treated at home? What happened to ampoules that weren't used? Were they put back on the shelf or destroyed? Who was responsible? How would anyone know if some weren't used and weren't returned?

Fiona wasn't available either. She'd gone to an important meeting in Edinburgh.

'I'm afraid that's confidential,' the receptionist said, when I asked for Fiona's mobile number. 'But I'll pass on a message.'

'Tell her, Mr Munro, *the lawyer*,' I added trying to up the importance-level, 'called and would like to speak to her urgently about the death of Tanya Lang.'

'The missing baby's mum?' the receptionist asked, interested now.

'I'm afraid that's confidential,' I said.

My next call was to the child day care centre in Jedburgh where I'd previously met with Megan. I wanted to confront her personally. I could have called the cops with my latest theories: that the Justice Secretary had had Tanya Lang killed to save disclosure of his affair with her, or, that his daughter had committed the crime so that she could steal Tanya's child. Either way I wasn't sure how well that would go down with the boys in blue. Not very, I suspected; especially if my speculations turned out to be a load of bollocks.

By the time I'd found the number, the nursery was closing for the day and the only person left was the manager who, no matter how hard I tried, was not inclined to reveal Megan's home address on the basis that I, 'could be anyone.'

When Grace-Mary popped her head in to say goodnight, I was pacing the room deep in thought and still pacing an hour later, as, with daylight already failing, I looked down on the street below: Jill. What was she doing in town? I grabbed my jacket, quickly locked up and ran after her.

By the time I was on the street, Jill was already a good fifty yards or so ahead of me, walking onto the cobbled area at Linlithgow Cross, on her way up to the car park.

In my experience, there are, generally speaking, two types of tripper. The first type stubs his toe (it is usually a he) on an upraised paving slab or such other defect, is momentarily off balance and, without looking around, breaks into a little run as though, actually, he'd been intending to go off for a short jog anyway. And he does, for a few steps, before deciding, nah, I'll just walk after all. Jill was the other type. She (and it is usually a she) caught a heel between a couple of cobble stones, turned about and glowered accusingly down at the defective pavement, as though perhaps expecting an apology. Jill checked her footwear and was about to march off again when she noticed me. 'Don't even try to apologise.'

'I'm sorry Jill, I'd no idea you and my dad had arranged to scatter Vince's ashes this weekend.'

She walked on.

'What brings you through here?' I asked, trotting to catch up with her.

'Keep moving,' she hissed.

'What's wrong?'

'Move!' she growled through clenched teeth. She stopped to adjust her shoe at one of the benches that surrounded the ornately-carved Cross Well, and I continued on, not sure where to go, eventually veering off at an angle and ending up on the High Street again. Two minutes later my mobile vibrated. It was Jill.

'Where are you?' she asked.

'Walking down the street towards the West Port.'

'Keep going, I'll meet you.'

I had reached the Water Yett when Jill's car pulled up on the opposite side of the street. I crossed the road. She reached over and opened the door for me. The moment I was seated she sped off.

'What's happening?' I asked.

'I've just been grilled for the last hour by the cops.'

'What about?'

'You.'

'What about me?'

'A certain detective inspector seems to think that we're an item. He also thinks that you might have some information on the whereabouts, dead or alive, of the missing Lang baby and he wanted to know if you'd told me anything.'

'That's ridiculous.'

'I told him that. I said even *you* wouldn't keep information like that from the police, would you?'

I hesitated.

'Would you? If you knew where the baby was, you'd tell – right?'

'I suppose it depends.'

'What could it possibly depend on?'

'How I came to know. There is a thing called client conf—'

'Robbie, this is a baby we're talking about. If you know—'

'I don't.' Obviously, the heat was on the cops to find the baby if they were scraping the bottom of the barrel by trying to have the defence agent's girlfriend spy on him. Not that Jill was my girlfriend. Something I had mixed feelings about.

'Where do you want me to drop you off?' she asked.

'Back where you found me would be fine.'

She made a face. I don't really want the cops seeing us together,' she said.

'Stuff them. I haven't done anything wrong.'

'Have you eaten?'

'Not recently.'

We were at Linlithgow Bridge by this time. Jill put the foot down and joined the M9 at the Lathallan roundabout.

'Why do I feel like I'm being abducted?' I asked.

'Don't flatter yourself,' she said. 'I'm taking you

back to my place. I'm going to make you some food and we're going to talk about Islay. After that you're going to see your father and sort things out.'

'I've already sorted things out,' I said. 'Malky is going to explain things to dad. He'll tell him about the big charity match and how much fun it would be to see his sons playing for Scotland—'

'And you seriously think he'll go for that?'

'He might. I've told Malky to buy him a bottle of something peaty from the Sacred Isle; oil on troubled waters, and we'll arrange to go to Islay in the Spring.'

'And *my* dad?' she asked.

I didn't know what to say.

She sighed. 'Spring it is.'

'Thanks.'

'It's okay. Islay was Alex's idea, and a good one, but it can wait. What happened to your face, by the way?'

'That,' I said, 'is a very long story.'

'Then tell me over dinner,' she said. 'I'm a slow eater.'

Chapter 49

Jill was a fantastic cook.

'I'm good at following recipes,' she said, watching me wipe the last traces of what she modestly called pasta sauce with a crust of bread. 'Must have been all that University training preparing ointments and poultices, all the things you never actually have to make when eventually you do become a pharmacist and work in the real world.'

'Same with law and all those ethics lectures.' I popped the bread into my mouth and washed it down with some of the red wine that Jill wasn't drinking because she was going to have to drive me home again.

'Not that Ally ever noticed. All he ever ate was carry-outs. That was when he was deigning me with his presence.'

Alistair Kidd. I'd almost forgotten Jill's ex-husband. They'd met during their pre-reg year at Boots in Edinburgh and married in their mid-twenties. He was a self-motivated, career-orientated pharmacist. The problem was so was she. When Jill was promoted over him, he hadn't like it. There were rumours of domestic violence. They'd taken an oath to remain together until death did them part and my dad had offered to accelerate the process should Alistair raise his hands to Jill again. The marriage lasted less than two years.

If Vince had been as disappointed as his best friend in his daughter's choice of spouse, he'd never shown it.

That was the kind of man he was. Except for their choice of whisky and an overly optimistic view of the Scotland football team's prospects in any competition, he and my dad were complete opposites.

'Bring your glass with you,' Jill said. 'I'll clear up later.'

We left the kitchen and went through to Jill's sitting room. We still hadn't touched on the subjects of my dad or the ashes-to-Islay trip. Over my bowl of tagliatelle and red pesto sauce I'd told her all about the punch to my face, Andy's mugging, the dead rugby player and the contents of Dr MacGregor's laptop.

'You've got to go to the police,' she said.

'With what? All I have is some highly confidential medical information about a lot of local worthies.'

'You've also got a real corker of a black-eye.'

'Somehow I don't think Dougie Fleming will be all that sympathetic.'

'Who?'

'The detective inspector who interviewed you. We're not usually on speaking terms. Not unless he's in the witness box and I'm asking him questions about his notebook and the confessions my clients keep blurting out whenever he's around.'

Jill poured herself some more sparkling mineral water and topped-up my glass of Chianti. 'Someone other than Dr MacGregor knew what was on that laptop. Whoever it is, is out to make sure that the information is never disclosed and, from what you tell me, it sounds like there are a quite a few possible suspects.'

'Definitely,' I said, 'but one stands out more than

the others, if for no other reason than he's hoping to be elected First Minister.'

'But why send a bogus cop to recover Doc Mac's laptop if you happen to be the Justice Secretary? Why not send the real thing?'

'Not all that easy. Even the Justice Secretary has to have a reason to seek a warrant and once the information on the laptop was in the hands of the Police, some cop would have it leaked to the press within hours.'

I reclined on the couch, drank some wine. Jill switched on the TV and then went off to make coffee. I hadn't told her the identity of the person from whom McIvor had contracted his STD. I still had a client charged with Tanya Lang's murder and I didn't want to reveal any potential defences. I couldn't help thinking it was a huge coincidence: Tanya Lang dead and Dr MacGregor's laptop destroyed in the same week? Quite a stroke of luck for the prospective First Minister.

Jill returned having switched the kettle on. The Scottish news came on the television, the headline being a possible sighting of baby Logan Biggam. A white couple had been seen with a black baby boarding a train for London and the police were following it up as a possible lead.

'It must be heart-breaking for the grandparents,' Jill said. 'And the baby's father too, I suppose – *if* he's innocent. Though I'd say that was a pretty big if.'

Not as big as it used to be, I thought. What did Kenny McIvor know about it all? He'd persuaded the Lord Advocate to turn a blind eye to his daughter's downloading of child-porn, but he'd need to do something pretty drastic to talk the LA out of prosecuting Megan for murder and child-abduction.

Jill sat down beside me and lifted the lid of my injured eye. 'I don't like the look of the blood in your sclera. If it doesn't improve over the next couple of days you should have a doctor look at it.'

'Don't worry, I'll keep an *eye* on it,' I said.

'Ah, Robbie, you are as amusing as you are handsome.'

'You must have thought I was not too bad looking at one time,' I said, countering her sarcasm. 'Anyway, let's not got there.'

'No, let's do go there. Do you know how humiliating it is for an eighteen year-old girl to stand hanging about a cinema foyer, waiting for a no-show date?'

'I believe you have mentioned it before.'

She laughed. 'I mean it about the police.' She put her hand on my forehead and tilted my head back for another look at my eye. 'And about the doctor.' The boiling kettle clicked off. Apparently satisfied that I was in no immediate danger, Jill was about to stand when I put my hand on her shoulder. My earlier urge to confront Megan McIvor was beginning to wane. I didn't even know where she was. Much better to stay where I was and have what was turning out to be a very pleasant evening with Jill. After all, I couldn't go charging about blaming people of murder and child abduction without some concrete evidence to back it up. Forty-eight hours ago I'd have been happy to accuse Kenny McIvor of Tanya's murder, now I was trying to shoehorn his daughter in the frame.

I gently pulled Jill towards me. I was taking a chance. Had Vince told me the truth? Had Jill always liked me? She'd had a funny way of showing it over the years. My actions met with no resistance. We moved closer, lips inches apart. Our eyes closed, or at least Jill's did and mine would have too, if not at that moment I turned my head involuntarily to see something on the TV. The front of Jill's face sort of bumped into the side of mine. 'Sorry,' I said, already on my feet and rummaging around on the couch for the remote and finding it behind a cushion. 'This could be important.'

'This,' Jill hissed, 'had *better* be important.' She jumped to her feet. 'And by important I don't include anything football-related.' She stomped off through to the kitchen and amidst the clattering of coffee cups I could hear her muttering to herself. I boosted the TV volume.

Chapter 50

On the eve of the leadership election, Kenny McIvor had withdrawn from the race.

'I am a man of principle. A man who puts the good of the Party before individual gain and the people before personal political aspirations. For that reason, I step aside and offer Angus Pike my full support as head of the Party and as First Minister of Scotland.' Much applause, but there was more to come. I'd heard the speech already, at Jill's house, and was listening to it again on the radio as we sped down the A68 to Jedburgh in Jill's car. *'In my new dual-role as Deputy First Minister and Secretary for Health and Wellbeing,'* McIvor continued, *'my first task will be to carry forward and make real my long-held ambition to put in place a level of Government funding appropriate to the esteem in which the Hospice Movement is held in the hearts of the nation.'*

The radio replay of the speech stopped there and the announcer went on to talk more about the re-shuffling of the Cabinet now that the leadership election was a fait accomplis.

I could remember the rest from the TV report: appointments and departures from the Government front benches, promises of new pieces of legislation – like there weren't enough laws already - and Fiona Scott stepping forward to be declared the head of the new Quango to oversee Scotland's hospices.

'They made Fiona Scott, Hospice Queen?' Jill said

'She'll be raking in about three hundred thousand pounds a year for that.'

'Long hours,' I said, remembering how Fiona had still been at her office the night of Vince's hospital-escape. 'Probably a lot of hard work involved.'

'Hard work? Going on junkets, sorry, *fact-finding missions*, being driven around in big cars, attending meetings about meetings?' Jill was going her dinger. 'It's a gravy train with a pension and a gong from the Queen at the end of the line. Hard work? Do me a favour.'

'She must know what she's doing. St Gideon's took good care of your dad,' I said, when Jill had paused for breath. 'And the hospice provision in this country certainly does need re-structuring.'

Jill grunted and ran a finger across the screen of her mobile phone. I'd left mine charging at the office.

'Any luck?' I asked.

'Yes, I've found it on Google Maps.'

We'd agreed that, notwithstanding my one and a half glasses of Chianti, I'd drive, while Jill tracked down the home phone number of the manager of the nursery where Megan McIvor worked. With some delicate persuasion and one or two white lies, she had managed to obtain Megan's address; something, I'd been unable to achieve earlier.

'I really hope you know what you're doing,' Jill said. 'We should have called the police if you're so sure about everything.'

I didn't normally work with the police. Or in certainties, for that matter. In my line of work there was usually a doubt lurking about somewhere and if there wasn't it was my job to create one.

'You are sure, aren't you?'

'Sort of.'

The idea that someone had murdered a young woman and stolen her baby was fine in theory. The problem was this wasn't the impeachment of Geordie Lyons the ginger-headed junkie: this was the daughter of the new Deputy First Minister.

'Sort of? You can't be sort of sure, you're either—'

'I'm looking at the evidence and I'm satisfied on the balance of probability—'

'Never mind all the legal jargon. What evidence do you actually have?'

'Actually, it's not so much evidence as—'

'A hunch?'

'Yeah, but a really strong one. Why would Kenny McIvor withdraw from the leadership race?'

'It's politics. There are millions of reasons. I hope you've got a better reason than that to drag me all the way to Jedburgh.'

'It's highly suspicious, if you ask me, but what really got me thinking was something one of the witnesses told me about Tanya Lang *having a darkie health visitor* and... well... Megan McIvor's coloured isn't she?'

'Don't go thinking *coloured* is anymore acceptable than *darkie*.'

'Well you know what I mean.'

'Black is what you mean.'

'Megan isn't black, she's more...'

'I'd stop now if I were you.'

'I think from the description given I can safely

assume that Megan was Tanya's health visitor and therefore would visit—'

'Families with problems, children at risk—'

'And elderly people. People like your dad with ampoules of morphine.'

'She wasn't a cancer nurse.'

'No, but if she was working in the community, she'd have access to people who were being treated at home. Think how easy it would be for her to get her hands on some diamorphine vials. I've still got a box full from your dad's house. You were going to pick them up.'

'Probably easier if you just hand it in at the Hospice pharmacy,' Jill said, 'but don't change the subject. I know Megan. She's a lovely girl. There's absolutely no way she would do anything so stupid.'

'She's a woman who's been wronged by her partner. Who loves children but can't have any of her own. Who clearly wouldn't have been thinking straight—'

'But straight enough to steal some diamorphine, kill one of her patients, steal their baby and make off without trace or suspicion?'

'Well, *I've* traced her now and *I'm* plenty suspicious.' The orange glow of street lights shone up ahead. 'Which way is it?'

Jill tapped the screen of her mobile phone to bring it back to life. 'It's a B&B. I don't have the exact address. Look for the High Street when we get there.'

We hit Jedburgh and found the turn off onto the High Street.

'What are you going to do when you discover that

you've got it all horribly wrong?' Jill asked.

'If I'm horribly wrong at least I won't have the Lothian & Borders homicide squad and Megan's dad to explain matters to. Where to now?'

'Go down a bit further and then turn right onto Exchange Street.' Jill moved the image on the screen with her finger. 'Then first right again onto Friarsgate and it's around there somewhere.'

Friarsgate ran parallel to the High Street. I found a small car park to the rear of some shops and left the car there while we set off on foot.

'How are you going to play this?' Jill asked, as we walked down the path to a big old stone-built house with a No Vacancies sign in the window. 'You can't just barge in and demand she hand over the baby.'

Despite Jill's reservations, that was my plan: sudden, unexpected confrontation. I rang the doorbell. An elderly lady answered. She was tall and stout. I thought I recognised her and yet couldn't quite place the face.

'Sorry,' she said. 'I'm not taking guests at the moment.

'We're here to see Megan,' I said.

'You must have the wrong address.' She wasn't a good liar. The old woman took a step back, her hand on the door. I put out my hand to stop it closing.

'I'm Mr Munro and this is Miss Green. We'd like to see Megan McIvor,' I said in my sternest voice. The woman wavered, then seemed to stiffen her resolve. 'How did you get this address?'

Jill pushed in front of me. 'We got this address because we're here as part of a criminal investigation.'

She gave the woman a velvet glove/iron fist smile. 'Now we'd like to speak to Megan McIvor, ma'am, or is it your intention to obstruct us in our enquiries?'

She was good. And I think it was the *ma'am* that swung it. That and the fact that neither of us had changed out of our work clothes and were still in suits. Mine was easily rumpled enough to be plain clothes and the old lady had no doubt seen attractive, smartly dressed female detectives like Jill on police shows on the telly. The door opened wide. We entered and were taken down a dimly lit hall to a room at the rear of the building, where we were invited to make ourselves comfortable on a particularly uncomfortable and ancient floral-suite, the backs of which were covered with yellowing, lace antimacassars. The rest of the furniture was mahogany, the wallpaper cream with a bottle-green fleur de Lyon motif. The place reminded me of an undertaker's waiting room. We stayed sitting there for around five minutes and might have waited a lot longer had we not heard the unmistakable sound of a baby crying, followed by general commotion. I ran out of the door. The baby was really exercising its lungs by this time. The noise was coming from the other end of the hall. I raced along, Jill close behind. A figure stood in the porch, coat on, collar up, clutching a blanket-wrapped bundle and, with the help of the old woman, trying to lug an enormous suitcase out of the front door.

'That was quick, Megan,' I called. The figure looked up at me. 'Last time I saw you, you were only ten weeks pregnant.'

The old woman manoeuvred herself in between us.

Megan touched her gently on the arm and handed over the baby. 'It's not what it looks like,' she said.

I nearly laughed. 'No? Then let's talk about what it doesn't look like.'

We returned to the funereal sitting room and I closed the door, leaving the old woman and child outside in the hall.

'How do you want to play this?' I asked, once we were all seated. 'You can hand yourself in, I can call the police or you can go on the run and wait to get caught. Just so long as you know that the baby is not going with you.'

'Can I at least explain?'

'Save that for your lawyer,' I said. 'You're going to need one.'

'You're a lawyer,' Megan said.

'But not yours. I'm acting for a boy who, right now, is in prison charged with the murder of the girl who you murdered and whose child you stole.'

That's how it looked to me. Megan discovers her fiancé's infidelity, fits him up with some child-porn out of spite, kills one of her patients and makes off with the baby she could never have. All she needed to do was lie low for a while. After that she could go anywhere: a black mother with her black baby.

Megan shook her head. 'I didn't kill anyone.'

I'd try and remember that when I was lodging Brandon Biggam's special defence incriminating her for the murder of his girlfriend.

Megan put her head in her hands and began to cry.

'Tears aren't going to help you,' I said. 'Jill give me your mobile, I'm calling the cops.'

Megan looked up. 'Wait, look I was going to take the baby back. Ask my aunt. This is her house. I would never want to get her into trouble. What I did was madness, I know that. I was in a complete mess. I wasn't thinking straight.'

I gave Jill a quick I-told-you-so look.

'My husband was having an affair. I was leaving him. It all happened so quickly. I knew one day I'd have to give Logan back.' Megan turned to Jill for support. 'You believe me don't you?'

I held my hand out. 'Jill, the phone please.'

'Hold on Robbie. She says she was going to give the baby back.'

'Jill, she killed the kid's mother. She stole diamorphine dry-amps and injected them into her own patient.'

Megan looked at me angrily, through teary eyes. 'That's a lie.'

'What did you tell Tanya, Megan? Did you say it was a vitamin shot?'

'Shut up, Robbie.' Jill went over and sat beside her, put an arm round her shoulders.

I'd had enough. 'Give me the phone.'

'No, let Megan explain.'

'This is not the time or the place to explain anything. She can talk to a lawyer once she's in police custody. In the meantime the baby is going back where it belongs.' Come to think of it, where was the baby?

Reading my mind, Jill jumped up and ran out of the door. Moments later she came back into the room holding the child, still wrapped in its blanket. Megan's aunt had worked some magic and he was sound asleep now.

'Just let me tell you what happened,' Megan said. 'Please.'

I couldn't deny I was interested to know how Megan could have gone so badly off the rails, and it wouldn't do Brandon Biggam any harm if she wanted to confess. 'All right,' I said. 'Just so long as you know that anything you say to me will be used in evidence if it helps my client.'

Megan snorted. 'Brandon Biggam? If that wee ned hadn't got Tanya hooked on drugs she'd be here today with her baby. I used to visit every few days to make sure how she was and he'd always be hanging about with his junkie mates. It was only ever a matter of time before she started using again.'

'So you decided to kill her and take her baby? Give it a better home – with you?'

'I first had my suspicions about Glen when I saw a strange yellow car parked outside our house.' Megan had decided to ignore me and was directing her words to Jill. She wiped an eye with the sleeve of her coat. 'Then once, when I was supposed to be away at a two-day seminar in Dundee, it was cancelled and I arrived home to find Fiona Scott in my house making herself comfortable. She assured me it was a professional call. It didn't look like it. And then there was the trip to London. Glen told me his friendship with Fiona was platonic, based on their mutual love of opera. I believed him; for a while. Until the late night phone calls started. No-one ever there when I answered, when he answered he always needed to take the calls in private and then rush away to an urgent case.'

A G.P. doing out of hours calls? That certainly was suspicious.

Megan got up from the couch and went over to where Jill was sitting. She hooked a finger around the top of the blanket and pulled it down for a better look at the sleeping baby. 'Then I found a necklace in the back seat of his car. It wasn't mine. It was as if they wanted to be found out or just didn't care.'

The baby sneezed. Jill gave him a shoogle and he stayed sleeping. Time was marching on. The clock on the mantelpiece was ebony inlaid with ivory. It showed nine o'clock. I had a feeling it was right twice a day.

'Megan,' I said, 'I know all this. I know Glen and Fiona Scott were having an affair and I know that you had your revenge. It was me who told your dad and he had the Crown turn a blind eye to the whole child-porn thing, but murder—'

'I didn't murder anybody and I didn't download those pictures.'

'Come off it.'

'Those pictures were the last straw.'

'Megan, it's so obvious that you planted them.'

'But I didn't plant them. I went after the person who did.'

Okay, so I hadn't seen that coming. 'And who might that have been?'

'Fiona Scott. It had to be her.'

'Why?'

'Because Glen was ending their relationship and she didn't like it.'

The woman was crazy.

'Oh, I see. It's okay for me to do something spiteful

like that, but not the great Fiona Scott?' she said, in response to my expression of incredulity.

Somehow, I couldn't see an ice-queen like Fiona Scott feeling sufficiently scorned over a romantic split to bother planting indecent images. And she'd seemed pretty cosy with Keith Haggerty at the rugby match. 'How would Fiona have known the password?' I asked.

'It was La Boehme, Glen's favourite opera. Do you think Fiona couldn't have worked that out during their long discussions about Luciano Pavarotti or whatever they talked about?'

She had an answer for everything. 'So why didn't you tell the police?'

'I was so surprised by the police bursting in, that it wasn't until I'd given my statement and they'd taken Glen away that I realised the truth and I drove straight to St Gideon's. I couldn't pluck up the courage to march in there and accuse her and so, I parked next to that little yellow sports car and waited for Fiona to come out. I must have waited for hours and after all that I nearly missed her because by the time she left the hospice it was dark and she left in a different car.' Megan was talking quickly.

Jill interrupted. 'So, what did you do?' Surely, she wasn't actually believing the story?

'I followed Fiona into Linlithgow and lost her at a right turn. It was dark and rainy. I drove around trying to find her again. I had more or less given up and was doing a three-point-turn at a dead end street when I saw her come onto the pavement outside Tanya Lang's flat. She was with a man. It was strange. Tanya stayed in a four-in-a-block that was being refurbished. Hers was the only inhabited flat at that end of the street and I knew there was nothing else down there but an electricity substation and a building plot. I parked. Before I had unclipped my seat belt, a car drove up, they jumped in and it sped off. I was going to follow and then I thought I'd go and see if Tanya knew what they'd been up to. I used to visit Tanya and the baby a couple of times a week. When I got to the door I could hear Logan crying. I knocked, but there was no answer. He kept crying and crying. I tried the door and it was open...'

Megan hung her head, long hair falling straight down onto her faded jeans. Jill jerked her head frantically, as though she was having spasms in her neck, until I realised that she was indicating her handbag. Inside was a pack of tissues. I opened it and gave one to Megan.

'Tanya was dead,' she said, eventually.

'So you took Logan and came down here?' Jill *was* actually believing the story.

I was less easy to convince. 'So, having possibly witnessed a murder you didn't think of calling the police?'

'I couldn't, they would have taken Logan away.'

'And what do you say was Fiona Scott's motive? Let's face it, you're trying to pin the blame on Fiona because of what happened between her and Glen. You're the one with a reason to kill Tanya, and I'm taking that reason back to his grandparents. Come on, Jill, we're leaving.'

Megan got up and stood between myself and Jill. 'No, please, leave the baby here with me. I swear I'll go nowhere. Just one more day with him while you check things out.'

'There's nothing to check out,' I said. We're taking the baby to see some policemen and you're coming with us.'

Chapter 51

It should have taken less than an hour and a half to drive from Jedburgh to Fettes Avenue, Edinburgh; however, I hadn't taken into account the need for a feeding stop, followed shortly thereafter by a nappy stop and then another nappy stop. Though there were other police stations on the way, including one in Jedburgh itself, I knew there would be a lot of questions to be asked, statements to be taken and lawyers to be called when we turfed up with Tanya Lang's missing baby. I thought that things would go a lot more quickly if we could do it all back in civilisation where we were guaranteed to meet some senior police officers, rather than have to wait for them to arrive.

'Can't we sleep on this?' Jill asked, not for the first time. 'It's not fair on the baby.'

'The baby's fine,' I said.

'Come on, Robbie. Give Megan a chance to get organised. She's told you what happened – what if she's right?'

'I'm not interested in what's right.'

'Really?' said Jill. 'Well, I am.'

'What's right or not is for a jury to decide. I've got a client in the jail awaiting trial for murder and I think there's an extremely reasonable doubt sitting in the back seat with a baby on her knee.'

That little speech shut Jill up, but only for a couple of miles. 'What difference is a few hours going to make?' she continued where she'd left off. 'This has all been so sudden. Things might look different in the morning.'

I didn't see how they could. 'We have a stolen baby that needs to be returned to its next-of-kin.'

'And that can wait until the morning. Look at yourself.'

I took a look in the rear-view mirror at a tired, stubbly face, pale apart from the livid area around my left eye that now had a yellow tinge to the edges.

As we reached the outskirts of the city, it was after midnight and Jill had scarcely let up. I yawned. The adrenalin rush from when I'd first seen Megan and the long-lost baby had long since departed my bloodstream. Maybe Jill was right. It would all be a lot easier to deal with in the morning. We were bringing in the Deputy First Minister's daughter to be charged with child-abduction and murder. It would take hours for the police to finish with us. Whether it was tiredness, Jill's powers of persuasion, Megan's sobbing or the smell of yet another dirty nappy, I allowed myself to be talked into dropping the two women and child at Jill's house.

'This is the woman who has already killed once for that child,' I warned Jill, as she alighted.

'Call me first thing in the morning,' she said. Through the rolled down driver's window she pecked me on the cheek, 'and don't worry.'

Chapter 52

But I was worrying. If Megan needed a chance to get herself together, I wasn't going to give her long. I'd catch a couple of hours sleep, shower, shave and be back through at Jill's place crack of dawn. On the way back home, I stopped off at my office to collect my mobile. Three missed calls; all from my dad; no messages. The last was only ten minutes old. I returned the call as I made my way back down the stairs and through the close to the High Street, where a few stragglers were making their way home from the pub.

'What time do you call this?' my dad asked.

'You've just phoned me.'

'That's right. I've been phoning you all night. Where have you been?'

'Working.'

'Don't give me that. Couldn't do it, could you? Couldn't come round yourself and tell me the Islay trip was off?'

'Malky—'

'Don't blame your brother.'

'I'm—'

'Trying to fob me off with a bottle of Bowmore?'

'Dad, I'm right in the middle of something. Can we talk about this some other time?'

'Like when?'

'Like not at one o'clock in the morning.'

'When then? We're supposed to be flying out

tomorrow afternoon.'

'Let me talk to Malky and I'll get back to you in the morning,' I said.

'Malky's here. And he's told me how determined you are to play in that Mickey Mouse football match.'

I could see what had happened. Malky had broken the news to Dad. The news being that the postponement of the Islay trip was all down to me.

'Let's sleep on it. Things will look different in the morning.' It was an argument that had worked for Jill. 'My phone's running out of battery. Speak to you later.' I cancelled the call and climbed back behind the wheel of Jill's car. I hated hanging up on my dad, still, he would see things differently once word of the baby had filtered through to him and he learned of my involvement in its recovery. Even if I wasn't playing in Sunday's match, we couldn't have flown off to Islay the following afternoon anyway. I had far too busy a day ahead of me.

I parked behind my own car and walked to my front door. I was looking for my front door key when I heard the click of high heels behind me. It was Fiona Scott, tight black jacket and skirt, black silk blouse and a single string of pearls. She folded her arms. Her lips were set in a thin red line. 'You wanted to speak to me?' she said. 'I was told it was *extremely* important.'

It was also one o'clock in the morning. I was feeling really stupid now. I hadn't expected Fiona Scott to take my message quite so seriously. I'd only been wanting some advice on how Megan McIvor might have got her hands on the diamorphine to kill Tanya Lang. It wasn't so urgent now that I'd made my move.

'I'm sorry to have bothered you,' I said. 'It's late and I know you've had a busy night—'

'I want to know what's so important.'

I supposed I did owe her an explanation after she'd taken the trouble of coming all the way to see me at that time of night.

'I'm making investigations into the death of Tanya Lang, you know, the local girl whose baby is missing?'

'I know who you mean,' she said.

'I'm acting for the man charged with killing her—'

'And?'

'I've received certain information,' I didn't want to leak Megan McIvor's name right at that moment, 'that the drugs used to kill her could have been prescribed to one of the hospice's patients.' Fiona raised an eyebrow; I'd obviously captured her interest. 'I'm going to the police first thing in the morning and they might want to ask you a few questions about drug security.'

Fiona shivered and hugged herself. 'It's cold.'

She didn't move. I looked around for a little yellow sports car that wasn't there.

'Could I come in for a moment?' She asked, moving closer. 'I'm sure it's nice and warm inside.'

My mobile phone chose that moment to rumble. My dad again. I dropped the phone back into my pocket, took out my front door key and the next thing I knew I was lying on my living room floor with someone kneeling down beside me. There was a stabbing pain at the back of my skull extending from above my right ear, stretching in a line of sheer pulsating agony down my neck and into the small of my back.

'Hit him again.' Fiona Scott's voice.

A hand seized my hair. Knuckles smashed against the side of my head. Light flashed and then darkness.

'Give me his arm.' Fiona Scott again, speaking underwater.

Someone grabbed my arm, rolled me over, ripped the jacket off my back. I knew I should be trying to get away, but my limbs wouldn't work. On my back, I looked up through watery eyes at the blurry figure looming over me and made out the craggy face and cauliflower ear of Keith Haggerty. He placed a knee on my chest, bringing his full weight down onto it, squeezing the breath from my lungs. He took my shirt by the cuff, tore the sleeve off, bundled it up in one hand and threw it across the room. Fiona Scott knelt down beside us. She was holding a syringe and a tumbler in one surgical-gloved hand, in the other a small white box. She took an ampoule, broke the top off and emptied the white powder into the tumbler that held a drop or two of water, repeating the process twice more. The pain in my head was so severe that the thought, like Tanya Lang, of being wrapped in warm cotton wool and never waking up again was almost tempting. Almost. Summoning all the force I could, I brought a knee up, striking Haggerty in the small of the back. The big man barely noticed. I squirmed, wriggled, thrashed my free arm wildly, tried to loop an arm around his head, gouge his eyes. He batted my hand away. The pressure on my chest increased. I gasped for breath.

'Hold him still,' Fiona hissed. Haggerty shifted his position allowing me to gulp in a lungful of air before he put an arm like a log across and around my body, pinning my arms to my sides. Fiona drew the water and diamorphine mixture into the syringe. She held the point up and squeezed the plunger, a single drip formed at the point. With the flat of her hand she smacked the inside of my elbow, looking for a vein. I strained to pull my arm away, trying to present a moving target.

'He's struggling too much,' Fiona said.

Haggerty jabbed a fist into my temple, but I was no longer feeling pain - I was fighting for my life. Fighting and losing. My mouth filled with blood. The point of the needle stabbed into the crook of my arm.

I didn't hear a key turn in the back door, or it open, but I did hear voices in the kitchen and one in particular. An angry voice. My dad's voice.

'Get in here right now!' he yelled from the other side of the door separating kitchen from livingroom. I heard the scrape of wooden chair legs across ceramic floor tiles as he sat down at the table.

The needle left my arm. Fiona put both hands, one on top of the other, across my mouth.

'Robbie!' My dad yelled. 'I know you're there, I saw the light on!'

Haggerty stood, literally a weight off my chest. I wrenched my head to the side, pulled away the hands clamped across my mouth. There were only two inches of wood between me and help. With a huge effort I barged Fiona aside and had almost clambered to my feet when Haggerty slammed into me, knocking me off balance and onto the floor again. He kicked me to the back of the head, booted me in the ribs. I tried to curl up into a ball.

'Try and fob me off with a bottle of Bowmore and some tickets to a kid-on fitba' match?' I could hear my dad bellow.

Haggerty grabbed Fiona, shoved her towards the other door. Suddenly, Malky was standing frozen in the doorway between kitchen and livingroom. 'Robbie?' he said, his eyes on Haggerty, six feet of carpet separated the two. That distance shortly became the length of Haggerty's arm as he stepped forward and planted a straight right into my brother's face. Malky fell against the door frame. Fiona ran across the room to the door leading out into the hall and the front of my apartment, where we had come in. Haggerty turned and lumbered after her, but never made it. A shove in the back propelled Malky forward into the room, sprawling down on the floor beside me. Something flew through the air, met the back of Haggerty's head and shattered. Twelve-year-old Islay single malt and broken glass rained down. He toppled forward, smashed his face into the light switch and slid down the wall. My dad strode into the room. 'Don't just lie there, he yelled at Malky. "Get her!'

Chapter 53

By four that morning, I'd had five stitches inserted in the cut below my left eye, in the middle of an even bigger bruise than before, and the back of my head shaved and two scalp lacerations glued.

Although the school-leaver posing as an A&E doctor suggested I stay overnight for observations, I opted to go home under the supervision of my father and brother and so left with a packet of painkillers and a head injury information sheet.

Scene of Crime had already been to take photos and swabs and only Inspector Dougie Fleming and a couple of young uniforms were waiting back at my place to take statements. Fleming was an unreconstructed forty-something police officer whose career had trundled on through the ranks, relatively unscathed by the inconveniences and procedural irritations of the European Convention on Human Rights. He'd been a cadet when Sergeant Alex Munro was in his prime. He'd been a quick learner. 'By the way, nice throw, Alex,' he said, snapping shut his notebook.

'Where are they?' I asked.

'Dubbed-up safe and sound. It will be Monday morning before that pair see the light of day through the tinted window of the prison van.'

It was another fifteen minutes before my dad and Fleming had finished catching up on police gossip and the detective inspector and his colleagues left.

'Right, you,' my dad said to Malky, who'd rescued an orphan can of beer from the fridge and was gently pressing it against the white plaster-strip across the bridge of his nose. 'Put the beer down and away to your bed. I'll stay up and keep an eye on Robbie.' He took the can from Malky and cracked it open. 'Are you feeling drowsy,' he asked me, after taking a long drink.

'Of course I'm drowsy?' I said. 'It's half four in the morning. I'm usually so drowsy at this time of night that I'm asleep.'

He grunted and lifted the head injury sheet from the arm of the couch. 'Well, you're not sleeping tonight. Have you got a headache?'

'Yes, because someone was punching it earlier.'

'Is it getting worse, though?'

I didn't think so. If anything, it was a lot better now that the painkillers were kicking in.

'Deafness?'

'What?'

'Very funny. Any blurred or double vision?'

He wasn't going to stop until he'd completed the list. It was easier to play along. 'No.'

'Any clear fluid coming out of your ears?'

'Nope.'

'Are you experiencing nausea?'

'Dad, really, I'm fine. Just let me have a few hours sleep.'

Satisfied at the replies to his questioning, former police sergeant Alex Munro finished the beer with another couple of slugs and, after crushing the empty can, made himself comfortable on the couch. In a few minutes, to my great relief, if not surprise, he was sound asleep and snoring.

I lifted the advice sheet. My dad had missed a few. Weakness in any part of the body? No – it was more *every* part of my body. Dizziness? Maybe a little. Unusual breathing patterns? No. Confusion? Not anymore. As I'd sat there in the Accident & Emergency, waiting to be stitched and glued, I'd been extremely confused. Confused as to why Fiona Scott would want to kill me. I'd thought about Megan McIvor and of Jill's belief that she'd been telling the truth and that it was Fiona Scott and some unknown man who'd killed Tanya Lang. It no longer seemed like such a leap of faith. But why kill her? Or try to kill me for that matter? The same reason Fiona had thrown herself at Glen Beattie. The same reason she planted child-porn on his PC. The same reason she phoned the cops and then sent bogus cops to recover what turned out to be the wrong laptop from the surgery. The same reason she'd had Andy mugged and me threatened. She wanted to erase the dirty truth about Kenny McIvor and heroin-addicted Tanya Lang. The destruction of that information, I was sure, had secured Fiona Scott a highly paid job as head of Scotland's Hospice Quango.

Jill would be fine. Megan McIvor's abduction of the baby had been opportunistic. She'd not murdered the child's mother. My dad let rip a salvo of sleepy snorts. I collected some essentials, put on my jacket, lifted my car keys and slipped out of the back door.

Chapter 54

Clearly, for some people, five-thirty a.m. wasn't such an alien territory as it was for me. JayJay Lang was already in work clothes and drinking a cup of tea in the kitchen when I arrived at his house. In the background, Mrs Lang, in an enormous pink dressing gown with matching towelling mules, was making sandwiches. There was a canvas bag on the table beside her. The top of tartan Thermos flask stuck out of the top.

JayJay stood in the doorway and took a moment to study the state of my injured face. 'What happened to you?'

'Doesn't matter.'

'Who is it Jay?' Mrs Lang wiped her hands on a tea towel and joined her husband at the door, trying to see past him.

'I've come to return this,' I said, holding out the envelope of cash that had been foisted upon me a couple of nights before.

'I told you, I don't want it,' JayJay placed a hand on the edge of the door. I put my foot in the way to stop it closing.

'Take it,' I said. 'You're going to need it.'

He pulled the door wide open and stepped towards me. 'Is that right?' he said, as though I'd challenged him to a fight.

'That's right,' I said. I shoved the envelope down the front of his hi-vis yellow vest. 'You've got things to buy - a pushchair, baby clothes, nappies; definitely nappies.'

He looked puzzled. His wife was quicker on the uptake. 'You've found him?'

'Safe and sound.'

Mrs Lang shoved her lump of a husband aside, stood on the toes of her slippers and threw her big, soft, pink, fluffy arms around me.

I drove JayJay and his wife to Corstorphine. On the way we talked about residence orders, adoptions, contact and other legal subjects on which I had very little clue. What I could say, with some certainty, was that if Brandon Biggam was the father, and even that was still unclear, the chances of a court placing baby Logan in his drug-dealing hands were zero to nil.

We parked around the corner from Jill's house. I'd phoned to warn her of our arrival and the child was freshly bathed and good to go.

'Look at the state of you. What happened?' Jill asked.

'Tell you later. Where's Megan?'

She'd gone. I wasn't hugely surprised.

After a tearful reunion, I packed baby Logan and his delighted grandparents into a taxi back to Linlithgow and rejoined Jill.

'Job done,' she said. 'Are you going to tell me what happened to your face?'

I gave Jill the short version of how Fiona Scott and Keith Haggerty had ended up in custody for trying to kill me. 'It's only a matter of time before the cops pin Tanya Lang's death on them too.'

'Megan was right then,' Jill said. 'And that makes me right for believing her and you wrong for not.'

'Let's just say I was unconvinced.'

'You mean wrong?'

'Okay, I was wrong, you were right. Megan isn't guilty of murder - just plagium.'

'I take it that's the smart Alec lawyer way of saying child-stealing? Give the woman a break. At least she's done the right thing now.'

'We made her do the right thing.'

'She was always going to give the baby back. We just helped, that's all. She's had a hard time. First she can't have children and then her fiancé cheats on her.'

'If you ever give up pushing pills, I can give you a job,' I said. 'You do an excellent plea in mitigation. Can you do one for me?'

'What do you mean?'

'I mean that long, cold, lonely wait in the cinema foyer twenty years ago.'

She smiled. 'It wasn't that cold and it was seventeen years ago. How's your head?'

I tilted my head forward to let her see the shaved section of scalp and glued laceration.

'Maybe whoever did the gluing should have practised on some Airfix models first,' she said, ending her brief examination. 'Don't ever go bald.'

She was so close. It would have been easy to lean forward. To kiss her. There'd never be a better opportunity. For one thing she'd never been less angry with me than she was at that precise moment. Did I feel lucky? She looked at me and smiled. I made my move.

A knock on the window. Jill turned her head. I

bumped my nose against her cheek. A face peered in at us from beneath a chequered cap. Blue lights flashed in the rear-view mirror.

'Stay where you are, sir,' said the uniform at my side of the car when I tried to get out.

The driver's door opened. 'Jill Green?'

'That's me,' Jill confirmed.

'Miss Green, I am detaining you under section fourteen of the Criminal Procedure (Scotland) Act nineteen ninety-five in connection with the abduction of Logan Lang.'

They took Jill to the architecturally-questionable building that housed Corstorphine's share of the Lothian & Borders Police constabulary.

Although I was actually in the police station and Jill didn't need legal aid, under the Government's new procedure the cops still had to call the Scottish Legal Aid Board advice-line, who then phoned me to tell me to make contact with the police to gain access to my client. If P.G. Wodehouse had never found it difficult to distinguish a Scotsman with a grievance from a ray of sunshine, he'd never have confused the Scottish criminal justice system with a well-oiled machine.

'Someone tipped-off the police. I think I can guess who.' I said, when, eventually, we met in an interview room. 'So much for giving Megan a break.'

'But you were with me. We found the baby together. She must know it's our word against hers.'

I didn't know what Megan was playing at. What I did know was that it was always a good idea to get your retaliation in first. I wished I hadn't taken the Langs to Jill's house. How would it look? As far as

Logan's grandparents were concerned, all they could say was that Jill was the woman who'd handed over their grandson. If the aunt at the B&B suffered an on-set of amnesia, suddenly the only person supporting Jill's defence was, as DI Dougie Fleming regarded me, her boyfriend.

'Don't worry,' I said. 'I'll have this all sorted and you out of here in two ticks.'

Jill risked a smile.

'First I have to go find you a lawyer.'

'You're my lawyer.'

'No, I'm your witness.'

I rapped the door to get out.

'Say nothing to the police. I'm going, but I'll be back.'

'When?'

'Before you know it.'

'Promise?'

'Promise.'

A uniform arrived and opened the door for me.

'Robbie,' Jill said. 'Don't keep me waiting.'

Chapter 55

Friday morning, five to nine, and a worried looking Grace-Mary was arriving for work. I overtook her on the stairs as I ran up them and into my office. I'd managed to get hold of Paul Sharp on his mobile and he was heading through to Corstorphine police station to see Jill. While she was being interviewed about the once-missing Logan Lang, I intended to take matters to a new level. If Kenny McIvor didn't get a grip on his daughter, the world was going to learn of his sexual indiscretions.

'What are you doing about your dad?' Grace-Mary shouted after me.

My dad, the Islay trip, the charity match had all paled into insignificance.

'Nothing!' I called over my shoulder. I met her in the corridor as I was making my way out again, the all important pen-drive, minus crisp packet, gripped tightly in my hand.

'Nothing? Wait, what happened to your face – this time?'

'Tell you later.' I started down the stairs.

'Have you been to the police station?'

I stopped, turned. 'Yes... how do you know about that?'

'Because Inspector Fleming phoned me at the house. He couldn't get an answer from your mobile or your home.'

'What's Dougie Fleming got to do with Jill?'

'Jill? I'm talking about your dad.'

'What about him?'

'Don't you know? He's been arrested.'

'Arrested?'

'For attacking some guy with a bottle.'

What was going on? Footsteps in the close. I could tell it was the cops before they came through the door at the top of the stair.

'Mr Munro? 'We're detaining you under—'

'What for?'

'A contravention of section five, two of the misuse of drugs Act nineteen seventy-one: possession of diamorphine.'

The duty sergeant should have filled in the detention papers at the charge bar, and I should also have been given the chance to have a lawyer intimated. Instead, on the instructions of Detective Inspector Dougie Fleming I was shoved in a cell. Typical of his tactics. Let me stew for a while. I sat down on the wooden bench. The world was falling in. First Jill, then my dad, now me, all in custody.

How would the Crown's jaundiced eye see the events of the last twelve hours? I knew very well that the same evidence could produce quite different outcomes when viewed from different angles.

Less than ten minutes later a key slid into the lock and the heavy door swung wide open. It was D.I. Fleming.

'Out.'

'What's happening?'

He didn't reply, just birled on a heel and marched

off down the corridor with me tagging along. If he was anticipating a question and answer session he was being overly optimistic.

'Where are we going?' I asked, as we passed the interview rooms.

'In here.' He pushed open a door which I knew from past experience led to the muster room; a small dingy room, lined with steel lockers and containing a sink, a table and an assortment of chairs. Surely, he wasn't actually going to try any strong-arm tactics. 'Sit.' He pointed to a chair. There was someone else in the room. My dad. He was drinking a mug of tea.

'Dad. What are you doing here?'

'Fiona Scott told Dougie that everything's your fault. That she came to see you and found you about to kill yourself with a massive dose of morphine.'

'I've had your flat searched,' Fleming advised.

My dad grimaced. 'They found that box of morphine from Vince's house.'

'Oh, I see. I tried to top myself, did I? Did I beat myself up too?'

'It gets worse,' my dad said. 'Apparently, I've arrived, got the wrong end of the stick and assaulted Fiona's boyfriend.'

Totally outrageous and yet I could understand how it might come across in court.

My dad took a slurp of tea. 'By the way, you're also a suspect in the Tanya Lang murder.'

Fleming nodded in confirmation. 'She was killed by a massive injection of diamorphine and you just happen to have a box full of vials. A witness puts you at Tanya's house around about ten o'clock the night she died.'

I wondered. Was that witness Fiona Scott? Or was Megan McIvor covering her tracks by sticking the boot into Jill and me?

'You can see how that all looks,' Fleming said.

I could and I also had a good idea how it all might appear to Hugh Ogilvie if a police report landed on the PF's desk. The Deputy First Minister's daughter and the head of the new Hospice quango would make fine Crown witnesses. Who did I have on my side to explain the drugs? My dad.

'So why aren't you arresting me for murder? Why are we having this little chat?'

'Because your dad has explained how you came by the drugs and his word has always been good enough for me. Plus, you've got an excellent alibi witness.' He jerked a thumb at himself.

Of course, the retirement do. The night Tanya died I was out with a bunch of cops, fiscals, lawyers and court officials. If Carlsberg did alibis...

'So for the moment I'm satisfied that you didn't kill Tanya Lang,' Fleming said. 'And if your dad wasted a good bottle of whisky by hitting it off the back of someone's head, I'm thinking it must have been an act of necessity.'

I was in danger of starting to like DI Fleming. I quickly snapped out of it.

'That still leaves the box of diamorphine that was found at your house,' he said. 'No matter how you carve it, you were technically in possession and unless you tell me, right now, what's going on, I'm going to charge you and hold you in here until court on Monday morning.'

I turned to look at my dad. So did Fleming. 'That okay with you Alex?' he asked.

'Fine by me,' said my dad. 'It's not like he was doing anything important this weekend anyway.'

Chapter 56

There was a lengthy process to follow when booking an appointment with any senior politician, far less the Deputy First Minister of Scotland. Even then, unless you happened to be a rich businessman with an open cheque book and a burning desire to boost Party funds, there were no guarantees. I slapped Jimmy Garvie's report down on the desk and suggested to Kenny McIvor's private secretary that she might care to fast-track the procedure. She didn't, not until I'd directed her to the appendix and the notes on her boss's STD.

'What do you want?' There was nothing happening in the Scottish Parliament that Friday lunchtime and McIvor was phoning from the back of his official limo. His secretary drifted off to a coffee machine.

'I have your medical records,' I told him.

There was a pause. 'I don't know what you're talking about.' There was no way McIvor would discuss matters over the phone.

'Then let me explain. I'd like to talk to you because I have these extremely private medical records that seem to link you to a young woman, a dead young woman, and a rather nasty sexually trans—'

'Where?'

'I'm at your office now.'

'No. Somewhere else.'

'How about my office?'

'One hour.' He rang off.

From the immense bronze doors at the entrance to St Andrew's House to the paint-peeling wooden door of my office took fifty minutes. A black limousine was parked outside, McIvor and his chauffeur were waiting inside. I told Grace-Mary to take the rest of the day off.

'You'll understand if Chris does his thing,' McIvor said, after I'd shown him and his chauffeur into my office. Chris fully extended the aerial on his pocket bug-detector then looked around the room for a place to set it up. He chose the highest point in the room, atop the summit of the files piled on Vince's old oak dresser-base. When he switched on the device, the series of multi-coloured lights down one side lit up and then dimmed leaving only the top green light and two red lights illuminated. The chauffeur grunted in satisfaction and then turned to me. 'Take off your jacket.' I did. He emptied the contents of my pockets, lining the various items along the edge of my desk. One of them was the folded copy of Jimmy Garvie's report. McIvor picked it up and began to read.

'Cell-phone.' The chauffeur held out his hand. I gave him my mobile. He knocked the battery out and then shoved it in a drawer. After that he patted me down, switched off my PC, disconnected my land-line phone from the wall and removed the tape from my hand dictation machine. 'Haven't seen one of these in years,' he said, looking at the tape as though it were an ancient artefact. He placed tape and machine in separate desk drawers, apparently not trusting them to be left alone together. He pointed to the bug-detector, now showing one green and one red light. 'If the green light goes out or another red light shows, let me know,' he said to McIvor, before closing the window blinds and leaving the room, shutting the door behind him.

'How many of these do you have?' McIvor asked, holding up the report.

'That's the only hard copy.'

'How many electronic versions?'

'One.'

'Give it to me.'

'Not yet. I want some information first.'

'Mr Munro, you have far too much information already; confidential information belonging to me, and if you do not hand it over this minute I am going to have you prosecuted for a breach of data protection.'

I sat down behind my desk. 'Would that be the data that says you had sex with a vulnerable, drug-addicted constituent of yours called Tanya Lang, grand-daughter of your old football buddy, Tam Fairbairn? Data that you caught something nasty and went to see Dr MacGregor who offered to hush things up by placing you on his very private patient list? It's not surprising, with data like that, you'd want your medical records back and Tanya Lang silenced. Was killing her your idea? Or was that Fiona Scott showing some initiative?'

McIvor looked at the closed window blinds. 'How much? How much to give me the records and forget the whole thing? Your friend. The one who wants to be a Sheriff. Why not you too? I'm sure it's not too late to apply, just put me down as a referee and buy yourself a wig.'

'Mr McIvor, all I want to know is who killed Tanya Lang because I'd like to prove it wasn't my client.'

'Your client?'

'Tanya's former boyfriend.'

'You've got to be kidding. You're trying to blackmail a Member of Parliament in order to save a drug-dealing ned?'

'It's called justice. You used to be secretary of state for it.'

'Even if I told you what I know it wouldn't do your client any good. I'd deny everything if you ever tried to bring it up. Don't even think about putting me on a witness list in the defence of Mr...'

'Biggam. And unless you give me what I want, I'm going to see that your sordid secret is published in every newspaper in Scotland.'

'Thanks, that's the sound-bite I needed.' McIvor stood. He pointed to the electronic device perched atop the files on the dresser. 'See that green light? That's the power light, but the one below it, the red one, that means it detects a bug.' He opened his jacket to reveal a tiny microphone clipped over the breast pocket of his shirt. 'This bug in fact. It's sending a signal to Chris who has a recording device. Chauffeur, bodyguard, counter-surveillance expert, Chris also knows how to edit a digital sound recording.' Using his nail, he pressed a tiny button on the microphone, turning it off. 'I have enough to prove that you attempted to blackmail a Member of Parliament.' He let the flap of his jacket drop across his chest again. 'Chris!' The chauffeur burst into the room. 'Call the police. Not the local mob. Ask Superintendant Forbes at Fettes to meet me here.'

Chris exited. McIvor sat down in the chair opposite me. 'It's not easy to get a warrant to search a lawyer's office, but I don't think I should have too much trouble now. I take it the electronic copy is here somewhere? On your PC? He noticed the bulging envelope on my desk, pen-drives spilling out. 'Or on a memory-stick perhaps?' He looked around. 'I'll bet the boys in blue enjoy a game of hunt the thimble.'

'It won't stop what's on it leaking into the public domain,' I said.

'Oh, I think it will. You decide a lot of police promotions as Justice Secretary, make a lot of friends. It's amazing how things can go missing - even in production rooms. Come on. Make it easy on yourself. Give me the data, before the police find it. Don't, and long after my medical records have vanished, you still won't have made a dent in your prison sentence.'

I dipped my hand into my pocket, removed the yellow and white pen-drive and held it out to him. McIvor took it, called his chauffeur back in and ordered him to tell the police to stand down. Chris did what he was told and left the room.

'There are definitely no more copies?' McIvor asked. There weren't and I told him so. He placed the pen-drive in the top pocket of his jacket. 'Good, but I'll be keeping my little recording just in case.'

'Now that you have what you want, will you tell me what actually happened?' I asked.

McIvor shook his head. 'No, but I will tell you this - I had nothing to do with Tanya Lang's death. I liked the girl. Her grandfather sent her to me for help, one unfortunate thing led to another, it's true, but I meant her no harm.'

He made to leave.

'I'm glad about that,' I said, 'because you'll make an excellent witness in the trial of her real killer.'

McIvor turned around to face me again, laughing. 'I've already made myself clear on that point. If you think I'm going to testify to save your client's worthless skin, then you are very much mistaken.'

'It's not only my client's skin that's at stake here,' I said. 'Your daughter's is too.'

'Don't be ridiculous.'

'Megan knows who killed Tanya. She found the body and stole her baby.'

'Nonsense. It said on the news that the baby's been found.'

'I know. I found him – with Megan. Still, there's no reason why anyone needs to know what happened. No reason for the daughter of the Deputy First Minister to go to jail for child-snatching. I can keep a secret, but it all depends on whether you'll tell me why Tanya was killed.'

McIvor whipped out his mobile. He tried calling his daughter, but without success.

I made another suggestion. 'Why not try your sister in Jedburgh?'

McIvor punched some more numbers. After an emotional exchange he replaced the phone in his pocket and sighed. 'It seems Megan has been very foolish.' He thought for a moment, eyes fixed on the floor where there were some faint stains; permanent reminders of historical coffee spills and Geordie Lyon's bleeding nose.

He unclipped the microphone from his shirt pocket, checked to make sure it was off and stuffed it into a trouser pocket. 'I'm going to tell you what I know and then I'm leaving.' He tapped the top pocket of his jacket where he'd put the pen-drive. 'But first I want your word that you'll not involve Megan, my sister or myself in the defence of your client.'

I agreed.

'Very well,' McIvor said. 'I've known Fiona Scott for a good number of years. We've served on countless hospice committees together. After Bill MacGregor's sudden death, I didn't know what to do. I knew that I couldn't let word of my... my problem with Tanya get out. Fiona was saying how much she'd miss MacGregor because she was down at the surgery a lot, keeping him up to date with the patients he'd referred to St Gideon's. One thing led to another and I asked Fiona to recover my records, not thinking it would be such a big deal. When she told me it was going to be difficult I told her that if she helped me out then, when my Hospice Bill became law, I'd recommend her for head of the new quango.'

'You let her plant porn on Glen Beattie's PC so she could stage a search of his surgery.'

'I didn't know. I never asked any questions.'

'But you did pass on information. After our breakfast meeting with Glen Beattie, you told Fiona that I had instructed an expert to analyse Dr MacGregor's old laptop.'

McIvor said nothing.

'Did you order Tanya's murder?'

'I swear I didn't know anything. I didn't *want* to know anything.'

'Come off it.'

McIvor ran his fingers through his hair. 'I knew nothing until... afterwards.'

'But Fiona did confess the murder to you?'

'She told me it was for the best; the girl was a junkie, an over-dose waiting to happen. Some respectable family would adopt the child and it would all be for the best in the long run.'

'So why did you resign from the leadership race?'

'The polls weren't good. Fiona wasn't happy. We both knew that if I lost the election the Hospice Bill would be binned. She told me she had my records, the only remaining copy.'

The ones violently removed from Andy's possession, I assumed. 'So you came to an arrangement with Angus Pike? You step down from the leadership race in return for him guaranteeing his support for the Bill?'

'There's no real harm been done,' McIvor assured me. 'It's a shame about Tanya, but it will all be for the best for her child. And whatever happens to your client, I'm pretty sure he deserves it.' He shouted on the chauffeur and then turned to me. 'You gave me your word. I expect you to keep it. I am a man of some influence and...' He tapped his breast pocket where he'd placed the pen-drive, as though reassuring himself it was all over. 'You have nothing left to bargain with.'

Chris the chauffeur entered. I lifted the bug-detector from the files on top of Vince's old oak dresser and lobbed it at him. 'Don't forget this.'

He caught it, retracted the aerial and switched it off. I suppose I should have felt flattered that anyone would think I held a stock of bugging devices; however, the whole bug-detector thing had been a complete waste of time. At Munro & Co. we lagged way behind in technology. We had to rely on older, though just as reliable, surveillance methods.

McIvor walked to the door.

'One more thing before you go,' I said.

'What now?' he asked, impatiently, turning around just in time to see me pull open the doors of the dresser and to watch D.I. Dougie Fleming clamber out on all fours. The detective inspector looked hot and sweaty, his face flushed. Suddenly, I remembered an apple left trapped in a locker at Polmont YOI. Once on his feet, Fleming dusted himself down, placed his hands on the small of his back and stretched.

'I thought you two were never going to stop,' he said, back-heeling the dresser doors closed one at a time. 'There's not as much room as you might think in there.'

McIvor spluttered like a teapot left on the gas. Fleming held up a hand as though stopping traffic. He flashed his warrant card. 'I have to warn you, sir, that on the basis of what I happen to have over-heard,' he made it sound as though he'd just been passing by, 'you are now a suspect in the murder of Tanya Lang and that anything you say will be noted and may be used in evidence.' He pulled the cord, lifting the window blinds and waved. At his signal two uniformed cops alighted from a car parked across on the other side of the High Street and began to jog towards my office.

Chapter 57

D.I. Dougie Fleming was odds-on to earn a third pip on his epaulette after nabbing Fiona Scott and Keith Haggerty for the murder of Tanya Lang and their subsequent attempt on the life of yours truly. What would happen to Kenny McIvor was less easy to predict, though I suspected he, along with his baby-snatching daughter, would escape prosecution and emerge as Crown witnesses one and two in HMA –v- Scott and Haggerty. Whatever happened, Scotland would very soon be requiring a new Deputy First Minister.

A blast of rain in the face brought me back to the moment. It was half past ten on a Sunday night. It wasn't Islay. It was a floodlit Hampden Park, Glasgow. The wind swirled about us, the grass under our feet was wet and muddy and the white paint of the centre circle was trampled and scuffed with the recent passage of countless football boots.

'Alex, would you like to say a few words?' Jill had recovered from her few hours in custody on Friday. An unpleasant experience that had ended around about the same time as the Deputy First Minister was taken into custody and an APB, or at least the Lothian & Borders equivalent, put out on Megan McIvor.

Jill passed Vince's silver urn to my dad. He cleared his throat and spoke the words of the bard. *An honest man here lies at rest, As e'er God with his image blest; The*

341

friend of man, the friend of truth, The friend of age, and guide of youth: Few hearts like his, with virtue warm'd, Few heads with knowledge so informed: If there's another world, he lives in bliss; If there is none, he made the best of this.

By the time he reached the last stanza his voice had begun to crack. He assembled a wobbly smile and offered the urn back to Jill. She shook her head. 'Goodbye Dad,' she said.

Alex Munro pulled the top off the Urn, turned his back to the wind and poured out the last mortal remains of Vincent Green, his best friend. The gusting wind caught the ashes and carried them off down the park where they mingled with the falling rain and returned to the emerald turf.

Malky signalled to the sidelines and a waitress from hospitality, black skirt whipping around her legs joined us. She was carrying a silver tray with glasses of whisky. We each took one.

I raised a glass. 'To Vince,' I said, and Malky, Jill and I drank ours. My dad looked ready to throw his down the pitch after Vince's ashes.

'You know what my dad would say if he thought you were throwing away good whisky,' Jill said. My dad knocked the drink back and as the rest of us followed him up the players' tunnel, Malky's ringtone: Blue Moon, sounded and simultaneously my own phone vibrated to announce an incoming text message. It was from Paul Sharp. *On second thoughts – do ask Malky.* The Sundays hadn't been slow in reporting the news on Kenny McIvor's demise. With only the Munro boys and dottery old Sheriff Larry Dalrymple down as referees on his application, I didn't think I'd be calling

Paul *m'lord* anytime soon.

'That was my boss,' Malky said, after a couple of minutes of listening and not much talking. 'Looks like I'm back on the buroo.'

On closer enquiry it turned out that Malky's producer on his radio phone-in had watched the Scotland Legends –v- Old Firm Old Boys game on some obscure TV station and been surprised not only to see Malky trotting out to captain Scotland, but also a close-up shot of his dead father sitting in the stand and shouting at the ref.

'Oh, cheers,' my dad said. 'You decided to bump me off so you'd have an excuse to come up here and play football?'

'It was the only way I could get a whole week off – compassionate leave. I thought we were going to Islay and then, next thing, Robbie had talked me into playing in the charity match. I never thought the Station would find out; Brighton's a long way from Glasgow. How did I know the game was being shown on cable?' He put his arm around my dad's vast shoulders. 'Looks like you're going to have a lodger for a while.'

My dad tossed his head, grimaced and emitted a loud groan of dismay. He was kidding no-one – he was delighted.

Inside the function suite the post-match party was jumping, the band was in full swing and Johnny Akbar was working the room. He came over and playfully nudged Malky, who'd scored from a last minute corner to equalise for the Scotland 'Legends' and draw the match three/three. 'Great goal, Malky,' Johnny shouted over the music. He ruffled my brother's hair. 'Of course, it's not easy to miss a head the size of yours from a corner kick.'

Malky introduced Johnny to our dad and by the time Jill had returned from stowing the now empty urn in the ladies' cloakroom, my old man was already regaling Johnny about the good old days, when they played *proper* football and you could actually brush against another player without them falling over and shouting for a penalty. When he started to bang on about Jim Baxter and footballs with laces, I allowed Jill to drag me away and we floated off in the direction of the buffet. Would I see her again after the night was over? I wondered, popping a cream-cheese-stuffed sweet piquanté pepper into my mouth. There was no reason to, other than, I now realised, I really wanted to.

'We should do this again,' I blurted. Not one of the better excerpts from that slim volume: the Robbie Munro book of chat-up lines. *Yeah, Jill, give me a shout next time you're spreading the ashes of a close relative.*

I waited for her to slap me down with a verbal wet fish. She didn't. Instead, she smiled.

Fortified by what I took to be a sign of encouragement, I continued. 'What I mean is, we should go out again... somewhere... sometime... when you're not too busy.'

'Have you seen Dr Zhivago?' she asked.

'No,' I looked around. 'Is he here?'

She laughed. 'The movie. They've digitally re-mastered it, I think, for Omar Sharif's eightieth birthday. It's showing at the Dominion next week.'

Dr Zhivago was a film I always tried to avoid; something easier said than done on bank holidays when it tended to crop up on one TV channel or another. Personally, I couldn't see the big attraction in watching a man with a moustache running about in the snow after a woman in a fur hat and taking more than three hours to do it. Even if that woman happened to be Julie Christie it couldn't compete with The Great Escape.

'Sounds great,' I said. 'Let's go.'

Jill looked pleased.

'Robbie!' Someone was shouting my name. 'Robbie!' Over the band tunes I heard it again; a female voice. Pushing her way through the crowded dance-floor, a figure trotted towards me on high-heels: Joanna Jordan, former Procurator Fiscal depute. She'd swapped her long, black, courtroom-gown for a short, white, cocktail-dress. 'Robbie Munro, what are you doing here?' she slurred.

'I—'

'C'mere.'

She pulled me aside. 'I never got that job with the Children's Reporter,' she whispered loudly in my ear.

'That's a—'

'Is your offer still open?'

'I thought you—'

'Cos, you know, I'm kind of desperate.'

'Well, that's er... fine. Give me a call Monday morning.' I tried to step away.

She grabbed my hand. 'Thanks, Robbie.' She pulled herself up on my shoulder and kissed me on the cheek. 'We'll make a great team!'

Jill was back at the buffet table laying a couple of prosciutto-wrapped asparagus tips on her plate.

'I'm free any night next week,' I told her. 'How

about Wednesday? We could go out for something to eat first.'

Jill mulled over the suggestion while she crunched into asparagus and watched as Joanna tottered off to from whence she'd come.

'Why don't I pick you up at your place - about seven o'clock?'

Jill finished chewing, selected the second asparagus tip and stuffed it into my top pocket. 'I've a better idea,' she said. 'Why don't I just meet you in the foyer?'

* * * * *

Continuing the Best Defence Series:

#4 KILLER CONTRACT

It's the trial of the millennium: Larry Kirkslap, Scotland's most flamboyant entrepreneur, charged with the murder of good-time gal Violet Hepburn. He needs a lawyer and there's only one man for the job – unfortunately it's not Robbie Munro. That's about to change; however, more pressing is the contract out on the lives of Robbie and his client, Danny Boyd, who is awaiting trial for violating a sepulchre.

Who would want to kill Robbie and his teenage client? And why?

While Robbie tries to work things out, there are a couple of domestic issues that also need his urgent attention, like his father's surprise birthday party and the small matter of a marriage proposal.

#5 CRIME FICTION

Desperate for cash, Robbie finds himself ensnared in a web of deceit spun by master conman Victor Devlin. What is Devlin's connection with the case of two St Andrew's students charged with the murder of a local waitress?

Enter Suzie Lake, a former-university chum of Robbie, now bestselling crime fiction author, who regards Robbie as her muse. Lois has writer's block and turns to Robbie for inspiration. She's especially interested in the St Andrew's murder and wants some information. How can Robbie refuse the advances of the gorgeous Suzie, even if they threaten to scupper his pending nuptials? And yet, the more Robbie reveals to her, the more he finds himself in a murky world of bribery, corruption and crime fiction publishing.

ABOUT THE AUTHOR

Willie McIntyre is married with four sons. He coaches youth football with East Stirlingshire F.C. and is head of criminal law at Russel + Aitken, said to be Scotland's oldest law firm.

Over the past twenty-five years or so Willie has represented clients from every stratum of society, charged with just about every crime known to the law of Scotland.

A 'Black Bitch', which is to say, a native of the historic Royal Burgh of Linlithgow, Willie draws heavily on his years in the criminal courts when writing his series of legal thrillers featuring criminal defence lawyer, Robbie Munro.

www.bestdefence.biz
wm@bestdefence.biz

5583841R00207

Printed in Great Britain
by Amazon.co.uk, Ltd.,
Marston Gate.